"EXCELLENT . . . GUEST AND HILL ARE CAPABLE OF POWER-
FUL INSIGHTS INTO HUMAN NATURE; CONSEQUENTLY, THE
READER REAPS A DOUBLE HARVEST. . . . THE CHARACTERS
. . . POSSESS COMPELLING DEPTH AND THE RELATIONSHIPS
BETWEEN THEM ARE REALISTIC AND COMPLEX."
—*St. Cloud Daily Times* (Minnesota)

Killing Time in St. Cloud
JUDITH GUEST and REBECCA HILL

"COMPLEX, ABSORBING, AND WELL-TIMED. . . . The
work of seasoned, confident, poised professionals."
—*Minneapolis Star Tribune*

"A MYSTERY THAT GOES BEYOND THE CONFINES OF A
SIMPLE WHODUNIT IN SPITE OF ITS SPECTACULAR CLI-
MAX. . . . A novel about contemporary mores . . .
about good ideas carried to extremes where they be-
come bad ones, about good people who need to control
life to the point where they become tyrants, about con-
trolling people who are pushed that one step beyond
their ability to manage and slip into madness. . . .
READS WITH THE EASE OF A MYSTERY SKILLFULLY
WRITTEN AND REWARDS WITH MORE THAN THE NAME
OF THE MURDERER."
—*Arizona Daily Star*

"GRIPPING . . . THE GRADUAL REVELATIONS NOT
ONLY ENRICH THE PLOT BUT KEEP THE READER
REEVALUATING CHARACTERS AND MOTIVES IN AN AT-
TEMPT TO DETERMINE JUST WHO THE GOOD GUYS RE-
ALLY ARE."
—*The Philadelphia Inquirer*

"EMOTIONALLY LACERATING."
—*Kirkus Reviews*

Books by JUDITH GUEST

Ordinary People
Second Heaven

Books by REBECCA HILL

Blue Rise
Among Birches

Killing Time in St. Cloud

JUDITH GUEST
and
REBECCA HILL

A Dell Book

Published by Dell Publishing
a division of
Bantam Doubleday Dell Publishing Group, Inc.
666 Fifth Avenue
New York, New York 10103

ISBN: 0-440-20427-5

Reprinted by arrangement with Delacorte Press

Printed in the United States of America

Published simultaneously in Canada

March 1989

10   9   8   7   6   5   4   3   2   1

OPM

When it appeared that Josephine could not, after a period of some years, bear him an heir, Napoleon divorced her and confined himself to governing the empire from the palace at St. Cloud.

1976

BOTH DOORS *of Simon's Plymouth coupe were locked. Charlie cupped one hand to the glass of the rear window and peered inside. In the crush and billow of pale crinolines he could make out a leg and one hand—the leg bare, the hand gripping something dark, a sweater. The girls had changed out of their prom dresses hours ago; what had Marty meant, then, she was going to the car to change? He raised his eyes to look past the granite boulders toward the flashlights. Along the far rim of the quarry the lights moved idly, catching the glint of water, the dim shapes of trees, the scissoring shadows of legs. Several weak beams were trained on the notched overhang where a figure crouched to dive.*

"Go, Bill!" Val's voice rose above the general clamor. Catcalls, hoots, cheers. Early June: the quarry water was icy. Stunts were for the very drunk or the very brave or the desperate. "You can do it!"

A brief flash of bare buttocks in the play of flashlights. He heard the echo of the splash. After that, yowls and screams. Hessel's head broke the surface. Somebody beat on the bass drum Nicky had swiped from the band room.

Charlie pulled a breath and lowered his head to the window again. A sudden stir among the petticoats, and Marty's face mashed against the glass, her cupped hand mocking his own. He jumped.

"Shit!" He shook off the scare and grinned at her.

She rolled the window down. "Hey, Charlie."

He showed her the two unopened beer cans he carried in one hand. "Supply's getting low," he said.

"Charlie, Charlie. How you do come through."
She put a hand out.

"Uh-uh. You have to open up."

She looked past his shoulder. "Where's Val?"

"Watching Hessel make an ass of himself."

"You don't care, do you?" She looked up at him. In the moonlight her face was squinty and puffed.

"Care about what?"

"She's your date." She shook her head slowly. "Guys. You can have it any way you want."

He was afraid to say anything. A breeze made the hairs on his legs stand up; he shivered in his damp cutoffs. He put one foot on the hubcap and leaned against the rear fender. This had been one long spring, long all the way. The drumming and shouting went on around the bonfire at the quarry rim. Shadows reached and wavered. The echoes, though, were the spooky thing, the way the sound hit and came back hollow again in the darkness.

"Is he back yet?" Marty asked.

"No." He leaned in at the window. He could smell the clean shampoo scent of the dark curls as they spilled and hid her face. "Come on," he said. "Better tell Uncle Charlie."

She took a swipe at her eyes with the back of her hand. "Is Uncle Charlie drunk?"

"For sure. How about you?"

"I want to go home," she murmured.

"Really?"

"Know what? I could walk in the door completely blasted, and as long as I got my veil on straight for six o'clock Mass, my mom would say not one word."

He couldn't think. Did she want to go home or not?

"If she yelled at me she'd have to yell at my dad. So she takes a pass." She pushed the dark sweater off her shoulders. The pale skin gleamed up at him. "D'you like my dress, Uncle Charlie?"

So she had changed back into the dress. This was a strange thing to do, but he said only the truest thing he knew to say to her. "You look beautiful, Marty."

"Mrs. Finch made it for me. I told her, I want something I can wear for the prom, and then the wedding. . . ."

He bent to look at her. She was crying hard, the way he could bear the least. Silently, as if something had grabbed her and was shaking her like a kitten. He set the beers on the roof of the car. She would never break, he knew it, but sometimes he believed he would break for her.

"No wedding," she said, "I can tell you that. No Chicago, no wedding, no Nicky."

He felt a hammering begin in his chest. "Open the door, Marty."

She sat very still. "I'm lousy company, Uncle Charlie."

He hooked an arm through the window and lifted the lock button, opened the door. He grabbed the beers and ducked his head, shoving the passenger seat forward with an elbow, climbing into the backseat. He didn't give her time to argue or time to move. He landed partly on her, and partly on a petticoat that puffed out on either side of his bare legs.

She started to laugh.

"What?" he demanded, laughing too. "What?" He seized her hand and slapped a warmish can into it. He opened first hers and then his own; the foam spewed and dripped. She scrambled out from under him, pulling at her slippery skirts. Beer poured onto the gray upholstery. He mopped at it with a wad of stiff nylon lace.

"Your brother's car," she said.

He gave up the effort. "What Simon doesn't know won't hurt him." He moved his leg over the wet spot.

Marty threw an arm around his neck. "You're more wasted than I am, Charlie."

"No Chicago, no wedding, no Nicky. Do you mean it?"

"I mean it."

This time when she cried he was right there. Comforting her was so easy; he had never known anything could be so easy. For the first time in his life he could do nothing wrong. He recognized magic when he stumbled into it. Pebbles dropped in the woods got devoured, fingers of fog pointed the way and were never there in the morning. What he remembered afterward was her wet face, shampoo smell, the slide of satin on his legs, how he got lost in the rasp of crushed net and crinoline, how desperate he was to stay lost. And then someone was outside the car, some other girl crying, but she was outside and he was inside. He shut his eyes and kept his arms wrapped tight around the one he wanted. Hessel was out there somewhere, let him take care of everything else.

1

SOUTH OF ST. CLOUD, where County Road 8 turned into East River Road, Nick Uhler barreled the red rental Ford up the blacktop as if what he had in front of him were fair weather. He had set the windshield wipers batting away the snow at full speed, and he took the curve where the road swung nearest the river the same way. This road would change names three more times before it delivered him to the downtown bridge. By then he would have made a few changes himself. As Arnie Palmer would say, he was about to improve his lie. Nick smiled to himself. He liked the phrase. It had style.

A sudden blast of arctic air caught the Ford sideways and sent sprays of snow whirling across the windshield. Great patches of ice glazed the asphalt; easy to forget how bad winter could be out in this wide open prairie. Nick set his teeth into his lower lip and goosed the accelerator. What the hell. You were driving blind half the time anyhow. When the rear wheels spun, he kept his foot on the gas while the back end fishtailed. He had passed half a dozen cars ass-deep in snowbanks all the way from the Cities, but this was St. Cloud. This was East River Road. The little car jerked and gave him traction again, shot him clear of the snow shower like magic. Nick grinned. Home turf advantage.

Not ten minutes before, he had pulled in at the Amoco truck stop off Clearwater exit and phoned the St. Cloud Hospital, just to make sure. Yes, the doctor was in. Not until he had that nailed down did he get back into the Ford and haul it over to County Road 8 with a big grin on his face. He was being careful, and he congratulated himself. Careful wasn't his strong suit.

Charm was what Nick did best, how could he not know that? He hadn't lived to the ripe old age of thirty in the heavy traffic that came down in the Windy City for nothing. To work charm you had to have opportunity. *The doctor was in.* Now, speeding down the narrow road that looped beside the Mississippi, Nick figured he, too, was in.

He didn't slow down until the green of the sign showed itself on his left through the blur of snowflakes. *River Haven.* That was it. He made the turn with no trouble. With luck everything would go as easy as this.

Elizabeth would be surprised to see him. Betsy Wetsy he used to call her back in high school. Got away with it, too, and with a lot more. Only now, the beautiful Elizabeth was married to Dr. Simon Carmody. Think of that! Simon Carmody scoring off Old Man Fallon. Nick didn't remember Charlie Carmody's big brother being that flashy. He must have done some fancy work to nail the prettiest piece of expensive goods around. Little Miss Betsy Wetsy was maybe the only thing in town Old Man Fallon didn't own lock, stock and barrel. No doubt it was the *Dr.* in front of Simon's name that helped his case. What if he, Nick, had had that going for him? *Dr. Nicholas Uhler.* Laughing, he nearly jerked the car off the road. But, really, what was so funny? In his own way he made people feel better all the time.

•

Out of the car and up the wide stone steps of the front porch. *Don't think about it.* His special talent was keeping it fresh—the most honest thing about him, as a matter of fact. And it paid off. Nothing ever sounded like a line until after, and that was long after, into dust-settling time.

The front porch was huge, bigger than the front half of the house he used to live in with his mother. Nick took in the beveled glass surrounding the carved door. In Chicago that glass would be sheer stupidity, but in the woods outside the grimy gritty granite city, who cared? Who'd bother? He pushed the bell. The look on her face when she opened the door made him know he'd been right all the way.

"My God," she said.

He gave her his best smile. "Do I get to come in?"

"Nicky, what are you doing here?"

"What do you think?" he countered. "I'm up from Chi Town to see my Bets—"

He started to make his move, but she was backing away. The rubber wedges of her shoes made small sticking sounds on the black-and-white tiles. And then he was looking at her middle, at the distended ball that jutted forward under a kind of tent. He knew his special grace lay in being able to pick up on the things women needed to hear, right down to the key words that would tumble all the locks. "Beautiful," he said. "You look just beautiful."

Her smile was faint. "I'm due the end of January."

"How is everything?"

"I have what I want."

And in that moment he knew she would come through for him. He always got the signal early. Early or not at all. He gave her the full bath—eyes looking straight into hers, voice like the velvet collar on her dress. "I almost didn't stop," he said.

"You shouldn't have."

"I stayed away from St. Cloud a long time because of you. Do you believe that?"

She laughed. "In a way." Then, dropping her voice, she said, "Simon's mother is here."

"Nellie? She's nuts about me. We're buddies from way back. Where is the little lady, anyway?" Smoothly he eased himself through the door and into the foyer.

"She's lying down. She lives here."

"Lots of changes, huh? Guess I've been gone longer than I realized."

She looked at him with those knockout green eyes. "I don't know why you're here at all. If I was going to hear from you, Nicko, it should have been before now."

"What are you talking about?"

"I wrote you a letter," she said. "Are you going to tell me you didn't get it?"

"What letter? When?"

She drew a breath. "I guess you have to keep on the move a lot."

"If I'd heard from you I would have come run-

4

ning. Anytime. You know I would. Twelve years, and I still can't let you alone."

"If only the things you do were half as convincing as the things you say."

He took another step toward her. "Listen. Let's get in my car and go for a ride. We'll talk about it."

"It's the same thing all over again, isn't it? You want something. Why not just ask?"

"Okay, I'm in trouble. I got a guy looking for me, and if I don't settle up, I'll have a couple of things missing from my body the next time you see me."

To his surprise she laughed. "What things?"

"I'm serious, Bets. I need five thousand dollars. I need it in forty-eight hours, back in Chicago."

He watched it take effect, not encouraged by the way those eyes grew and grew. Christ, this was a small town. Five thousand didn't have that many zeroes in it as far as he was concerned. "Five thousand," he said again. "Baby, you got *lamps* in this place worth that much." He reached for her, pulling her to him, feeling the round shape of her stomach against his hip. This time she didn't move away. Still, her arms stayed at her sides.

"Nicko, I'd help you if I could. I don't have anything to give you."

He held on, while his eyes roamed the hall. Through the doorway he could see small red and blue rugs on the polished floor. He could see a carved antique table next to a marble fireplace. Under the table was a long-haired gray cat, its yellow eyes blinking in the half-light.

"Jewelry. Don't you have a ring or something? I could get it back to you after a little while. You know I would."

"Everything is in the safety deposit box."

"Since when?"

"Since I lost my mother's emerald bracelet last April."

"You didn't have insurance?"

"Of course. But my father was furious all the same. So Simon decided—"

"Yeah, okay, I get it, I get it." He tried to keep the small flare of anger contained in his head, keep it so it didn't reach his fingers where he was slowly working over the back of her neck.

She pulled back then to stare at him. "Do you get it? I wonder."

"Bets, I'm desperate. You got a checking account, don't you?"

She shook her head. "Not with five thousand, not even close."

"All right, then. What about Tom?"

"No. Not a good idea."

"Why?"

"Because. He's my brother. He'll want to know what it's for."

"It's your money, isn't it? Your trust fund. Just tell him it's an emergency."

She looked away from him, then let her eyes close.

There it was, the little collapse, the swoon that would line his pockets. Again he pulled her to him.

"You'll have to take me to the office," she said, her voice muffled against his chest. "I'm not supposed to be driving."

He helped her into the blue wool coat. "We're going for a spin," he said. "You haven't been with a driver this hot since 1976."

2

IT WAS STARTING TO SNOW again. A dusty covering lay on the cement ledges of the building across
the street. Tom Fallon picked up the telephone in
response to the blinking red light on his desk.

"Hi. Just a quickie. I wanted to remind you
about the centerpiece. Brisson's. It's all paid for, so
don't let them charge you twice."

Jeanne's voice came at him—high and very
brisk, in her checking-off mode. He could almost
see the list in her hand. He turned his chair around
to face the window, tilting it back so that he could
rest his heels on the wide, wooden ledge.

"Why don't you have them deliver it?"

"Honey, you go right by there on the way home.
I didn't think you'd mind."

"I don't mind, but the delivery's free. I could be
home setting out the luminaires—"

"The luminaires are out. They just have to be
lighted. The booze is on the back porch, the hors
d'oeuvres are in the refrigerator, the bar is set up,
everything's done."

"What do you even need a husband for?"

"I told you. To pick up the centerpiece." A tiny
silence. Then a burst of laughter. "Tommy, you
know me. I can't help it."

7

"It'll be fine. You give great parties, Jeanne."

"Not without cost. Do you know the songs well enough?"

"Listen, I know every carol in that book backward and forward. Ask the girls if you don't believe me. Anyway, everyone'll be stewed and singing nice and loud."

"Tom, if you let me down on this, I'll never forgive you!"

"Wife, I'm telling everyone at the party how you doubted me. And tomorrow morning I expect to be paid for my efforts."

"What does that mean?"

"Never mind."

A pause. "You won't forget the flowers?"

"Nope. I won't. See you about six."

He hung up and swung around from the window. He was in the mood for a party. He flexed his fingers and ran up and down some imaginary scales. *Ready or not.*

The door to his office opened wider and his secretary stepped inside. With Chris was Elizabeth. She offered her cold cheek as he came around the desk to embrace her. "Sweetheart, how are you?" he asked. "Feeling okay?"

"Fine." She made a small, dismissive gesture. Then her hands fell to the spot where her belly protruded beneath the blue coat.

"Come sit down. You want some coffee? I haven't seen you since—"

"Thanksgiving. Not that long. No coffee, thanks."

Two weeks. He tried to think back. A hectic day, as it always was with Dad; trying to keep peace between him and anyone he decided to pick a fight with. Erin this year. She had made the mistake of telling him that she wanted to get her ears pierced. He had raved on about that all through dinner, until Tom had finally picked up a turkey leg and threatened to pop the old man if he didn't leave her alone.

"She's seven years old, Dad, for Pete's sake!"

"Exactly! So why does she want to get herself up like some cheap gypsy tramp with things dangling from her ears?"

"Not cheap, Dad," Jeanne said. "Believe me."

To hell with them if they wanted to argue the day away. After dinner he and Simon had retired to the den to play chess. Had Elizabeth looked so pale then?

He said, "Isn't it too cold for you to be running around town?"

"I'm not running around town. Anyway, I wanted to see you."

"You're going to see me tonight. Aren't you?"

"Yes, of course. This is . . . something else." She settled heavily into one of the upholstered leather chairs. Tom leaned against the desk. *Oh, shit,* he thought. *What now?*

"Tommy. If I needed money, would you give it to me?"

He looked at her pinched face, wishing suddenly that he were sitting behind his desk, where he could at least feel that he had some advantage. "Goddammit," he said wearily.

She was not a time waster when she knew what she was after. "I need five thousand dollars," she said.

"Five thousand." He had said it as neutrally as he could. A sudden flush of color came into her cheeks. In contrast Tom felt his own energy level begin to drop. He got up and moved to a new position behind the desk. He meant to wait her out. He was always meaning to wait things out, but it was not in his character to be patient. A liability in a lawyer, he knew that. It had been shown to him on a number of occasions. "What in hell do you need five thousand dollars for?"

"I can't tell you."

This moved him suddenly to action; he began to pace in front of the window. "Well, okay, let me guess. Christmastime. You want to buy Simon a present. Or maybe it's Dad. Yes, that's it, I'll bet. Or something you need for the baby. . . ."

Elizabeth stood up. "Tommy. No lecture, just an answer. Yes or no."

"Why no lecture? Just waltz in and ask good old big brother, no explanations necessary, what the hell, he's loaded. Well, news flash, I'm not. I don't have an extra five thousand lying around, and I can't just pull it out of the trust fund without a reason. What am I supposed to tell the executors?"

Her face went pale again, and she sat down in the chair. "No lecture and no questions. I don't care what you tell them."

He walked quickly to her side. "Elizabeth. Are you all right?"

"I have a problem to solve. That's all that's wrong."

"You sure?"

"I'm sure."

Something about the firm set of her shoulders, her matter-of-fact tone, made his heart contract.

"This'll be over soon," she said. "I'll make it up to you, Tommy."

He put out a hand. "All right. But after Christmas we need to have a talk. After the baby's born."

She nodded and covered his hand with hers.

"Because this is not a gift, understand? This money is not a gift." He went to his desk, wrote the check, and held it out to her. "Promise me you'll hold it until Monday. Please. I want you to think this over. Will you do that?"

Without a word she came to him, slipping her arms around his middle. His own arms went around her shoulders, and he returned the hug with the familiar sensation of joy and shame. Another black mark against his soul; another secret to be kept from Jeanne. Jesus, would he ever be out from under?

She pulled away, then, lifting her head to look him in the eyes, "You are the dearest thing in the world to me."

He marveled at the sweetness of that child's face. But she was no child; she was twenty-nine years old. And married, so why should he still be the dearest thing in the world to his sister? It was just that they had been in league for so long. Secrets were a way of life. Too many things had to be kept out of their father's grasp. Looking into Elizabeth's china-doll eyes, he had a sudden, brief spasm of grief for their mother. If she were alive, Elizabeth would not be here in his office, he knew that. His mother would have known how to handle his sister, would have known how to handle everything. And then he would not be always trying to figure out how to mother her, and always, always failing at it.

"You look tired," he said. "Do you feel well enough to come tonight?"

She laughed. "I wouldn't miss a party for anything, Tommy. You of all people ought to know that."

She was folding the check carefully between her fingers. She slipped it into her pocket as she walked toward the door. And then she was gone.

Tom went to the window to stare down at the traffic on Fifth Avenue. Foot traffic, mostly; not many cars moving. A red car idling next to the curb. He tried not to feel he'd been had, tried also not to worry. What good would it do?

After Christmas. Things would be better; less hectic. And maybe it was nothing to worry about, after all. *Tom, you dreamer, you.* He could almost hear his father's voice in his ear. Well, he knew a number of ways to banish that bad luck charm. He checked his watch. He had twenty-five minutes before his next appointment. He caught sight of Elizabeth on the icy sidewalk below—hatless, her coat blowing open. *Give it up, Tom. You can't button her coat for her.* He turned away from the window.

3

NICK SMOKED THREE CIGARETTES while he kept
the Ford's motor running. Parked outside Tom's
offices he watched people blow by in their cars. He
watched pedestrians, with their facemasks and
padded coats and long scarves, walk unseeing past
his window. Christ, St. Cloud was the perfect spot
for crime. Nobody saw anybody in the winter
weather, and if you did see them, you couldn't
recognize them. In the wintertime this was the
perfect place for every crime except rape, and
rape didn't interest him. He could never see the
angle. Sex? Jesus God, he'd never needed much
leverage for that, and besides, there was no money
in it. A low-life way to go, no money and no class.
What was keeping Elizabeth? Relax, now, relax
and wait it out. Shit, it was a waste of time being
nervous, nobody was going to pay him for that
either.

He watched two old women go by, clinging to
one another for balance in their long down coats,
looking like stuffed marshmallows and steaming
their breath out the top. They made him think of
the nuns at St. Dunstan's. So handy with their
snappy little foot-rulers. It was a real job to imagine them naked, but that's what he'd spent his

time doing in kindergarten. Did other kids do that? Maybe he was an oddball. Actually the nuns deserved it, for the time they had made him take down his pants in Sister Agatha's office, then called his mother. What was his mother supposed to do? She had cried. From then on, for every whack of the ruler he ever got from them, he said in his head, *I've seen you naked!* And he never cried. Why was what they did to him so different from what his old man used to do? Figure that one out.

A furry-jacketed woman crossed in front of his car, wearing a thick scarf wrapped around her throat and head. Who could tell if she was even human? When it got this cold you forgot about everything else and dressed for survival. Exactly. So maybe he'd stay put and wear his snowmobile suit around St. Cloud until he could figure something out. Just go walking around this pedestrian mall the city fathers were so proud of. Killing time with all the city mothers. After all, Chicago was a long way away.

When he saw Elizabeth come through the doors of the old red-brick building on the corner and stand looking for him, he moved to put the car in gear. *She* looked human, all right, the wool coat gapping open around her middle. God, he should've rented a Cadillac. But her old man could do that for her. A big car wasn't what juiced her.

He held his patience for once, waiting while she got in beside him. "How'd you make out?"

She didn't say anything for a few breaths. Then she wriggled her hands inside her coat pocket and brought out a wrinkled check.

He took it from her fingers, careful not to snatch it, and looked at the numbers. Five thousand, all right, made out to Elizabeth Carmody. He ran his eyes over Tom's signature. All those spiky Fallon flourishes, just like the old man. A family with bucks! Sweet trait in a woman. He slipped it into his pocket.

"A personal check!" He nearly sang it. "That's one hell of a big brother you got yourself. This calls for a celebration, am I right? Is the old caramel-corn place still going?"

"Nicky, I haven't been there in years."

Her face told him that was a mistake on Dr. Simon's part. "Then it's caramel-corn city, right after we go to the bank."

She leaned back against the seat. "Tom asked me not to cash it right away."

He pulled out the check and looked again. Tom the fuckhead had postdated it. December eleventh, next Monday. He slapped the steering wheel with both palms.

"What? What's the matter?"

"Nothing. Just a little problem, about a one-minute problem."

"Nicky, take me home."

"Tired? I can fix that. You know I can." From the inside pocket of his overcoat he drew out a small rolled plastic bag. She had her eyes closed, so he opened one of her fists and closed her fingers around the bag with its small red caps.

Her eyes came open. "I don't want them."

"Make you feel better. Absolutely guaranteed."

She looked at what she held in her hand. "Not with the baby. I don't want anything."

He took the bag and pushed it into her coat pocket. "Keep them for later. A little present from Nicky, okay?" He put the car in gear and started

15

forward. "You just endorse the check for me. I'll take care of the rest."

"I don't have a pen."

He drummed his fingers on the steering wheel, a continuous rhythm. "I'll take care of that too."

•

In the St. Cloud post office he stationed himself beside the change-of-address blanks and the ballpoint pens on chains—thievery was all around you. He was just in step with what the world expected, is all. When all three clerks were busy with their patrons he gave the pen he was pretending to use a quick jerk, and walked out the double glass doors. He'd left the car parked right in front beside the yellow curb line, and when Elizabeth saw him heading straight for her, she rolled down her window. He grinned and handed her the pen with its short tail dangling. She looked at it and laughed. *All right!* That was more like it. She signed and he walked back into the post office to the table. On the face of the check he added one slanting stroke to the date, changing December 11 to December 4. The four looked a little skewed, but it would pass. He turned the check over and, underneath the scrawl of Elizabeth's signature, wrote *Nicholas Uhler*. Then he approached the last lady in the line, one in a fur coat with brown-paper-covered packages. He leaned inside the orbit of her perfume.

"Could I trouble you for change for a dollar?"

Gallantly he offered to hold her packages while she rummaged her purse for change. Here was one of those good Minnesota ladies who took on responsibility the way locomotives took on water. One more minute of search and he waved away her efforts. "I'll settle for two quarters," he said, handing her his dollar.

She blushed with uncertainty, turning to point across her own bulk. "I think there's a change machine in the box area—"

But Nick was keen on the beauty of his gesture. "I'd rather have your quarters."

"But—"

"No, no, I insist." He liked himself and her better as the flush of confusion and pleasure deepened on her fat face. Happiness so cheap and he knew how to give it away by the raft-load. Why can't a guy make an honest buck at what he knows how to do?

He fed the change into the copy machine in the lobby. On the other hand, who would have ever believed you could walk into a town you hadn't seen for twelve years and walk out again with some of its oldest and best money? The machine whirred and glowed green and he made copies of the check, front and also back, where his and Elizabeth's signatures looped and sloped. He examined the second copy as it arrived in the slot. His name and Elizabeth's. *What's wrong with this picture?* Nothing he could see.

He folded the photocopies and slipped them inside his coat, then put Tom's check in his opposite breast pocket. He gave both places an affectionate pat. A check for five thousand was a thing of beauty. He never did like to let something beautiful slip through his fingers.

4

SIMON FINISHED HIS ROUNDS, making a note to
check back on the young woman in 412. He didn't
have time tonight, but on the other hand if he
didn't do it, one of the nurses would get to her first.

He glanced at his watch. Five thirteen; he'd be
late getting home. He let out a shallow breath and
then felt his jaw set. Thinking of his teeth then,
about the layers of enamel he was grinding away
every night of his life, he felt a sudden panic that
reached all the way down to his groin. It was all
like this, surfaces grinding away down to where
the nerves would sing like nightingales baked in a
pie. Blackbirds. Singing of the heat, the caking
down of fluids, bird flesh into meat pie.

He let his jaw hinge open, worked it loose.
When the pie was opened . . . Seven years of surgical practice, and he knew how the body worked.
Nothing like the bloody-minded German Catho-
lics for teaching you that.

The young woman in bed 412A had the kind of
fairy-tale beauty he used to imagine in his adoles-
cent fantasies. A pale princess with streaming
black hair; he'd be the knight with the white lance
kneeling at her feet. This vision had so occupied
him all through high school that dating seemed

beside the point. The farm girls he'd gone to school with were big strapping blondes with rosy cheeks. All that German blood. Built for this part of the country, all right, with the musculature for getting up and chopping wood for a morning's kettle of coffee. Not exactly princess material. This woman—a girl, really—was the exception. Fragile and petite, like Elizabeth. He had a sudden thought of his wife, lying in bed early in her pregnancy, deathly afraid of throwing up. Nibbling saltines, even though a saline mixture would have worked faster. She shouldn't have been having salt. You couldn't tell her anything, though. He felt his jaw set again.

"Miss Brandon?" He glanced at the chart. "Susan?"

She had been waiting for him. Her great eyes pooled and filled as she stared up at him. He noted the small blue patches underneath each eye as tears slid down her cheeks.

He sat on the foot of her bed. "It's all right."

"No, it's not," she said dully. "I've still got it, don't I?"

"You were lucky. You could have killed yourself and the baby."

She covered her face with her hands and began to sob quietly. Simon pulled a clean handkerchief out of his pocket. Leaning forward, he handed it to her.

"I don't care!" she said. "I don't want this damn baby. I shouldn't have to have it if I don't want it!"

"I agree," he said. "But there's a better way than the one you tried."

The girl took her hands away from her face.

"Look, this is a Catholic hospital," he said. "And

you're going to get Catholic counseling here, whether you want it or not. When the nurses are through with you, and if you still want an abortion, you call the Family Planning Service. Marty Voigt's a good person to talk to. Can you remember all that?"

The girl blinked away the tears, nodding. "Marty Voigt," she whispered.

"The number's in the book. The nurses will give you the Birthright number, but you remember the Family Planning Service," he repeated, getting up. "Matters of faith you can settle afterward, in the confessional if you need to. Medical matters won't wait."

He heard the nylon rustle as Sister Ernst's shoes squeegeed to a stop behind him. He made a note on Susan Brandon's chart and handed it to the nun. "First priority for this young woman is rest. No visitors for twenty-four hours."

"Of course, Doctor, but the priests are making their rounds. A few minutes is all—"

"Absolutely no visitors for twenty-four hours until we see that she's clear of infection." Looking at the broad, impassive face, he recalled Sister Ernst's particular stubbornness. He rarely had to think about using a bedside manner, except with hospital staff. Now he made his voice almost tender. "There's plenty of time, Sister."

"But this is Father Precant's night. He does parish visiting on Tuesdays."

He kept his expression steady. He watched Sister Ernst's eyes flicker down.

"He'll stand at the door and give a silent blessing, then."

"That would be good of him."

21

•

Five forty-seven. In the dark Simon pulled up in
front of the small convenience store on Wilson,
parking directly in front of the door. The walk
hadn't been shoveled yet, but the steps were clear
under the small overhang. He took them two at a
time.

Inside the storm door was the front door of a
house, which is what the place had been until Boz
Voigt opened up a neighborhood market in his
own living room thirty years ago. Now the store
took up all of the ground floor and Boz let Marty
use the sloped upper story as an apartment. The
OPEN sign, with its clock and hands, flapped
against the door as Simon shut it behind him.

He picked up a *St. Cloud Daily Times*, rolling it
automatically as he turned up the aisle to the ho-
siery display. His eyes flicked down the color
chart: nude, suntan, black.

"Need any help?" Marty Voigt came down the
aisle toward him, carrying a carton of disposable
diapers.

"No," he said, and heard the tone that he used at
the hospital. "Thanks, anyway."

She could probably lay hands on exactly what he
was looking for, but the point was, he could deci-
pher the system himself. That was what systems
were for. He checked the backs of the packages;
pictographs of weight against height.

"I saved some of that special tea for you." She
handed him a box of cranberry tea. "It was going
fast."

"Thanks." Again, his tone was short, and he
tried to soften it. "Sorry. Tough day."

"You know it." Marty Voigt had a very pretty

smile, a healthy glow to her skin. For what seemed like the first time he noticed the mop of dark curls around her face. When he had been looking for a princess to rescue, she'd been invisible—much too young. Yet Elizabeth was younger. He'd bided his time, that was all, and married late. Married Elizabeth! After the knight had carved a place in the world, it seemed he did get to claim for himself a real princess. So, as far as he was concerned, Marty Voigt was still invisible.

"A few minutes ago the service got a call for me," she was saying from the register. "A Susan Brandon, from the hospital."

They were alone in the store; he shouldn't have been surprised that she'd mention a referral. Still, he didn't want to discuss it now. "Can we talk about this another time? This really has been a long day."

"Sure. Sorry." She reached for the package of tea and rang it up.

Damn. Now he'd hurt her feelings. He hadn't meant to do that. He liked her well enough, it was just that he didn't have time for all this.

"Thanks for saving that for us, Marty," he said. "I'm trying to keep Elizabeth off caffeine entirely if I can."

Forgiven. Marty was all concern now. "She's all right, isn't she?"

"It's a struggle. I wanted her in the hospital where Ken Rice could keep an eye on her, but she wasn't having it."

"She should take care of herself."

"Yes. Well, she doesn't want to give anything up. You know how it is. I've got my opinions, but I have to live with her." He stopped himself. What would Elizabeth think of this conversation? "People have to make their own decisions. That's what it's all about, right?"

"Last time I heard," Marty said, picking up the other package. "Four dollars even."

Simon handed her the bills and picked up the bag on the counter.

"Merry Christmas."

"Same to you."

•

In the driveway he checked his watch: six ten. Thirteen minutes from the store to the house, even with ice on the road. Not bad.

Reaching into the glove box he pressed the switch on the garage-door opener. Nothing. All the machinery in the world, half of it in continual disrepair. This morning the lateral X-ray apparatus, this afternoon an overhead spot in the OR. Minor things, not his job. Simple housekeeping regulations would take care of the light problem; the policies existed, but the light bulb didn't. So what could you do?

He pulled the sheepskin glove from his right hand and reached again, pressing hard. The big door jerked, then rolled up smoothly. He saw Elizabeth's Camaro, parked in the exact spot where it had been this morning. *Good girl.* She hated not being able to drive around by herself. Thank God Ken Rice had taken the rap on that one.

He picked up the small paper bag and retrieved the opener from the glove box. Climbing out, he shut the door of his car with care. A good, solid door, it closed almost of its own weight. Nothing gave away a history of cheap cars like somebody who got out of your Lincoln and slammed the door like it was the lid on a garbage can.

In the utility room he opened the cupboard and took the screwdriver from its holder.

"Simon, is that you?"

"It's me, Ma."

He pushed past the spare flashlight batteries on the lower shelf to the ones he needed—double A's. He dumped the opener unit and the box of batteries on the dryer.

"I wish you'd speak up when you come in. I never know who's in this house with me." Her voice grew loud as she came to track him down. "Sometimes I feel like I'm in a shopping mall, trying to keep an eye on all the exits."

"You don't need to do that, Ma."

"Who says I don't?" She came to look over his shoulder. "What's that you've got there?"

"Nothing."

"No need to bite my head off."

He shifted his feet, bending to unscrew the plastic cover of the opener.

"If you ask me, the two of you have no business running off to a party on a bitter night like this. I've told her. Now I'm telling you. What's that?" She was eyeing the box of tea. "A proper cup of tea is a comfort. This stuff tastes like boiled grass."

Simon grinned. She was in a worse mood than he was. It helped him to relax. He said, "It's better for her, Ma. You know that."

She avoided his eyes and shook out a linen dish towel that had been lying next to the wash basket. "All this care that has to be taken," she grumbled, as if to herself. "She's only pregnant. It's not a disease. Don't they teach people that in medical school?"

He sighed. "Take these stockings up to her, will you? Tell her I'll be up in two minutes."

"And don't think I can be seeing where she is every living minute of the day. She takes a notion and she's out the door, you know. I get up from my nap today and no Elizabeth. Gone for a good half hour. Then, who comes trudging up the driveway? Out for a walk, she says. What if she'd taken a fall at the mailboxes? Who'd know it? Nobody can look after a person who won't use the sense God gave—"

He put a firm hand on his mother's arm. She shook it off.

"You pay too much attention to some things," she said darkly, "and not enough to others. Ever since you started growing up."

"What is it you're trying to tell me?"

"You know very well. You were fifteen years old when I begged you not to go with your dad—"

"Oh, Lord."

"You wouldn't listen. And what happened? In that freezing rain you sat in a duck blind all night, you sat in an open boat all morning, and the next time I saw you, you had double pneumonia."

"And you nursed me three weeks, night and day. . . ."

" 'Don't worry, Mother,' you told me. 'We've got the tarpaulin, and we can build a fire. I dipped the matches in paraffin,' you told me. Paraffin! For all the good it did, with Mike Carmody soused up like a Christmas fruitcake."

"Hand me that battery, will you?"

"All your father ever taught you was to kill

26

things and then track muddy boots across my carpet. And to cut up a living fish—is that a lesson to pass on to a child?"

He set the battery between the prongs and snapped the case back together.

"Your brother showed more sense than you did that day. Seven years old, and he knew not to leave the blind in a rainstorm. And if he hadn't been there to give you his dry jacket, you would have died, Mr. Paraffin Matches. Your dad would have got you killed a hundred times." She shook her finger at him. "Fifteen years old. I put a stop to it."

"Except we're still talking about it."

But she turned away, her mouth drawn tight.

"You're invited to this party, you know," he said. "I don't see why you won't come along."

"It's not my kind of party."

"What does that mean?"

"Nothing." She picked up the package of stockings.

He followed her into the kitchen with the *TV Guide.* "Let's see if there's a movie—"

She snatched the magazine from his fingers and slapped it down on the table. "I can still read, thank you."

Simon looked hard at her. In quite a different tone he said, "Take the stockings up, Mother."

She lifted her chin. Oddly enough this was her signal for giving in. She clutched the package to her bony chest. NO NONSENSE. He could read the label just above her arms. Her hands showed blue veins across the knuckles. "That's one thing your brother Charlie knows," she said.

"What?" he asked, caught again. God, but she was good at that!

"What to pay attention to."

•

He went up the stairs loosening his tie. Slipping off his shoes, he chose another shirt and tie and headed for Elizabeth's dressing table.

She sat in front of the mirror, putting on eye shadow. Among her cosmetics he caught sight of a half-empty bag of caramel-corn. He fought down the feeling of irritation as he kissed the top of her head.

"I thought that was you," she said. "Your mother is generally much more quiet when she comes padding up on her search-and-destroy missions."

"Where did that popcorn come from?"

"Jeanne and the girls, the other day."

He stared at his wife in the mirror. He saw her pink flesh pushing out around the black brassiere. *Edema. Getting worse.*

"I wish you wouldn't snack," he said calmly.

"You wish I wouldn't snack. You wish I wouldn't drive. What else, Simon?"

He bent to kiss the crown of her head. She ducked.

"I don't mean to fuss." He sighed. "I just can't help myself, you know that." His eyes held hers in the mirror. He reached into his pants pocket and brought out a wine velvet box. "Look what I brought you for tonight," he said, opening it.

Seated on white satin, the gold bracelet with its five large cabochon diamonds sparkled.

She snapped the box shut. "I've decided to wear something cheap. Something nobody wants to take away from me."

28

"Elizabeth. We've been all through this. You agreed—"

"I didn't. I wasn't consulted."

"You agreed that this deposit-box arrangement was the only way to keep peace in your family."

"There is no peace in my family." Elizabeth pushed her shoulders back and nestled into his body. Tears filled her eyes. "Simon. Why did you marry me?"

He let his hands drop to her shoulders. "What a question. Because you were the prettiest girl I'd ever seen. I wanted you all to myself." In the glass he saw himself grow solemn. "I still do."

"And when there's three of us?"

"These things happen." He smiled at her then, and pushed her gently forward until she sat straight. "Besides, there already are three of us, remember?"

She gave her rosy chest two puffs from a crystal atomizer. Then she puffed a shot in his direction and he jumped back. "Goddammit!" He brushed at his shirtfront. "You're unpredictable tonight, aren't you?"

Putting her hands on the vanity top she pushed herself up off the chair. Simon watched her walk away, meaning to inspect the veins on the backs of her knees. But she was wearing stockings already; pink shimmery stockings.

"Sweetheart," he said, "I sent Mother up—"

"Support hose," she shot back, without turning. "They were black. I'm wearing pink." The last word came out like the top note of a piano keyboard. "You don't get to prescribe my underwear, Doctor. It's not a goddamn funeral we're going to, it's a goddamn party!"

She stood glaring at him, her eyes brimming again. Simon raised both hands. "I'll meet you downstairs. Take your time."

He got out of there. On the stairs he fought down the knot of feeling. He had to get hold of himself. A tricky balance: husband, physician. He had to get it right.

5

"AH, YOU'RE HERE!" cried Jeanne gaily. "Come in, you two, it's freezing out there!"

Elizabeth embraced her, glad of her sister-in-law's warmth. Yet she felt herself being passed too quickly on. Tom stood ready for her coat, and some defiance made Elizabeth throw her arms around her brother and hug him fiercely. All the while he held her, she could feel him trying to make way for Simon. She hung on anyway. She and Tom looked foolish, she supposed, since that came so easily to them both. Brother and sister now both had short, portly figures with round bellies. She started to giggle. She needed somebody to hold on tight to, somebody to keep her on the ground. All the way in tonight Simon had listened to *All Things Considered* as though the discussion of inner-city police and domestic violence could have the slightest bearing on their lives.

"Two turtledoves!" Jeanne said. "Where's the partridge in the pear tree?"

Elizabeth felt tears rise. She dropped her arms. Right in front of Tom and Jeanne the tears let loose. She clapped both hands to her face and rubbed them away. She saw Jeanne's look.

"These long days, you know." The voice was Simon's, the hand on her shoulder, Simon's.

Taking a deep breath she forced herself to smile. "The old prepartum blues, right, Doctor?" Looking to Simon for support. He nodded for her. "I'll just take my coat to the girls' bedroom, all right?"

"Fine," Jeanne said.

She started down the dim hallway. The doorbell rang, and Tom gave his nervous laugh.

"Molly will ask you if the baby is here yet!" he called after her in a cheery voice. "Same old suspicious Molly."

She took a quick right into the bathroom and closed the door. At the basin she ran cold water and splashed her face. Her mascara had run, and she'd smeared her pink lipstick. She stared at herself in the oval mirror and felt a ripple of shock. She looked *tartish*. That was the only word. No, her father would have others: painted gypsy whore. What had she been thinking of, with her makeup job and pink stockings and pink crystal beads?

Well, she had been thinking that she felt young, felt *good* tonight, for a change. That had been Nicky's doing.

Her stomach gave a turn, and she sighed. She no longer knew if that turning feeling was herself or the baby. She looked at her smeared, pouty mouth as another tear spilled down her cheek. She picked up a tissue and went to work on both.

She knocked softly on the closed door at the end of the hall, then turned the knob and pushed the door open. She heard a scurrying and a scuffling as two small bodies dived into their beds. She laughed.

"Hey, you two, it's only me."

The girls sat up in their beds and shrieked, then dived back under the covers and swam to the footboards of their beds.

Elizabeth sat on Molly's bed and waited until the giggling subsided. She arranged her stomach to cause her the least discomfort. "No chase games tonight," she said.

Erin, the elder at age seven, sat up and fought her covers down around her. The form in the other bed turned and lifted, then after a search, finally fell off the edge. Elizabeth caught her breath, but Molly rolled from underneath the counterpane and got to her feet. She made for her aunt like a streak.

"Did you have the baby yet?"

Elizabeth laughed, looking into the girl's earnest face, lighted by the Donald Duck night-light beside her bed. Erin had Fred Flintstone. "Not yet," she said. "Want to feel it move?"

The girls came to her at once, their small, eager hands roving her belly.

"I feel it!" Molly squealed.

"Do not!"

"Shhhh," Elizabeth cautioned them. "Listen, I came to ask a favor. Is it okay if I leave my coat in here while I'm at the party?"

"Sure!"

33

"Put it on my bed, Auntie Elizabeth!" Molly patted a place.

She stood and sorted out her things. "My hat and this long scarf and my mittens will go on Erin's bed," she said. "And this big, woolly coat goes on Molly's, how's that?"

Molly looked up at her. "Erin gets three things, I only get one."

"But the coat is a very big thing."

Molly frowned at the items stacked on Erin's bed, and Elizabeth remembered herself and Tom, back under all those Christmas trees of childhood, counting presents. What mattered was the number, not the size.

"Wait. Let me show you something," she said. "I've put my beads in my coat pocket."

She found the side slit and drew the necklace out. The glass facets glittered in the combined light of Donald Duck and Fred Flintstone.

"Pretty!" Molly breathed. Erin came to look and Elizabeth placed the necklace over each girl's head in turn. *They* were young enough to find it beautiful. She loved the way the small heads grew still, waiting for the honor of wearing a grown-up's jewels. She'd coveted her own mother's necklaces; the feeling came back. All feelings came back sooner or later, that was the trouble.

In a brisk voice she said, "Now both of you— back into your beds! And when the party's over, I'll come in and kiss you while you're sleeping."

"I won't be sleeping," Erin said. "I'll be guarding the stuff."

"Me too," Molly said.

She laughed. "You two are a big help. I'm counting on you for that when the baby comes."

She blew them each an extra kiss from the door. Coming down the hallway, which now seemed bright around her, she felt melted with affection for her two small nieces. This was the sanest, richest feeling of all. Oh, she could hardly wait to have a child. *A baby!* As long as she got to trade these rotten feelings in on one of her very own, then okay.

•

She entered the living room, squinting, noting with a decided lurch in her stomach that people were smoking. She held her breath and headed through the knots of familiar faces. Letting out her breath to say, "End of January," to the question that followed her through the room. Yes, the baby was due January thirtieth. "Great!" she said again and again to the other question. She wanted the baby so much. She was feeling great if she could forget the tight pulling of her tendons under its weight, if she could forget the pushing of the baby in its bubble of water up under her ribs, if she could miraculously free herself from this terrible sense of fatigue. If she could get away from the cigarette smoke.

Millions of women got pregnant every day, and they had discomfort like this. They lived. Millions of them always told you how happy they were for you and how they never remembered the pain of childbirth afterward. "It's worth it," they always added. So which way was it? Did they remember or not? Elizabeth remembered. "It's worth it" was becoming a phrase that she hated.

She made it to the kitchen, brushing past Jeanne, who stood next to the microwave oven, holding a tray between two red oven mitts. Elizabeth opened the storm door and held it wide, taking deep breaths of cold air. Her stomach stopped its fluttering. When she was fourteen she'd thought she would be a nun, bride of Christ. She had made herself a circlet of thorns from the bushes along the riverbank, and had kept it under her pillow. Every night she had faithfully pricked one of her fingers with it. That was before she found out about real pain. Before Nicky.

"I used to love to smoke," she said to Jeanne. "Can you believe that? God, I used to love a lot of things."

"Don't worry, it all comes back." Her sister-in-law looked down at her own plump figure and the tray of food she carried. She smoothed a strand of her blond hair away from her face. "Even the shape comes back—if you want it more than you want stuff like this. It's worth it."

Elizabeth smiled. Jeanne could tell her it was worth it, because *she* didn't pretend there was no such thing as pain, no such thing as cost. She just counted it all up and went on. If you wanted something badly enough you went for it and you found some way to balance what you lost. Her sister-in-law understood that. Still, there were limits with Jeanne. She had found that out too.

Elizabeth watched her balance the tray in one hand and pick up one of the little rumakis by its toothpick, watched her pop it into her mouth.

"Those actually smell good to me," Elizabeth said. "You know, there are times when I think I'll never be hungry again. At least, not for anything I'm allowed to have."

And suddenly there was Nicky's face before her. She shifted her gaze to the crucifix on the wall over the oven. Jeanne had one in the entryway, too, and another—this always struck Elizabeth as embarrassing somehow—over the double bed where she and Tom slept. But Nicky's face! Whatever was she doing, letting Nicky's face appear in Jeanne's kitchen? Good Lord, she wasn't going to cry again, was she?

Jeanne said softly, "I need to take these out while they're hot."

.

"Okay, everybody! Listen up!" Tom had taken the floor. "Time for the Christmas carols."

A happy murmur and general movement toward the organ followed his announcement. Across the room Elizabeth recognized Bill Hessel, the deputy sheriff. Bill and Tom had been friends since high school. He stood off in one corner, his dark head bent in conversation with a man she didn't know. Elizabeth made her way over to them. If her father were here, he would be making sure the guests did as they were told.

"The boss says it's time to sing," she said.

Bill looked up at her and grinned. "Hi, Elizabeth."

"We're having a fine time right here," the other man said.

The first minor strains of "What Child Is This?" hung plaintively in the air.

"*After* the singing." She caught Bill's arm and led him across the room, not looking behind to see if the other man was following. Gathering the stragglers: why did she think this was her job? Only the force of years, she guessed. She was her father's daughter, after all.

Standing next to Bill as Tom played, she kept her arm linked through his.

> *. . . whom angels greet with anthems sweet,*
> *while shepherds watch are keeping. . . .*

Such a beautiful song, so sad. It made her feel sad.

She stopped singing, to catch her breath. Bill's arm felt solid and comforting, and she gave it a squeeze.

"Okay!" Tom shouted, when the song was over. "You name it, I can play it."

" 'God Rest Ye, Merry Gentlemen'!" A voice rose over the others and Tom swung into the tune, bouncing on the round antique stool, playing the clown. They sang it at the top of their lungs, and Elizabeth, riding on the energy, felt that she loved this crowd, loved this party! She would have another one after the baby was born and invite these very same people, and it would be wonderful all over again!

They broke, laughing, and Jeanne was there with another tray of hot hors d'oeuvres. "C'mon, open your mouth and shut your eyes and live a little," Jeanne teased Simon.

Across the organ his eyes caught Elizabeth's and held. Did he refuse because of her, to set a good example? She hid her cup of rum punch behind this year's photo of Erin and Molly perched on Santa's lap.

Bill Hessel had returned to the corner and was sitting with Val. Elizabeth made her way over to them.

"Your husband can really belt it out!" she said, in what she thought was a friendly tone.

"How are you, Elizabeth?" A cool, tempered smile. Was Val annoyed with her for standing with Bill during the singing? Well, this couple wouldn't be invited to the postpartum party. She felt a giggle bubbling up inside her. And then, Simon was at her elbow.

"I brought you a drink," he said.

Sparkling mineral water in a wineglass, a thin slice of lemon floating on the surface. She took a sip of its coldness. As he started to move away, she went with him.

"Having a good time?" he asked, slipping an arm around her shoulders.

"I am. How about you?"

He raised his eyebrows, gave her a quizzical grin.

"I'm ready to leave whenever you are."

"What kind of answer is that?" Everything hit her so hard these days. "I don't want to go yet, Simon."

"Fine. I just thought you might be tired."

"Do I look it?" she asked, and before he could answer, turned away. She set the mineral water down on the coffee table and circled the room, smiling at every gaze she encountered, joining in when there was laughter, even though she had no idea what she was laughing at. At last she found herself near the entrance to the kitchen, and she pushed her way through the door.

What did she want, then? More of Tom's rum punch? Something more to eat? She was alone in the kitchen, and she leaned her head against the cupboard, closing her eyes, wrapping her arms tightly around herself. Yes! She wanted everything. She was starving for everything in the whole world. And that made no sense, made her feel like a spoiled little girl. Because she had everything, didn't she?

The door opened behind her and Tom's voice, not a baritone, but that clear tenor, was full of concern: "Everything okay, Pidge?"

The old nickname, from another time. She felt tears under her eyelids again.

"Fine, just fine."

She gave his fingers a squeeze, grinning at him.

"You sure?"

"Positive."

He went to the refrigerator, rummaging, coming up with four bottles of beer. He held them up by the necks, in one hand, as if waiting for her applause; then he was gone. She stood still, watching the door through which his back had disappeared. Then she moved to the black glass door of the microwave and opened the latch. Lifting them by their toothpicks, she could easily remove three rumakis with each hand.

6

NELLIE CARMODY OPENED HER EYES and felt the weight of the remote control in her hand. She set her teeth into her thin bottom lip and slowly prized her fingers off the oblong. Lord, this arthritis would kill her. She squinted at the screen, looking for the whereabouts of her favorite show. A seated man with silver hair went on talking and talking about something. Was this Johnny Carson? Surely not. Johnny Carson was a *young* man. What show was this?

She closed one eye and tried to see the little blue numbers on the TV. Too small. Who could read those teensy numbers made out of little straight lines? Not her, not her old eyes anymore. If they wanted you to know what time it was while you watched TV, why didn't they use clocks with hands to point the way?

She laid her hands on the padded arms of her rocking chair and rocked, forgetting about the bottle of sherry until it tipped forward and made three liquid glugs onto the carpet. She got her fingers around it and righted the thing. By then her hands shook and her heart was pounding like the Sheriff of Nottingham on her old ribs. What was that terrible noise? Not thunder, not now in the middle of winter—was it the garage door? Her mind grew terribly clear. She found the screw-cap on the table beside her knitting. She thrust it on the bottle and turned her glass upside down over the neck. Setting these inside her knitting bag, she packed them with skeins of wool.

Time to spare. She pulled a roll of fruit-flavored Tums from her cardigan pocket, and pushed a tablet around the inside of her mouth with her tongue. She picked up her bottle of fingernail-polish remover and, with an expert ear tuned toward the garage, opened the bottle and sprinkled a few drops in the area of the sherry spill. By the time the big automatic door came rumbling down, and then Elizabeth's high heels came clicking over the kitchen tile, she had the thumbnail and three fingers of her left hand clear of any trace of polish.

"Mother Carmody!" Elizabeth called out.

Nellie watched her totter across the carpet, catching those spindle heels in the shag loops. She frowned as the girl leaned over her chair back and patted both of her shoulders. She drenched another cotton ball.

"Off goes the pearl polish," Elizabeth said. "Well, how was everything else?"

She peered around at her daughter-in-law. The foolish pink face was more nearly white. Nellie narrowed her eyes. That her handsome son, with all the world to choose from, could have ended up with such a whey-faced creature! Even in pregnancy Nellie Carmody had kept her color.

"Friday night hasn't a thing worth watching, as you well know," she snapped.

"I hope you weren't too bored. It's a big lonesome house." Suddenly Elizabeth leaned on her chair, and the rocker groaned backward.

"Let go! What do you think you're doing?"

Elizabeth sucked a breath as she landed on the floor behind the chair. She started to giggle, and then to Nellie's consternation the giggles turned into sobs.

She heard the back door bang. "Hush!" she commanded.

But the girl's voice rose and fell, like singing.

"What are you thinking about, carousing till all hours? Simon, get yourself over here and get her upstairs!"

Her son wore a deep flush that reminded her of Mike Carmody.

"This is the month of December in the state of Minnesota!" she informed him in the hard voice that used to have some effect on his father. "There's nothing but ice and irresponsible drunkards on the roads! I want to point this out to you *children*!"

Simon bent and helped Elizabeth to her feet.

"I'm here to care for the baby that is to come!" she scolded. "Not three babies on my hands, thank you ever so kindly, I don't have the patience."

Elizabeth went up the stairs, leaning heavily into Simon. The sight of her son's arms around this girl filled Nellie with a bitterness that she could not name. Who would take such care of her in her lifetime?

She heard Elizabeth say, "I'm sorry, Simon, I'm sorry."

"I'll put some good strong tea on the fire," she called after them. "I've nothing better to do!"

Sorry was as good as Simon was going to get.

What a prize his little rich girl had turned out to be! Him who had wanted all his life to help humanity; she remembered him getting chased by his brother and that ruffian friend for saving picture-puzzle people. What a ruckus that had been! Simon was her little man; she'd sent him out to the garage in the rain to see about Charlie and the other. In no time all three had come running in, right through her kitchen, mad and dripping wet. Simon had their pieces, the little boys said, from their Indian war-puzzle. Simon denied it. But she'd found the pieces in his pocket when she went to do the wash, just the warriors' heads saved out. She knew then he'd be a doctor. So early on, his thought was to keep people from trouble and pain. Now here he was, with a spoiled wife on his hands. There was one could use help, all right.

She filled the kettle, banging it against the steel sinks as she tried to lift the heavy thing to the countertop. Too much water, the girl only needed a cup. But then maybe Simon could do with one, and come to think of it, she herself. A proper pot of tea. She poured water out into the sink, in a fury at the way her old hands shook. Finally she got the kettle over to the burner half-full of water, and the burner dialed up to high. She was too old for such as this. If her sherry had been nearer than across the half acre of this kitchen and den, she could have done with a drop. As it was, she closed her eyes and leaned with her back to the stove, to quiet herself while she waited for the water to come to the boil. Why did life go on and on? Where was Michael Dean Carmody and what had he meant by stealing off to death like the coward he was, leaving her to face all this by herself? It was not what she had expected at all.

When she opened her eyes it was on the sound of her son's hard fast footsteps on the landing, his voice screaming to her, and a kitchen full of steam.

7

THE HOSPITAL had never seemed like a very friendly place to her, but tonight was different. Even the light seemed different; warmer, somehow—a soft glow spilling across snow-covered lawns; all the windows lit up, welcoming her.

Funny how quickly things can change. One minute you are frightened and trapped, alone with your illness; then, suddenly, all of the knots unravel; a smooth, gentle slope of pain-free time rolls out and you are full of peace and goodwill. Elizabeth felt relaxed, drowsy. She lay with her eyes closed, thinking back over the evening. Wonderful party. Wonderful. She'd loved the singing best of all. Bill Hessel. Tommy, her big brother, at the reed organ. When had he learned to play so well? And wherever had Jeanne gotten that lovely instrument? Leave it to Jeanne to haunt every antique dealer in town until she turned up just the right piece. Clever, clever girl.

Tucked into the high bed, the sheets cool against her cheek, she had a sense that everything was moving very fast, but quietly, so quietly. And, except for Simon, she hadn't yet seen anyone she knew. Where was Dr. Rice? Ken. She wished that he were here with her now. He'd been so worried about her. She wanted him to know how well she felt. It would be good to see his boyish smile, those pink cheeks that always looked as if he'd been out in the cold. "He's a sweetheart," she had told her mother the other day. No. Not her mother. Jeanne, maybe. Yes, that was it. In one of their long, cozy talks in Jeanne's kitchen over cinnamon tea and muffins.

How she admired Jeanne's cleverness. The ease with which she took care of Tommy's house. It was like having an older sister, almost. Or her mother back. Almost, but not quite. Jeanne had her own ideas, her own way of seeing things. It's hard on people if you tell them things they don't want to know. She and Jeanne had grown apart lately. Why was that? She wasn't sure exactly. She'd have to fix it, though. Very soon. She wanted them to be close again.

This was how it would happen: Jeanne would come to see her in the hospital, bringing a gorgeous, thick baby-blanket woven in pinks and blues. To take the baby home in. A lovely day, cold outside, but the room would be sunny, full of flowers. Jeanne would tell her how beautiful the baby was—"just like his daddy!"

Thinking of that, Elizabeth smiled. She loved making pictures of the future. She had been doing it all her life. When she had first noticed Simon at the charity ball—was it eight years ago?—she had pictured him driving up on summer weekends to the lake cottage, seen the wedding reception on the lawn, even envisioned the two of them living in the Tudor house beside the river—all, all in that space of time it took him to walk across the floor and ask her to dance.

There had been a long while when she could not get a picture of a baby. How disquieting that had been; in her dreams she had seen Simon's handsome face always in profile, turning away from her, hiding from her. The side view of his head reminded her of a Roman coin—a patrician look that she had associated with her father. Well. She would have a new vision. Starting this very hour.

For instance, she could see Jeanne's blanket wrapped around the baby—she knew it would happen. And something else she knew—a secret almost too good to keep: it was a boy. She was certain now. Simon had wanted the amniocentesis done, but she had refused. There is always danger; why take any chance? Why have the test if you don't intend to do anything? And she wouldn't have. She wouldn't let this baby go. No matter what.

Simon will understand and he will forgive. I wanted us to have this baby. Don't be afraid, Simon. It will be all right. She should tell him that. But she was suddenly so tired, too tired to talk just now. Just thinking about this small person about to enter the world made her smile. The name she'd picked out for him: Patrick Simon Carmody. Patrick for her grandfather Fallon. Daddy will be so pleased. She had felt the baby moving inside her all through the singing tonight. He would be musical. Handsome, too, with dark hair and liquid brown eyes. . . .

They had never told her anything about the first one. Not even the sex. Better that way, they said. It's over and done with. A healthy baby. They had found it a good home.

And with that thought the golden light that

wrapped itself around her turned suddenly cold. The room itself was too cold, too quiet. She could hear her own heart beating; the baby's too.

Earlier, lying helpless and in pain across the bed, she had heard Simon talking on the phone, his voice low and urgent: "I'm sure she's in labor, Ken." She had wanted to contradict him, tell him there was something else going on, that it did not feel like labor at all. But if he were to ask how she knew that? No. Let him think what he wanted.

And there he was suddenly, staring down at her. Not his handsome self tonight. Or was it tomorrow already? She had somehow lost track of time. Maybe Ken Rice could help her find it. Both of them here, now; Simon still wearing his sport jacket from the party, and Dr. Rice in his hospital greens. Simon's face was white and strained. She wanted to tell them both to go away, she had important business here, she didn't have time. . . .

But they were both talking to her. It all sounded mushy and blurred. Talk slower, she wanted to say.

"We're going to take the baby, Elizabeth."

Take him where? No, you can't do that. He belongs to me. You can't take him, it's not fair. Not both. You can't take both of my babies and leave me with nothing. I won't let you.

It was Ken Rice telling her this in his soft voice; that young, young face. Too young to be a doctor, she had always thought, always meant to tell him. All the things she had meant to say were gathering inside her head, waiting to be sorted and spoken aloud at last.

There was too much going on here. The pictures were coming faster, now, and she was so very,

very tired; it took all her strength just to keep her eyes closed, in order to pay attention. Where was her daddy in these pictures? *Daddy, don't let them do this.* It isn't right to do this. A baby needs his own mother, his real mother. Somebody has to think about the baby this time. Who will think about the baby?

8

"I DON'T BELIEVE IT," Jeanne said. "Tom, it can't be. . . ."

Tom brushed past her, going down the stairs to the kitchen. "I've got to call Dad," he said.

She pulled her terry cloth robe more tightly around her, tying the belt. Her hands felt heavy and clumsy. She followed him down the stairs.

Glancing up at the clock on the wall, she saw that it was just after six. The ringing telephone had wakened them only minutes ago; yet it seemed to her that weeks had gone by. Tom had already dialed the number, was waiting for an answer. He stood with his back to her, facing the windows, drumming his hand on the gray countertop. Then, abruptly he hung up.

"Damn! He's got it turned off. I'd better go."

"What are you going to do?"

"Pick him up," he said.

She followed him back up the stairway as Erin came out of her room below. She had on her white shortie nightgown with the red hearts and red ribbons at the neck and wrists. Her face was flushed from sleep.

"What are you guys doing?" she asked.

Jeanne stopped at the top of the stairs. "Aunt Elizabeth . . ."

"Is she having her baby?"

No need to upset the children at this point. They didn't know anything for sure, did they? And it wasn't going to happen, it just wasn't.

"Yes," Jeanne murmured. "Go back to bed, Erin."

"I'll tell Molly!" Erin ran back into the bedroom and Jeanne went down the hall. Tom stood in his stockinged feet, pulling the green sweater over his shirt.

"What should I do?" she asked. "Should I come with you?

He shook his head. "I'll call you."

"As soon as you get there."

"Yes."

She went with him to the door, where Erin met them.

"Tell Aunt Elizabeth I love her lots," she said.

Without speaking Tom took his daughter's shoulders, pulled her to him in a fierce hug. Then he was gone. A moment later Jeanne heard the garage door go up, heard the muted roar of the Karmann-Ghia as he backed out. Why was he taking it? So cramped, if he was picking up his dad. . . .

She went to the stove and turned on the fire under the tea kettle. Again she glanced at the clock: ten minutes after six. She couldn't believe it. Only ten minutes had gone by since they'd been in here? Twenty since Simon had called from the hospital to say that Elizabeth was in trouble.

"Mom, I can't get Molly to wake up!" Erin

called. Jeanne went to the door of the dining room.

"Let Molly sleep, Erin!" she said.

"But I want to tell her about—"

"You can tell her later."

This wasn't happening. That's all there was to it. She wouldn't believe it, she just wouldn't. She had stopped things from happening before by simply not believing in them. She would do it again.

She got down her favorite cup—the one the girls had given her for Christmas last year—with the snow scene painted on it: JOYOUS NOEL in bright red letters. All of the evergreens had little yellow stars on the tops; a yellow half-moon hanging in a navy-blue sky. She took a teabag from the porcelain jar on the counter. Cinnamon Rose. Dropping it into the cup she poured boiling water over it; watched it brew, trying to think about only this, the fragrant tea steeping in her own warm, safe kitchen, while, outside, a gentle snow was coating the bare branches of the trees.

She had stopped the thing with Tom and Louise, hadn't she? Easily, oh, so easily. By refusing to believe in it. A friend—or someone she thought was a friend at the time—had told her about it, and at first she hadn't known what to do. But later, after she had thought it through, it was obvious. Nothing would happen, because she would not allow it. She and Tom had their life, and they would continue to have it. It wasn't necessary to become hysterical, or to confront Tom, or even to care about it; it wasn't necessary to do a thing but to go on as before. And she had done just that. And soon after, she had felt things changing with them; Tom stopped working late and became more attentive; they planned the trip to the Bahamas with the girls; he bought himself that toy car of his, and, in less than a year, Louise and Paul had moved to Virginia. She never doubted that she had done it. She would begin this moment to believe things right, to make things right.

"Mama." Erin stood in the doorway, her blue robe thrown over her nightgown. She had on loafers and long wool socks.

"Erin, why are you up so early? Go back to bed, now. I'll call you as soon as I hear anything." Jeanne blew into her teacup. The rose-colored liquid rippled gently.

"Molly won't wake up, Mama."

"Honey, why do you want to wake her up? It isn't even six thirty yet."

"Something's the matter with her," Erin said. "I can't make her answer me. And she's breathing funny."

Carefully Jeanne put the cup down.

"What do you mean, 'breathing funny'?"

"Snoring, sort of. She sounds like Grandma did. And her skin's real cold—"

Jeanne ran, still insisting with some part of her mind that she would not panic. There was no way in the world for anything to be wrong. It was impossible. With her alone here in the house, trying to hold things together, this was too much. As she lifted Molly's limp arms to carry her into the bathroom, she was thinking, Mary, Mother of Jesus, how could both of these things be happening? She struggled against the dead weight, bending over, trying for some leverage. Her hand caught in a length of beads around the little girl's neck, and the string broke, scattering pink crystals across the floor. Even as she sat on the edge of the bathtub, with Molly across her lap, rubbing the child's limbs, splashing her forehead with cool water, she knew this was a punishment, someone else's punishment that she had stumbled into.

9

TOM STOOD OUTSIDE THE EMERGENCY ROOM,
holding his father's overcoat in his arms, stalled
here in the hallway after what had gone on behind
those heavily padded doors. It was over. Simon
had left with Dr. Rice. Only one nurse and an
orderly remained, seeing to whatever duties were
theirs. Or maybe keeping an eye on the old man.

He had tried his best to get his father out of
there, but Terry Fallon seemed frozen to the spot
after his outburst.

"This is your fault!" Hurling the words at his son-
in-law, not caring who was there to hear. "You
knew she wasn't able to go through with this! You
knew how dangerous it was! Why didn't you stop
it? You saved your baby boy and you let my daughter die!"

Simon hadn't flinched. His voice was hard, a
match for the old man's. "It wasn't my choice."

But his father had gone on raving until Ken Rice
had finally intervened. Rice had told the orderly to
let him stay behind with the body. Everybody
seemed to accept that Elizabeth's father was out
of his head with grief, but Tom himself felt brutal-
ized, involved in some sordid way. He had left the
room with the blood pounding in his head. Now,

59

standing here, he felt his face again grow hot with shame.

So this is how the day begins. Down in the main lobby a fifteen-foot decorated tree filled the front windows. Fake, of course. Fire regulations. It was all going to be fake from now on, wasn't it?—everything from the garish garlands of tinsel across the city streets to those perfume ads on television —they were never on at any other time of the year, so what did that mean? Christmas was sexy?

Oh, Elizabeth, I don't believe this. I saw you in the kitchen last night. We laughed, and you were happy—weren't you?

Yes, and what about the tears earlier last night? Where do they fit? This baby she wanted so much, born to her, never seen by her—what was going to happen to it? He couldn't think about that now; it made him weak to think of it. He had to concentrate on something else. He had to call Jeanne and let her know.

He found the public telephone next to the elevators. But he couldn't make the call. He stood staring down the hallway at the doors to the emergency room, seeing them open suddenly. The orderly came out and behind him came his father. Even from this distance he read pain in those gestures—the handshake, the pat on the orderly's shoulder—Terry Fallon was a politician; if he behaved badly, he knew how to repair the damage. *Some things you can't repair, Dad.* He turned and took the stairs to the first floor, to the tiny chapel off the main hallway.

Empty this morning. Good. He didn't want anyone else's grief. He saw the ceramic Virgin Mary beckoning before the altar. *No, thanks.* The door to the confessional was ajar. He flung himself inside and slammed the door. Pressing his face into his father's tweed coat, he let the tears loose. *I don't know what you thought you were doing, Elizabeth, but I don't blame you.* They were just alike. He could understand that she needed some magic in her life. And it was all right, wasn't it? If you were careful not to cause pain to those you loved. If you didn't expect them to pay for it.

Oh, God, he hated confessions, still remembered the day he'd told the priest about the blackboard erasers he'd taken home and hidden away because he'd loved the silky feel of their wooden backs; the night he'd necked with Helen Morrison out behind the junior high gym, until he'd gotten so hard he thought he'd done himself permanent injury—Christ, had he really told old Father Michael about that? Must have been one of the last times he'd been inside that booth, the one that had always smelled so mysteriously of Oreo cookies.

He wiped his eyes roughly with his hand. *This was not my fault. Nothing I have done caused this to happen.* But he couldn't buy it. Somewhere, somehow, the blame would eventually be brought to rest; Simon would be off the hook, and his turn would come. It was now that span of time between when you first felt a blow and the actual pain of it set in. He knew the pain was coming; his body was gathering in, preparing.

Suddenly he was on his feet, seeing a replay of the scene outside the emergency room—his father shaking the orderly's hand, the pat on the shoulder—whatever had he been thinking? He knew his father. Those gestures belonged to the catalogue of moves for passing a bribe.

He left the chapel on a run, keeping his eyes away from the winking Christmas tree. He had to get the old man out of here, get him where he couldn't cause any more trouble.

When he reached the emergency room it was seething again—a fresh set of nurses, doctors he didn't recognize. He looked around the hall for his father; no sign. But he knew he had been right, for there stood Bill Hessel, unshaven and in his shirtsleeves, a notebook in his hand.

"Your dad had someone call me—"

"He shouldn't have done that. Bill, they couldn't save her, they couldn't stop the bleeding. . . ."

The doors swung open. His father stood staring at him. "Where have you been?"

"Downstairs."

"Tom, go in there. She needs you. She shouldn't be alone."

"Dad, why did you—"

He saw the two doctors striding toward him and felt a flood of relief. Then it had all been a horrible mistake; she was still alive. No, that wasn't possible. Yet he would be willing to believe it. *Let her be alive, let this whole thing just be a nightmare.*

"They don't know how it happened," his father was saying. "What can you tell them?"

"Tell them . . . ?"

"Molly's in a coma. Jeanne brought her in. Tom, what the hell went on at your house last night?"

Molly? He felt lightheaded. He couldn't take it all in. *His baby girl.* The doctors were at his side then. They were leading him toward the doors.

His father made as if to follow. "Do you hear me, Tom? I expect an answer from you!"

Again the blood pounded in his head. He swung

around. "Get back!" Turning to Hessel, he commanded: "Keep him out! Keep him away from me!"

He dropped the overcoat and pushed through the double doors.

10

"THANK GOD IT'S NOT SNOWING," Nellie murmured under her breath.

The remark didn't seem to call for an answer, so Charlie Carmody said nothing, merely stared out the side window of the limousine at the bleak winter landscape sliding by. The monotony of it—white hills backing up rows and rows of black tree trunks—wore him down, made him feel trapped; a familiar feeling in his hometown.

"At least it's a decent day. It could've been dreadful weather, bad driving."

She seemed to be talking mostly to herself. Her gloved hands lay limply in her lap. Charlie glanced across at Simon; his brother was looking older than his thirty-seven years this morning—eyes hollow, a tense line around his mouth. He held a single sheet of folded paper in his hand; he would unfold and consult it, fold and return it to his coat pocket. On the ride from the house into town, Charlie had already seen him do it a dozen times.

"Make sure the Taylors get invited back, will you?"

"I will," Nellie said.

"Everyone knows about lunch in the parish hall?"

"Father Mark said he'd announce it."

Simon nodded, again folding the piece of paper in half. "Tell Tom to invite anybody they want to back to the house."

Charlie leaned forward. "Anything you need me to do, Si?"

Silence; his brother looked over at him, almost as if he were angry; then the look passed, and he shook his head. The limousine turned the corner at Eighth Avenue and pulled up in front of the Cathedral of St. Mary's. A man in a black suit stood waiting at the curb, his hand extended to open the car door. Nellie gripped Charlie's arm tightly; a flicker of fear went across her face.

"It's okay, Ma." Charlie patted her hand.

For a moment she seemed about to soften; then her back went stiff and she fixed him with a look not unlike his brother's. "I'm fine."

Simon was already ahead of them, out of the limo and halfway up the stone steps. The man in black called to him softly as Charlie handed his mother out. Simon stopped and waited at the top step, so that they could enter the church together.

Through the wooden double doors that led to the main seating area Charlie glimpsed a huge sea of people. *The house was packed.* He censored the thought immediately; this wasn't a sporting event.

"Nellie, Nellie, I'm so sorry. . . ."

A tiny woman in a gray, feathered hat caught his mother's shoulder and the two embraced, pressing their cheeks together. Charlie recognized Mrs. Finch, from "the old neighborhood," as his mother called it now. But, Jesus, she looked *ancient.* Was it possible?

Mrs. Finch reached out: "Simon, dear, I'm so sorry. . . ."

"It's all right."

His brother's voice, brusque and businesslike, dropped like a curtain between them, and Mrs. Finch's hand fell to her side. Charlie was growing used to the flat, perfunctory tone; it was all he'd heard since he'd arrived. Simon issuing orders over the phone, accepting condolences, explaining Elizabeth's death. At first it had struck him as bizarre, but the whole thing was bizarre—Elizabeth gone; that beautiful, vivacious girl his brother had married—gone for good. And he, Charlie Carmody, back home. He had never expected to see this place again, had hoped he would not. What had he been thinking? Death is what always brings you back.

"Charlie. Good to see you." A balding, gray-haired man took his hand, pumped it, moved on without waiting for a reply. He saw, then, that they were standing in a receiving line of sorts—the Bereaved Family—and, that, closer to the door, the Fallons were gathered in a second, separate group. Terry Fallon stood next to his son, Tom. *The family that prays together looks alike.* Did Tom's girls have that same wide forehead, that ruddy Irish complexion? Or were they softer and more blond, like Jeanne?

Last night Simon had told him about Tom and Jeanne's daughter, Molly—that she was in the hospital in critical condition, and they still weren't certain how it had happened. "It was some kind of drug poisoning," Simon had said.

"Drug poisoning? From what?"

67

"Apparently Elizabeth had some pills in her coat pocket."

"What kind of pills?"

"Can you get into this suit of mine?" Simon had pulled the blue pinstripe out of his closet and tossed it on the bed. "Here's a clean shirt. Take whatever tie you want."

"What kind of pills, Si?"

"I have no idea. Nothing she got from me." Said in that same emotionless tone as Simon turned to face him. "I have an extra overcoat, if you think you'll need it. In the downstairs closet."

With that he had left, and Charlie had stood alone in the cream-and-beige bedroom, trying on his brother's clothes, trying not to lose track of what was real. He couldn't stop himself from looking around for Elizabeth—her with the coy grin, mischief deep within those wide green eyes. The way she was in high school—a bright image that nothing could tarnish. *Oh, God, Elizabeth, what's this all about? Because it just can't be what it seems.*

The organ was playing softly now, signaling the services about to begin. His mother nudged his arm. From out of nowhere the casket had materialized, taking up half of the lobby, it seemed, covered with fresh flowers, wheeled on a low dolly, steadied front and back by the altar boys. The priest walked ahead of the coffin. Simon followed behind it, with Terry Fallon next.

"We go in now," his mother whispered to Charlie. He took his place beside her in the procession. From the corner of his eye he caught a glimpse of a woman entering the lobby. She wore a camel-hair coat, and her black hair hung in a thick fall to her shoulders. He couldn't see her face as she bent to fumble with the clasp on her purse, but he knew her in that instant: Marty Voigt.

•

The priest was young; he was the one who had married Simon and Elizabeth, Nellie Carmody whispered to Charlie. Good-looking, too, with a commanding voice. The guy would go far in this business. Charlie, feeling a twinge of guilt, pulled his attention back to the eulogy.

". . . we are called from this life not because of any merit of ours, but according to His holy design. Elizabeth rejoices in the chance her child has been given . . . she goes to the holy life . . . but she will be ever present in his. . . ."

Charlie felt his brother's body stiffen beside him; his mother's face was in her handkerchief. He steeled himself, staring ahead down the narrow aisle toward the altar. He could never make sense of these talks. *A uterine hemorrhage.* What kind of holy design was that? Was Simon buying it? He glanced at his brother—the familiar, hawklike profile. Buy it or not, Simon would make it through all of this. He was tough. His strength had gotten him through med school, gotten him set up as head of surgery at St. Cloud Community. And this baby, hanging on for dear life at Simon's hospital, would make it too. His mother would say it was Carmody blood. *And you, Charlie? You've got that blood. What's it ever done for you?*

He shifted slightly in the chair, as Simon raised his head and looked at him, or looked through him. He seemed unaware that anyone was sitting there. Charlie switched his gaze to the choir loft, empty today. He wondered if the choir was as good as it used to be. He remembered them as a huge swarm of crows, sweeping down the aisle in their black robes. Above and behind the marble altar the brass pipes of the organ were gleaming dully in the light.

"Pray for Elizabeth," Father Mark was saying, "and for all of us in this short and difficult life. . . ."

Behind him Terry Fallon broke into barely controlled sobbing. Charlie felt a shudder go through him; he would be bawling himself if they didn't end this thing soon. What would Elizabeth think of that? *Not your style, Charlie,* she would have said. *Not your style at all.*

•

A bitterly cold and windy afternoon. Charlie shivered in Simon's pinstripe suit. It was snug on him, and he had decided against the vest, thinking he looked too much like a Mafia hit man. Now he wished he'd worn it, and the gray overcoat Simon had offered; he was freezing out on this hill.

Odd how vividly he remembered this spot; he and Nicky and Marty used to barrel the old Ford V-8 through these winding graveyard curves at night, just cut the lights and scare hell out of each other. A long time ago. Elizabeth had never been part of that, though. She didn't belong in their crowd. Or so he had thought at the time. Nicky had had other ideas.

The cars were parked down the rise from the grave site, and up the other direction, as far as he could see. He spotted a girl he had known from high school, Ginny Heller, hanging on to the arm of someone who looked like he might be an ex–football player. *Was* an ex–football player. Jesus,

Cliff Jones. Ginny Heller had married Cliff Jones? Next to them he recognized two more people from his high school class—Don Malin and Angie Wold. What the hell, didn't anybody ever think of leaving town? And they all looked *old*! Had it happened to him too? He touched the bald spot on top of his head, smoothing the hair down—a habit he had lately developed. The spot wasn't all that noticeable; he drew attention to it with this gesture, and was annoyed each time he caught himself.

Lifting his eyes to the other side of the circle, he caught sight of Marty Voigt for the second time. Her coat was buttoned up high against the wind, her hair loose, blowing about her face. What was she doing here, anyway? She had barely known Elizabeth in high school. Why come all the way from California for this funeral? He stared hard at her for several moments, willing her to look his way, but she did not. Was it possible she hadn't recognized him? Again he touched his hair.

The service was mercifully brief. Father Mark said a short prayer; then, Simon stepped forward and lifted a long-stemmed white rose from the funeral spray. Holding it over the grave, he hesitated, then let it fall.

The group assembled around the coffin silently followed suit, then began moving toward their cars. Taking his mother's arm Charlie started toward the limo, keeping the camel-hair coat in his line of sight. He would get his mother settled, then go find her and say hello.

Ahead of them Simon slipped on the icy path. Instinctively Charlie reached out, but Simon was already down. Crouched there on his hands and knees, he pushed Charlie's hand away. He knelt motionless on the snowy ground, head lowered, while behind him the crowd slowly stumbled to a halt.

"Let's get to the car," Charlie said gently. "Si. Let me help, okay?"

Simon waved him back. "I know," he said, "I know." Brushing himself off he slowly got to his feet, looking down at his hands. His face was a mask of grief. "I've cut myself," he murmured, wiping the blood off onto the sleeve of his over-coat.

Beside him, their mother began to wail softly into her handkerchief. Simon looked at her, then turned and walked away, down the hill toward the line of cars.

11

THE GATHERING AT SIMON'S HOUSE went on into the late afternoon, the mourners moving from room to room, carrying drinks and plates of food. They had eaten the luncheon at the church but still seemed to have room for more. The liquor was moving too.

Charlie was tending bar at the kitchen counter. He was surprised at the number of people who stayed around, had not thought of his brother as the social type. But then, he hadn't thought of him as the type to marry Elizabeth Fallon either. Well, what did he know? They were seven years apart, he and his older brother—Simon in junior high when he went to kindergarten. By the time he was in high school, Simon was interning at Cook County.

Maybe these people were mostly Elizabeth's friends. She had always been at the center of things. Funny how he kept seeing her riding that float, on top of the fake mountain in the St. Cloud Winter Parade—the Snow Queen, dressed in white velvet from head to toe, waving to all of her loyal subjects on St. Germain Street. When Simon had written to say he was getting married, that parade had flashed across his mind. Six years ago, wasn't it? Six or seven. He knew because he hadn't been able to come to the wedding. But then he wouldn't have, in any case.

"Charlie Carmody, my God." A rosy-cheeked man in horn-rimmed glasses approached and put out his hand. "Bill Hessel. Been a long time. Lotta years."

A voice from the past. Charlie smiled, shook the hand that was offered. "Hi, how are you?"

"Great, great. How about you?"

The picture he got now was of Bill Hessel, class clown, calling out for a pizza on the chem lab telephone while Mr. Litke was out of the room. He started to laugh out loud; caught himself.

"Where you been hiding, Charlie?"

"Around. Out West. Montana, Wyoming."

"Yeah, I remember. You wanted to be a cowboy, didn't you? Sounded like a great idea to me at the time."

"At the time, yeah."

"So is that what you're doing?"

Charlie glanced over Bill's shoulder at Terry Fallon, who was standing in the doorway of the kitchen, talking loudly to a gray-haired man. Terry was crashed. Charlie had already made him a number of Scotches, each time trying to go light on the booze, until finally the old man had given him a look. "You paying for this stuff?" A hard edge to his voice. After that he poured the shots the way Old Man Fallon wanted. Hell, no, he wasn't paying for it, nor did it matter to him who got stiff.

"I hear they're using motorcycles."

"What?"

"Cowboys," Bill said. "Using Hondas and Yamahas. Saw it on television."

"Is that so."

The two men were talking about little Molly
Fallon now; the friend was trying to calm the old
man down. Charlie wanted to get close enough to
hear what they were saying, but Bill Hessel wasn't
through yet.

"You planning on staying around here for a
while?" he asked.

Charlie shook his head. He was seeing the words
criminal and *stupid* form and spew from Terry
Fallon's mouth.

"That's a good-looking suit. Nothing like a nice
pinstripe." Hessel reached out to finger his lapel.

"It's Simon's," he said. "Want me to ask him
where he got it?"

"Nah, that's okay." Bill's hand dropped to his
side. "Seen Nick lately?"

Too pointed to be an accident. Charlie looked
straight into that innocent, grinning face. "What's
it to you?"

"Nothing. Not a thing. Just curious."

"What are you doing these days, Bill?"

"For a living?" Hessel smiled. "I'm a cop.
Stearns County Sheriff's Department."

"That's what I figured."

"Sorry about your sister-in-law." Hessel clapped
him on the shoulder and moved off, and Charlie
reached down to grab a beer from the bucket at
his feet. He opened it and took a long swallow.
Turning back he had a view of Fallon, gesturing
wildly with both hands, one still holding his drink;
he was clearly out of control. The other man's
hand was moving to rescue the glass.

". . . no one's fault, Terry, it's one of those
tragic things. . . ."

Fallon was shaking his head. "Oh, it's somebody's fault, all right, you can believe that. And you can believe I'll find out whose."

They left the doorway, then, the friend's arm around the old man's broad shoulders.

"Hey, I'd know that face anywhere." Ginny Heller was suddenly standing at his elbow, her arm linked to that of the stocky man beside her. "You remember Charlie Carmody, don't you, Cliff? My husband, Cliff Jones."

Charlie said, "Ah, yes. The cheerleader marries the tight end. The way life oughta be." His tone sounded hostile in his ears, but the couple before him just grinned; they were not in the least offended.

"We haven't seen you since graduation," Ginny said. "Where'd you disappear to?"

"The army," he said. "Then Arizona."

"Really. What do you do out there?"

"Lot of different things. Mostly carpentry work."

Cliff reached into his back pocket and took out his wallet. "Well, we've been pretty busy." He flashed a snapshot of four stocky boys, all with Ginny's grin, her red-gold curls. Charlie admired them as Cliff detailed their talents and clever ways.

"You married yet?" Ginny asked.

He took another swig of beer and shook his head. This town had a way of conducting an assault on his nerves; he always had the uneasy feeling that something was coming, something he wouldn't like.

"Hey," Cliff said, "that reminds me. I saw Marty Voigt at the cemetery. She looks good."

"Is Marty back in town?" Charlie asked. "Living here, I mean?"

Ginny shrugged. "I didn't know she ever left."

•

A long-haired gray cat lay by the hearth, its yellow eyes gleaming. Charlie stared into the dying fire as he stretched out his hands toward it. Now that the people had gone, the house felt cold again. He bent to stroke the cat, and she arched her back, turning her head to look up at him.

"Her name's Pearl." Simon had come into the room, and was standing by the door. "You like cats? I don't, really." He walked to the bay window, closed the drapes, and switched on the lamp. "Did Mother go to bed?"

"Yeah. She was pretty beat."

"I'm worried about her," he said. "She's drinking again."

"That why you moved her out here with you?"

"It was Elizabeth's idea. She thought it might give Mother something to do. With the baby coming and all . . ." Simon turned away from the window, gestured toward the fire. "Cold in here. Throw another log on, why don't you?"

Charlie bent to do so, and the cat quickly ran and hid under the wing chair. "Terry Fallon was sure putting the booze away today," he said.

Simon shook his head. "Doesn't surprise me."

"What's his problem?"

"His problem is that he thinks he runs the world. It confuses him when things don't turn out the way he plans them."

"I don't get it," Charlie said.

"Do you have to, Charlie?"

This was the way of their conversations. Always

the stopper that short-circuited things. "No, I guess not."

"When are you going back?" Simon asked. "You have a job out there?"

"I've got work. Enough to keep me going."

"Nothing permanent, though."

Jesus, he hoped this wasn't going to be lecture time. He was too old for that, wasn't he? With Simon you never knew. He stoked the fire, keeping his back turned.

"I meant, do you have any real plans for yourself?"

"None at all," Charlie heard himself say cheerfully as his brother moved toward the fireplace, directly into his line of vision.

"I had to know."

"No doubt."

"You asked if I needed anything. I need to renovate the house."

"Why? It looks okay to me."

"Not this one, the old place. I want to get it fixed up." Simon looked down into the fire. "I won't go into my reasons right now."

"Are you asking my permission to sell? I told you before, you can do what you want."

"Not sell it. I want you to do the remodeling for me. You could move back in and live there while you worked. I'd pay you, of course. I don't expect you to do this out of the goodness of your heart."

That was all it took. "Now, that's a laugh. Charlie Carmody with goodness of heart. You want me to stay around, Si, just ask. I know I owe you."

Simon frowned. "You don't owe me anything."

"No? What about the lawyer's fees?"

"Forget about them. Look, we're square. You don't need to feel guilty about any of that."

"Thanks. What else don't I need to feel guilty about?"

"Charlie, it's your problem. Quit trying to make it mine. I'm not up to this."

Charlie put the poker down, resting the handle against the gray stone. "Sorry. It's just . . . Hessel got on my nerves today."

"You mean you let him get on your nerves."

"He knew, Si. I could tell by the questions."

"So what? Hessel's a jerk."

"Yeah, but how does he know?"

Simon shrugged his shoulders. "You can't live your life worrying about who knows and who doesn't. You made a mistake and you paid for it. You've got to make your own peace."

Here was the lecture at last; he did feel better for having heard it. Still, not something he planned to endure on a regular basis. "There's plenty of good carpenters in this town," he said. "I'll help you find one."

"I don't want them. I want you."

"Why?"

"Do I have to have a reason? Does Terry Fallon have a reason for going to Hessel about those drugs?"

"Is that what he did?"

"Hell, yes! He needs to blame somebody for all this, doesn't he?" Simon leaned his head against the mantel. "I know how he feels. Things didn't exactly work out the way I planned either."

Charlie stood for a moment. The scene in the cemetery slid into his mind—Simon on his knees in the snow, the look of bewilderment on his face.

He started forward, then stopped himself. He knew his brother. A physical gesture would not be welcome here. "I'm sorry." They looked at each other. At last Charlie said, "I'll go over and check the place out tomorrow."

"Thanks."

"But I can't stay long, Si."

His brother nodded, as if he understood.

12

A CLASSICAL PIECE ON THE RADIO. Marty almost recognized it. The piece was a celebration of spring, but it always reminded her of Christmas. The dark side of Christmas; people without their loved ones, or exposed in some loss. The photograph on the front page of today's paper showed a family whose house trailer had burned with all their holiday presents inside. The couple and their children were huddled together on a neighbor's couch, looking so sad. She could almost see the photographer posing the shot: "Okay, now. A little sorrow and despair, that's the ticket." And their Christmas presents, bought and wrapped weeks before and stored in a closet. They were so efficient, it was hard to believe. She herself had never bought a present more than a day in advance, never wrapped one until the moment before she gave it away. Particularly baby presents; buying early just seemed like tempting fate.

Anyway, those people would get it all back. Someone would start a fund, some dealer would contribute a van complete with cable TV and a microwave, and the town would feel blessed in holiday spirit: that was the way it went. But people needed more help than that if they were going to make their lives work. A different kind of help.

She stood behind the counter, slowly turning the pages of the newspaper, waiting for eleven o'clock—closing time on Saturday night. It was ten thirty now, business as usual at this hour, which meant no business. So cold this month that TV weathermen were saying every day, "Remember your survival kit. Keep it in the trunk of your car." A northerly wind had blown into town yesterday, along with six inches of snow. The streets were very nearly empty. Anyone willing to brave the subzero temperatures to go to the grocery store had long since done it. She'd had her last customer about an hour ago—Ed Bruner, their neighbor, getting his daily supply of fresh milk.

Voigt's was one of the last markets in the state still selling milk and cream in glass bottles. The myth was that it was somehow better than the stuff that came in cartons. Bottles had become a status symbol—one that her father was not above taking credit for. But Sauk Rapids Dairy made the decision.

She had cleaned the dairy case and covered the meat trays. The day-old bread was stacked on the counter for the Sisters of St. Benedict. Nothing more to do except close out the register and set the alarms.

Turning to the hot plate behind her, she poured the last cup of coffee, then went for the cream bottle she had hidden behind the wheel of cheese. She doled herself out a generous shot, averting her eyes from her reflection in the glass. She knew she was putting on weight. She would make a New Year's resolution, but that still gave her two weeks.

She tore the envelopes of sugar, stirring them into her cup while she read her horoscope:

CANCER. *Get involved with charitable organizations. Recycle old possessions. One of your secrets may be disclosed.*

Day-old bread to the Sisters. That took care of the first two items. And there were few secrets left at this late date.

She glanced again at her watch: ten forty. These last minutes always inched by. She thought about the novel waiting for her upstairs beside her bed. On the nights she worked she would turn on the electric blanket before she left. Her bedroom was ten degrees cooler than the rest of the apartment. Crawling into that warmed bed would be a treat.

She reached beneath the counter for the bank bag and opened the register. She counted the bills first, then the checks and finally the change, entering the figures in the accounts book. Slipping the money into the cloth pouch, she put it beneath the counter. She would lock the drawer before she left.

She had inherited the accounting aspect of the business from her mother. Boz was careless about money. It seemed to be the one thing Josie Voigt had been put in complete charge of, hence the one thing Boz could respect his daughter for, without feeling threatened.

A quick sweep of the aisles, and she would be finished. She was anxious to get to her book, to sink against the pillows and lose herself in the drama of someone else's life. As she swept around the meat case, she heard the door open, felt at once the icy pull of air down the narrow aisle. She gathered her red sweater together.

A man stood facing her at the end of the aisle. He was dressed in gray cords and a khaki jacket, with a gray wool scarf slung around his neck. Smiling at her, stuffing his gloves into a jacket pocket, he said, "What d'you know? The first place I look."

"Hello, Charlie."

"How are you, Marty?"

His voice had changed; it was deeper and huskier than she'd remembered. Everything else, though—the dark, curly hair, the straight nose, those high cheekbones that squeezed his eyes almost to slits—all the same. Marty took a breath against a sudden tightness in her chest.

"Fine," she said.

"Been quite a while, huh? How long?"

"I haven't kept track."

"Twelve years." He ran a hand through his hair. "So. What've you been up to?"

"I'm at the university. Part-time."

"Teaching?"

"Getting my degree."

"In what?"

"Social work."

"Social work."

She moved to the front counter with Charlie following, shuffling his boots along the wooden floor.

"I should do that," he said. "Go back to school, I mean." Surprised at his own observation he laughed. "I should do a lot of things."

"Better get started, then."

He unzipped his jacket. "I saw you at the cemetery," he said. "Thought you might come back to the house after the funeral."

"No. That wouldn't have been right."

"Why not?"

"I really didn't know her. It just seemed . . . it was such a sad thing." She felt suddenly very awkward; busied herself, replacing some packages of film that had fallen from their display hooks. She wished he would take the hint and go.

He leaned toward her, with both hands on the counter. "You closing up now? I thought we might go somewhere for a drink."

"I don't drink," she said.

"Then how about a cup of coffee?"

"It's eleven o'clock. I get up early on Sundays to go to Mass."

"It's twenty below. It's against my religion," he mimicked. Then, raising his hands: "Another time, maybe. I'll be around. I'm doing some work for Si out at the old house." He pulled on his gloves. "I forget how cold it gets in this town. Couldn't start the car this morning. Somebody saw me with the hood up and stopped to give me a jump. Wouldn't even let me pay him. Nice guy."

"This town's full of nice guys," she said. "We hardly need any more."

A small silence. Then he inclined his head and, turning away, headed for the door. When she heard it close behind him, she quickly locked the cash drawer and set the alarms.

She had seen Charlie at the funeral, all right, had seen him and had kept carefully out of range. It wasn't hard; only those first moments at the church had felt dangerous. Yesterday at a busy corner near the university, she had been waiting for the light to change when a car had zoomed alongside, missing her by inches. She had stood there with her heart drumming in shock and fear, just the way it was doing now.

She hurried up the flight of stairs to her apartment on the second floor. The lights were on in the small kitchen, her day's dishes still in the sink. She had been living alone for a long time now. She was used to it; it was what she wanted. But she remembered a time when it hadn't been. She turned on the hot water tap, filling the sink nearly to the brim and squirting soap over the pile. She liked doing dishes the last thing at night. Liked starting each day fresh without having to face any of yesterday's mess.

What kept playing across her mind was Simon's blurred face at the grave site, his body sprawled on the frozen ground. He'd be alone tonight, and alone for a lot more nights, and it would not be what he wanted at all. How sorry she felt for him. How impossible to take in the idea of Elizabeth out there on that hillside, and her baby somewhere else. She suddenly felt the presence of all those tiny souls brought into this world, innocent of how they got there. Trying to look out of the window into the darkness, she saw her own reflection coming back at her.

Her bedroom off the long hallway was cold. She was shivering by the time she had undressed and slipped into her white flannel nightgown. She crawled under the covers and lay still. Tonight she didn't feel like reading.

Burying her head under the pillow, she forced herself to relax. She wanted so much to trust herself. That was crucial, wasn't it?

13

"WHEN I WAS A KID," Boz said from the breakfast table, "I never went to church. Never felt like I missed anything either."

"What are you grumbling about now?" Marty reached behind her to the toaster on the counter. She tossed one piece of toast onto her father's plate, buttered the other for herself.

"Every single Sunday. Never a break. Never time off for good behavior. No, she hasn't heard of good behavior."

"I've heard of it. I'm waiting to see some."

Boz stuck his knife into the cherry jam and slathered it over his toast. He looked very dapper in his tan slacks and white turtleneck and the jacket she'd picked up for twenty dollars at a garage sale. A real find—Irish tweed. Marty poured his coffee first, then hers.

"What time did you get home last night?" she asked.

"Who wants to know?"

"You usually whine about church when you've been out late."

"Listen, missy, that's not your business. But since you ask, I had a couple of beers at the Wedge

87

and was home by twelve o'clock. Kinda blows your theory, don't it?"

Marty laughed uneasily. "I guess." This conversation and a hundred others like it made echoes in her head. Was she turning into her mother, after all?

"So it looks like I can whine if I want to, since I'm the one ready to go."

He drank his coffee in triumph, playing to invisible audiences. Besting her in an argument always put him in a sunny mood. At sixty he was still very much a little boy—husky and strong, a charmer, with the German appetite for good food and drink. He liked having Sunday breakfast at her apartment, even if it meant Mass at St. Mary's afterward. Or maybe he liked the ritual for the same reason she did: an automatic check on Saturday night. And didn't that sound familiar too? She lifted his steak, eggs, and hash browns out of the oven.

"Ain't you having any?" he asked. "You always eat. You upset about something or what?"

She shook her head.

"Sure?"

"Listen, mister, that's not your business." She imitated his tone, just a shade prissier. His turn to laugh; only he didn't.

"So how much did we take in last night?"

Their usual Sunday-morning discussion— whether it was worth it to stay open past eight o'clock on Saturday night for the handful of customers they saw.

"Fifty-two," she said. "Not counting the videos."

"Which makes . . . ?"

"Just under a hundred."

88

"See?" He sat back, smiling. "I told you. Miss Marks show up?"

"Of course. She wants to know why we don't carry that new brand of flavored seltzer-water."

"Ah, she thinks she's a yuppie. That old lady'll try anything just because it's new. Me, I like to wait till they get the bugs ironed out."

She laughed at the idea of bugs being ironed out. Her father treated the business the way he did the rest of his life—the Fates were in charge. It made things so simple. It didn't matter if he was the first to carry a new breakfast cereal or soft drink or snack food; they'd either prove themselves over time or they wouldn't. Meanwhile, if somebody wanted to go to Byerly's or Coborn's and didn't mind that they didn't get the personal service or couldn't find their way around, so be it. And it had worked. His customers were many and loyal, and they took a lot of scolding from him about being frivolous. "Quit watching that TV!" he'd holler. "You been using this brand of soap for years and you like it fine, why change?" What people would put up with from Boz Voigt continually amazed her. But then, she herself had been putting up with his bullying for years.

"Better get dressed, missy," he said, looking at his watch. "We're gonna be late again."

•

Her paisley print hung on the back of the closet door; the one she had worn to the funeral on Tuesday. She hesitated before pulling it from its hanger. Silly. It was just a dress.

Pulling on her stockings she thought about herself and Boz, how joking and teasing came so easy for them. She could only remember one real conversation, and that was years ago. He'd been so sure the Fates did him a service by moving her back to town the same year her mother became so ill. Sure enough, after the funeral, he'd fallen completely apart. She finally drew the line. She moved out of his house and into the apartment above the store. She said he would either pull himself together or the store would be up for sale. He'd been furious.

"You could do a lot worse with your life than this!" Slamming his fist down on the table. "Missy, you already have!"

"That may be," she had told him. "But I'll decide what I'm doing with the rest, and it won't be running the store while you sit around and drink up the proceeds."

"Ever since you joined AA you think everybody's a drunk!"

"Dad, I'm telling you where I stand. Take it or leave it."

The only time she had really stood up to him. Her acting like an adult seemed to be his cue for turning into a little kid. He had cried and begged her for another chance. He would do better in the future. And he had. He confined his drinking to Saturday nights, and she had her schedule worked so she got to her classes and her meetings with no trouble from him. All to the good. Yet, here she was, still.

She cast a critical eye toward the mirror: good enough, if you didn't look too closely at her waistline; her dark hair was smooth and shiny, her legs trim in the patent leather pumps; they were her best asset, she had always known this. *Marty, you've got great legs.* An echo from the past. She picked up her purse from the dresser. Thinking about the past was what old timers did. She had a way to go before she was in that league.

•

"I'll park the car, Dad. You get out."

"You just drive around, girl. I can make it from wherever you park this little tin can of yours."

Marty knew what he was up to. Better to brave the cold than to have to stand alone in the alcove of St. Mary's. Certain people in the parish looked down on him, was his view. "They'll buy from you, but it's something else again to speak to you in the center aisle."

Halfway down the block she spooned the little Datsun neatly into a parking space, and she and Boz hurried for the doors.

They were later than usual, but so were a number of others. The group waited patiently in the lobby for Father Mark to finish his Bible reading. The smoky odor she always associated with the Mass hung in the air; rather, it seemed to have penetrated to the very foundations of the building, the wood and limestone steeped in it.

Beside her Boz looked at his watch and shook his head. He claimed the priests started early every Sunday, setting people up to feel guilty. Yet for all his talk, Boz was the one who had insisted they start going again. She hadn't wanted to. But now she was grateful for this ordering of her week, to have the hour to relax and make a kind of peace with herself.

The doors opened and they moved forward. They usually sat in one of the pews near the back, but this morning they had to go down the center aisle, past the small table that held the communion chalice. Marty slipped into the row, knelt briefly, and unbuttoned her coat. She kept her eyes on the huge Advent wreath suspended from the ceiling, with its three purple candles and one pink. Had it been there during Elizabeth's funeral? She couldn't remember.

Father Mark raised the book over his head, and the folds of his purple robe fell to his elbows.

"This is the Word of the Lord," he intoned.

"Thanks be to God," Marty murmured with the others.

Her eyes wandered past the pink-and-gray granite columns to the ivory walls broken by the wooden door of the confessional. Below the grill-work a sign lettered in gilt: BE NOT ASHAMED TO CONFESS THY SINS.

Directly in front of her a man in a gray jacket had his arm around a young blond woman. Ahead of them Marty saw Mrs. Carmody, with Simon seated next to her.

"We are the Lord's creation," Father Mark was saying. "We are *not* gods."

Where was Charlie? She knew the elevator feeling in her stomach had to do with him, even though he wasn't present.

"What we need to do," said Father Mark, "involves remembering. A *re-membering* of our lives, a putting of them into a new and different order. To be transfigured in this way . . . can be a good thing. . . ."

Amen, she thought.

•

The clerestory windows in the high ceiling normally filled the interior with light, but today it felt damp and dark inside the church. Beside her Boz sighed and pulled back the sleeve of his tweed jacket to let her know the homily was running long. Marty expected him to stand up some Sunday and give the high sign directly to the priest. She turned her eyes back to the altar, where Father Mark was indeed winding down.

"Let us proclaim the mystery of faith."

As they went down the aisle to receive the Eucharist, she noted how few people drank from the communal chalices. She herself did not partake. It wasn't the wine, or even the idea of germs so much as a reluctance to get that close. What she felt when she came here each Sunday was her *aloneness;* something she wanted to hang on to.

". . . We pray for the sick," Father Mark was saying, "and for little Patrick Carmody, who was given the gift of life by our Lord and by his dear mother. We pray for his good health today. And we pray for the dead, especially for Elizabeth Ann Carmody, our sister, called to a holy life. . . ."

After the services she spotted Mrs. Carmody and Simon standing with Dr. and Mrs. Hilliard. Simon's eyes were fixed on a spot over the moving heads of the crowd. His face looked drawn and pale.

Boz had hold of her arm, steering her toward the door. Gently she freed herself.

"Just a minute, Dad." She worked her way through the crowd until she stood facing Mrs. Carmody, who squinted up at her.

"Who is it?" Mrs. Carmody asked, her voice faint.

Simon bent his head. "It's Marty Voigt, Mother."

"I just wanted you both to know, if there's anything I can do . . ." Marty began.

"So kind of you," said Mrs. Carmody. Her handkerchief was crushed in her fist. She was leaning heavily on Simon's arm and for an instant Marty caught an oddly sweet scent in the air. Her perfume? Then Father Mark joined them and Nellie Carmody turned to the priest and pressed her handkerchief to her eyes.

"I'm sorry," Marty said again, feeling suddenly out of place. "If she'd like a ride to the hospital or anything, I'd be glad to . . ."

"Thanks, Marty." Simon gave her a brief smile as Boz came up behind her, nudging her arm.

"Are we ready?"

And then she and Boz were out the door, walking quickly to the car. He couldn't wait to let her have it.

"There you are, sucking up to that old bitch, I can't believe my eyes!"

"Dad. She's suffering."

"Tragedy is no excuse."

Marty opened the car door and slid behind the wheel, reaching over to unlock the door on the passenger side. "You don't believe in charity, is that it?"

"Charity is for the poor. Nellie Carmody never heard of the poor, not since her doctor son went and married a Fallon. She never heard of a lot of things she used to be right in the thick of."

That odor she had smelled back inside the church; it hadn't been perfume. She looked at Boz, who had climbed in beside her and was now staring gloomily at the windshield.

"So where do you think Charlie was?" he asked.

"Don't he believe in church?" He let her start the engine before his voice came at her again, full volume. "Don't be coy with me, now. I saw him goin' into the store last night."

"Then you must have seen him leave." She waited while the defroster melted the thin glaze of ice on the windshield.

"What's he doing in town anyway?"

"What do you think? He came for his brother's wife's funeral."

"That was Tuesday."

"He's doing some work for Simon—"

"*Work.*" Boz gave a snort. "Charlie Carmody's got no concept of work."

Turning to look behind her in the traffic lane, she pulled out of the parking spot. The windshield wipers slapped at the last bit of glaze.

"You've changed," he said. "But he hasn't. I seen him up to the Wedge last night, downin' beers, makin' noise, like he was still in high school."

"Like you?" she asked.

He pretended not to have heard. "I wouldn't give a nickel for that guy's chances in this world, not a single nickel," he said. "Him and his old buddy, Nick, just a pair of small-town losers."

She guided the Datsun around a barrier set at right angles to the curb. The barrier appeared to be guarding nothing; why did they have to screw up these roads in the winter? Didn't people have enough to contend with?

"Somebody ought to neuter that son of a bitch Uhler."

"Dad, we just left church."

"Don't he deserve it? Marryin' you, takin' you off to Chicago, gettin' you pregnant?"

"Why are we talking about this now? Twelve years ago, when I needed—"

"I swear, Marty, if you even think about breaking my heart again, gettin' yourself hooked up with some faithless charmer—"

"Guess where I learned that?"

"All I know is you ran from that whole scene, missy. And that ain't the same as being done with it."

"It's done. Nick and I both made our mistakes—"

"Oh, maybe I missed it. Was he there, then, when you was so sick and that baby died?"

She pulled the car sharply over to the curb. "You're right," she said. "I have changed. I won't put up with this anymore. Now, either shut up or get out of the car."

Her father stared at her.

"I mean it," she said, realizing that she did. She waited while they stared at each other. Then she pulled back onto the road. He never knew when he had gone too far. Now he sat, hunched behind his coat collar, eyeing her in a worried way.

"All right, then," he said at last. "We won't talk about it."

As if it had been his idea, and he had merely been waiting for her to think of it.

14

SIMON FLIPPED HIS LAST CHART CLOSED. He pushed the ballpoint pen into his breast pocket and slid the clipboard into the color-coded slot beside the nurses' station. Blue for completion, records into the file: his evening rounds were finished. He leaned with both hands on the wall for a moment. Routine was so important. He hated these junctures where the thing was to decide what he had to do next. What was the normal thing to do next? He would like to do the normal thing. If he had to be seen—and in a town this size that was it, you were eternally seen—he would like to be seen behaving as normally as possible. But there was no way to do this right. Elizabeth was dead. His wife was dead, the baby was alive. Simon's face clenched tight. He didn't want to be this man in pain. He'd rather be anybody else.

"Good night, Dr. Carmody."

"Good night, Doctor."

He nodded, and the two nurses gave him fleeting little smiles when they passed. He could hear them begin to whisper to each other, and his face burned. The sympathy people had for him was a killing force, didn't they get that? Those sad looks —they made him want to run screaming out of the building and into the river. How did anybody think he would get through this if they kept breaking him down? Did they have to see him fall down in grief every day of his life before they were satisfied?

Count your blessings, his mother kept saying. Well, he could count them on one finger tonight, maybe two. He was not at home in his empty bed, and the nurses' station was for once deserted. There was no one he had to smile at or give comfort to or keep his face organized for.

A blessing, then, that he could stop and rest these few seconds at a transition point and decide what he had to do next. See the baby? Go and check the respiratory unit, make sure the tubes keeping that provisional life in its balance were properly connected and functioning. Because you couldn't trust anybody—and that's what gossip said about him these days, he knew it. He'd been around this town too many years not to know. What kind of doctor would allow his pregnant wife to die? Well, what kind of doctor, and what kind of wife?

Elizabeth pregnant, Elizabeth dying in the delivery room, that bloody fountain of surprise. Hemorrhage! He had been worried about the wrong thing! Her toxemia—oh, she'd taken chances! The quantities of sodium, caffeine, sugar —not his fault! But in the end it didn't count, didn't even matter. The autopsy was brief and explicit. Cause of death: uterine hemorrhage.

But this other business, the sedatives Tom's kid had got into, where had they come from? From Elizabeth's pocket. Where had she gotten them? Elizabeth's pocket, the necklace, the plastic bag.

What kind of wife? Simon chewed his lower lip, and did not see that he had come to a full stop in front of the nursery glass. Maybe he actually ought to go over to Pediatrics first, check on the little girl in the coma. Tom's little girl: of course he knew the name. This was no time for the brain to cave in —*but dammit, Elizabeth! How could you be so careless? With a child, with your life, with mine!*

This could have been prevented. He hadn't been careful enough, hadn't been *thinking*. Her name—what was it? "Molly." He said it aloud with relief. "Molly."

He wasn't alone. Standing in the boxlike hall not five feet away was a woman in a tan coat. Staring at him.

"Marty," she said. "It's Marty Voigt, Simon."

Simon felt his body curl into a posture of defense. "Yes, of course. I saw . . . your coat. Is it visiting hours still?" He felt the hot tightness in his forehead and knew he had turned violently red. How he hated that, hated having everything show.

She moved closer and put a hand on his arm— he held himself from flinching.

"I was just leaving," she said. "I'm sure you'd like some privacy."

He stepped toward the window where a nurse stood between the double row of babies. The ones in the front slept, all but two of their heads turned in the same direction. Their faces were shut down, their bodies still. His baby was in the back row, in one of the tented isolettes along the far wall. Simon stared hard, trying to see anything that denoted life, but there were just the tubes going out from the glass box, attached to the monitor. He didn't want her here. He also didn't want to be left alone.

She went to the glass, tapped her fingernail on the surface.

"I came to cheer him on. He's so tiny to be landed with so much trouble." She looked away. "I hope you don't mind."

"Mind what?"

"Me being here."

"Of course not."

He couldn't make her out. Something about how young she seemed, or how vulnerable— Marty Voigt didn't often strike him as vulnerable. She was attractive, but that reserve she had didn't go over with everybody. He himself appreciated it. Behind the counter at the store or across the table at the Family Planning Board meetings, Marty Voigt was all business. In a way he counted on her for that.

She lifted her face and her eyes were deep brown, emotional. "Can I ask you how he's doing?"

Simon lifted his shoulders. "He's making steady progress, normal for premature delivery. Seven weeks, that's significant . . . we're watching for respiratory problems, but—he's doing fine."

Her relief was immediate, her bright gaze fixed on his face. Clearly she wasn't thinking about him but about the baby. All right, he could use a break. In his careful professional voice he rattled out information he'd gotten from the pediatricians that morning. Oddly enough he started to relax. This was the closest he'd got to anything that felt like comfort—the sheer command of information made him feel grounded again.

"I've been wondering who I could ask," she murmured. "I didn't want to bother you."

"It's no bother."

"I mean, you have enough to think about, Simon."

In that moment he wanted to strike her. So she, too, meant to flush him out for the emotional payoff. What was it about women, that they wouldn't let up until they got their pound of flesh? He'd watched his mother work Charlie over when he was little and in the wrong, which is where Charlie stayed most of the time. The kid could never figure it out. He'd break a lamp and lie about it, try to hide it, then she had him. She'd keep hectoring until he cried. And that seemed to satisfy her; nothing else. She had to make him break. Simon never forgot it. He made sure nobody ever got that kind of hold over him.

Seemed as if his brother had come to the same conclusions by a different route. That was true, wasn't it? Charlie was no family man. And instead of staying out of trouble, he stayed right in the thick so he could practice what he knew best: toughing it out. Well, what they both knew was that when people had you, they really had you. No accident, either; a woman would follow the spoor of tears like a bloodhound.

He felt himself going red again. "We have a board meeting coming up, right?"

"Next week."

"Anything new?"

"One letter recommending we give ourselves up to the grand lottery of fertility. One asking us to really think about why we hate life so much."

He felt a corner of his fury coming loose. "What

is with these cranks? It's called the Family Planning Service, don't they get it? Right in the phone book: a planning service. Nothing more."

"I guess people don't want to see it that way."

"What if this were the Middle Ages?" He was warmed up now. "Back when mothers got rid of babies they didn't want by rolling over on them? Smothering them in the marriage bed?" He ran his finger under the edge of a hand-lettered sign taped to the door. NO ADMITTANCE. "How about when orphanages farmed them out to killing nurses? That's planning for you. Now that we have the capability to make intelligent choices and the medical knowledge—" Why was he babbling so? "The carelessness! That's what ruins people's lives! When the truth is," he finished, "some people don't deserve to have babies."

Beside him she hesitated, then whispered, "It feels odd to be talking about this in here. With all these little ones." She opened a hand to the row of small heads beyond the glass.

"Right," he said. Stupid of him to have started that. He saw that Marty's gaze was rooted to the floor, and the silence again made him want to break and run. He looked to the nursery attendant for interference, but her back was turned.

"I've never thanked you for what you did for me all those years ago," she whispered. "That mess."

"Oh. Well." His mind reeled, and he moved away from her to get some room. "Long time ago." And she *had* been young then, blank as paper. Emaciated and—it began to come back. The question remained, why did she want it to come back? Why bring this up? "Don't thank me,

Marty," he said. "I never think of it. That's the truth."

"I shouldn't," she said, her voice low. "I know I shouldn't, but I still do sometimes."

What did she want from him? Absolution? He couldn't do it, didn't have it. Not for himself, not for anybody. He calibrated his tone. "Listen. Don't think about it anymore. That's my best advice. As a doctor, I'm telling you."

As a doctor, every inch the professional, he sent her off. She seemed relieved as she walked out of the nursery corridor, back to the main business of her life with Dr. Simon Carmody's best prescription for not thinking. It was the one people needed, since thinking led them away from whatever clarity they could have and straight into the murk of feelings. Which was an excellent way to avoid the job of thinking about your life, planning what to do next. What he couldn't understand was why Marty Voigt or anybody else put themselves through misery, and then wouldn't let it go!

Oh, he could understand it if he lent himself to the pathological view. And wasn't that his business? He *had* to know how to do that, or in this town he couldn't conduct a conversation on the street. Let alone a hospital corridor.

He walked inside the glass enclosure and at the sealed-off isolette labeled BOY CARMODY, he bent and took a careful look. The respirator hummed, and the infant inside the lighted cube looked red and chafed, its dark hair plastered to the pulsating skull. Tubes in the nostrils, monitors pasted to the chest, eyes closed, fists tiny, the wrinkled legs unlikely as bent pipe cleaners coming out of the diaper. It was surely vulnerable, it was surely the last real part of Elizabeth that would remain in his life.

Simon cupped his hand over his own paining forehead. So as a matter of fact he did understand, and perfectly, now that it was put so squarely before him, why it was Marty Voigt might be here, awash in feelings, looking out for this baby.

15

THE LITTLE WHITE LIGHTS spread like a succession of nets over each of the slender mountain ash trees in the mall. Christmastime. But the netted feeling made Tom's stomach faintly queasy; staring out his office window, all he could think of were caterpillar nests up in the trees at the lake. Gauzy triple-wrapped nests, squirming with life. Millions of caterpillars, and then, one year, army worms that dropped continually from exhausted leaf-stems. Nights in the cabin you could think the sound outside was a hard, slow rain, unless you knew.

He watched the familiar tall figure, leather topcoat buttoned up to the neck, move briskly through the wads of shoppers on the mall below. Tom did not move; he didn't notice any particular variation in his feeling, which was blankness, and the tepid wish to get back to the vision of the cabin. He could do better than caterpillar nests. He could place everybody just as he wished to see them: himself a decently trim twenty-seven, standing on the end of the dock. At the horizon Elizabeth cutting through lake water with that efficient backstroke. He could look down to see

Molly grinning up from inside a magic black circle of inner tube.

"See me swim? I'm swimming, Daddy."

He heard his secretary's voice, musical and low, and was for one clear moment sure that she stood behind him on the dock. He would erase everybody else, turn and fall into her arms. This had almost happened when he realized it was too late; a masculine murmur answered hers in the reception area. Tom took his feet off the bottom drawer of the desk.

He was out of his chair by the time Simon appeared in the doorway, leather coat laid somehow formally over one arm. Like a waiter. Shocked again by how *perfect* his brother-in-law could look. Was this what got to Elizabeth? He shook Simon's hand.

"Come on in. Didn't Chris offer to take your coat?"

"She did."

"Well, have a chair. I've got a pot of coffee in here . . ." He left the sentence in midair, looking for a sign.

"No, thanks."

Perfect manners, too, and yet why did it sound so rude? Tom went to the warmer and stood with his back to Simon while he poured himself a fresh cup. His job here was decorum. He was a lawyer. Simon had made an appointment. That is why they were in a room together, just keep that much straight. Keep the resentment, or whatever the hell it was, reined in tight. It was true about wanting somebody to blame.

Tom held the hot cup between his palms. "How's the baby?"

Simon regarded him carefully. "Doing well."

"Good. Well, I knew that, I guess. Jeanne told me. She stops by the nursery every morning. . . ."

"This has been very hard on Jeanne, I know. She's trying to look after everybody, taking care of herself last. . . ."

"She's got me to do some of that."

"Of course. It's the strain. And of course, your father doesn't make it easier for her or for the hospital staff—for anyone, really."

"Right. I know." Tom leaned against the windowsill and watched Simon's mouth move and make words. What was he getting at? What was anybody getting at anymore? He couldn't keep track. He wished he could look out the window and it would be summer, he could look out and see the lake spreading out in front of him with its white stabs of sailboats.

When Simon stopped talking and looked at him, Tom shook his head slowly. "I'll tell you the truth. I feel like I'm half out of my mind. I don't know what I'm saying or thinking. How are you, Simon?"

Simon colored. "Doing well."

It was such an obvious, helpless lie that Tom almost forgave him everything. He watched as Simon twisted his hands, the long reddish fingers interlaced. *Million-dollar hands.* What a crazy thing to be thinking, but you think crazy things. He did, anyhow. He surely did lately. *Red pills in a plastic bag, Simon. Where did they come from?*

Simon cleared his throat. "I came to ask you something about Elizabeth."

Tom felt his own color rise. *Here it comes, here's*

your turn at bat. Five thousand dollars, Tommy, where did the money come from?

Simon's eyes darted to Tom's and away. "I need your help with this. I want to do something. Legally, that is. I want you to help me set up . . ." He settled one hand around his mouth, as if he would fix its expression that way. He began talking through his hand. "I've been thinking what there is to do, what Elizabeth would . . ." He stopped, and after a moment cleared his throat again.

Tom pressed fingers and thumbs to his own temples. "Take your time," he murmured. Seeing himself telling Jeanne that night, *He's in worse shape than we are. We still have each other, we still have Molly. So far, so far, so far!*

Simon cleared his throat. Tom watched him pass a hand over his eyes, then spring up out of the chair.

Halfway to the window Simon turned, the color mottled on his cheeks. His eyes were hard. "Dammit. I don't care what your father or anybody like him thinks. I don't care what Terence Fallon says in this town about me or—"

"Simon. My father—you know him." Tom felt his chest gather like a fist. "My father is overwrought. We all are. Please let me apologize on his behalf for *anything*—"

"For *everything*?"

"—for *everything* he might have said. I'm sorry. We are all scratching for a way to hold on. I am sorry you have this added burden."

With his hand Simon cut through the air between them. "All right. All right. I don't even want to talk about this. I didn't come here to enter into this discussion and if I was in *my* right mind I wouldn't have."

"I will make him stop. I will ask him—"

"No. I don't care about that. What I want to do is *do something*. I want to put something in motion here. I want to donate a facility in Elizabeth's name, a temporary residence for people whose children, you know, are hospitalized. The Elizabeth Carmody Family Shelter, I think she'd like that. I'd renovate that house I have off East River Road. I just want you to set the thing up—we can iron out details later, can't we? I want to get this on paper and get some action started. Will you do that? Help me do that?"

The tears had welled up. Tom shifted his weight on the chair to reach for the handkerchief in his back pocket. All he wanted at this moment was the use of two words.

"That's great." His voice cracked anyhow.

16

SHE MADE IT A POINT TO PUSH through the double
doors at the end of the maternity corridor ahead of
Marty Voigt. She had allowed the girl to drive her
in that small car and to help her out of the passenger side in the parking lot, and to hold open the
big doors at the hospital entry. But then, in the
building where her son saved lives every day,
Marty Voigt had grabbed her arm and dragged
her over to the elevators, right in front of the
receptionist! That rubber mat just inside the big
hospital doors was a hazard, she was surprised nobody had broken their neck—she'd already got
her balance back and decided to say something to
Simon by the time Miss Voigt laid hold of her.
Then, before she could even think, she'd found
herself deposited inside the elevator and the girl,
without consulting her at all, had punched the
button that said four. That was fine, that was all
very kind she was sure, but here in the place
where her son was chief of surgery, Nellie
Carmody was not just some old lady on a visit.

"We turn left out of the elevator." A voice like
syrup.

"I've been before." She made her own voice
cold, and when the door slid open, she shook off

the girl's arm. Marty Voigt would simply have to see where she fit in.

She hurried up the corridor in order to arrive at the nursery window as much alone as could be managed. She patted her hair in place. To her great relief the big dark-haired nurse turned and saw her—one of the Maccobbee girls, it looked to be. Miss Maccobbee smiled and went straight to the bassinet marked BOY CARMODY.

Nellie stole a glance sideward, but Marty Voigt had thrown herself against the glass, like a cheerleader at a hockey rink. "He's got his eyes open!"

Nellie allowed herself a glare of inspection. *"His* name is Patrick Simon," she pronounced. "After his father, and Great-grandfather Fallon."

The Maccobbee girl wheeled the little cart directly in front of them, and Nellie nodded her thanks. But instead of leaving and going about her business, the nurse gave a silly wave. Nellie saw Marty Voigt wave back. She peered at the name on the nurse's chest, the way an honest citizen would note the license plate of a suspicious automobile.

"Did you go to school with Ellen Maccobbee?"

That smooth face turned pink. "She's just seen me here before. Yesterday, when Simon was here. Ohh! Look, he's yawning!"

Nellie made her back a little straighter. *So that was it.* In a severe tone she said, "Babies need sleep. They need some peace too." She would have put a finer point on it, but out of the corner of her eye she'd caught sight of someone coming through the double doors. Dark hair, a head that ducked forward, then the heavy feet.

"Charlie!" It came out more heatedly than she

would have wished. She looked about to see if anyone else had heard, then fixed her son with a stare as he came jauntily jackbooted, still in his work jeans with the mended pocket, treading down the clean hall.

"Hi, Ma, how's our boy today?" He wore an idiot's grin. "Hello, Marty."

"Charles," she said, cooling her voice to notify him, "I thought you were working this afternoon."

"I was, I was working. I'm taking a break, okay?"

"If you'd thought to let me know, we could have saved Miss Voigt a trip."

"It was no trouble," Marty Voigt said. "Hello, Charlie."

"The kid's sleeping, eh?" Nellie's younger son pushed his face up to the glass just above the bassinet, and plopped his big elbows on the wooden rail. "Just taking a break, right, little guy?"

"His eyes were open before."

"You saw 'em? What color?"

"Blue," she said. "Beautiful blue eyes."

"All babies are born with blue eyes." Nellie meant to make something clear to both of them. "His will turn brown before he's six weeks old. Simon's did, turned brown like my father's. *Your* eyes stayed blue as the day you were born, Charles."

"I could have changed them if I really wanted to, Ma." He swiveled his head and gave her that round-eyed look meant to pass for innocence. "I was just waiting for the right time."

Nellie let out an audible sigh. "I may as well see the nurse in charge, since I'm here." She turned and walked down to tap on the glass of the nursery enclosure. Miss Maccobbee looked up and came smiling to the window. Yes, the baby was taking his fluids well; no, he wasn't being handled by anyone apart from the nursing staff; yes, Dr. Carmody had been down that very morning. Did Mrs. Carmody wish him to be called?

"No, no, that wouldn't be necessary." She was gracious and she could see the nurse, young as she was, appreciated her concern. Everyone knew that when Patrick Simon was ready to go home, it would be Nellie Carmody who'd have the care of him.

Cutting her eyes back at Charlie, she turned to walk the other way. As for Marty Voigt, she needn't think she'd be nuzzling up to Dr. Simon Carmody without anybody taking notice. Nellie was shocked by the brazen nature of modern girls, for once and all. She'd never been taken in by Elizabeth Fallon; what high-school girl ever left St. Cloud for four months except for one reason? And it wasn't to go to convent school, thank you; some of us weren't born yesterday. We know soiled goods when they come under our noses. But try to tell Simon that! You'd think a son wouldn't turn on a mother who had only his good in mind. Well, she had never said another word, of course. Simon was a grown man, he made his own bed to lie in. Still, the daughter of Terence Fallon was a different kettle of fish from one of Boz Voigt's! If Simon didn't think to know it, she would tell him what to think.

She found herself standing before the sign and arrow for Pediatrics. What a small world this was; to think Terence Fallon had two grandchildren in this hospital to her one. The poor man. Decent people had to offer one another what comfort they could.

•

She found the room number without difficulty, though no one seemed to be about. She put her head just inside the door of the child's room. There in the dim light she could see Jeanne Fallon's blond head bent to the white of hospital sheets. Had Jeanne always been a blond? Nellie thought not. Jeanne's mother was a Schwab, and all the Schwabs were brunettes. Oh, but the poor woman was kneeling in prayer at the bedside. Without quite meaning to Nellie let out a small sigh, and Jeanne's head lifted. Weary blue eyes found hers.

"I'm so sorry," Nellie whispered. "Don't let me disturb you."

Jeanne got to her feet and came to the door.

"No, no, don't trouble to come out. I just came to pay my respects, please don't trouble yourself."

"Mrs. Carmody. How kind of you to stop. You're here to see little Patrick, of course. How's he doing?"

"Climbing up every day. Soon ready to go home."

"What a blessing."

"Yes, and your little one, is she still—"

"Still in a coma." Jeanne turned to glance over her shoulder. When she turned back, she blinked as if to recall who she might be talking to.

"I went to school with your father-in-law," Nellie offered. "You might just tell him Nellie Carmody stopped by. I'm know he's suffering."

"Yes. I'm afraid it's been very hard these past

few days. I worry about Terry. First Elizabeth gone, and now . . ." Her voice went faint.

"There's nothing harder than seeing your own child go before you. Oh!" Nellie gasped, "I'm so sorry, I didn't mean you, I meant Terence, losing his one and only daughter, I didn't—"

Jeanne patted her hand. "No, no. It's a thought I live with. Mothers have to face these things, don't we? If it's God's plan to take Molly now, then He'll do it, and we have to accept."

"Why, yes. I guess that's so." Nellie crossed herself as Jeanne went on.

"Molly is ours only through His grace. We have to keep remembering that. We have to be prepared to give her up."

Nellie fidgeted. "The Lord giveth, the Lord taketh away, all right. But"—she dropped her voice to a whisper—"have they told you . . . ?"

"They don't know. All we can do is prepare. That's what I told Mrs. Mathews yesterday. I asked her if little Victor would stand as altar boy in the event . . ." She paused. "He and Molly have known each other since they were babies."

"Well. Our prayers are with you, up at our end." Nellie nodded again toward the nursery, and took a step back.

"Thank you."

"You know Simon's right here in this hospital, if you need anything."

"Thank you, Mrs. Carmody. I've been meaning to come down and see the baby, but it's hard to leave Molly—"

"No, no," she said swiftly. "Don't trouble yourself. He's just fine, he'll be fine." With that she backed away and fled down the hall. How eager she was to lay her eyes on the solid healthy flesh of one of her own!

Outside the double doors of the nursery she was surprised and pleased to find Charlie by himself, waiting for her.

"I can take you home," he said. "If you're ready to go."

"I'm ready." She drew her first easy breath. "Where's Miss Voigt?"

"Ma, her name is Marty. Why not call her that?"

His voice had a queer sound, and he would not meet her gaze as they turned to walk down the corridor together. In fact, Charles Dean Carmody was wearing a face that looked like he was hiding something. How well she knew that look!

"I had a long talk with Jeanne Fallon," she said, glancing at him sideways to appraise his grasp of that fact. "The poor thing is white with agony. She won't leave that child's bedside, of course, and who knows when she's had an hour's sleep? Then there's another child at home—" she shook her head. "It's a terrible shame on this family, Charlie, but it's shame on the Fallons too." She lowered her voice. "It wasn't me or Simon taught Elizabeth Fallon to leave drug-pills in her coat pocket!"

Charlie stopped to look at her. "How do they know that for sure? That the pills were in Elizabeth's pocket?"

"The older girl said she saw them, but she didn't know the young one got into them—"

"What kind of pills? Do they know that yet?"

"Don't you listen to things? They know from the blood work what kind they were." She dredged her brain trying to bring out the Latin words Simon had rattled off to her over the dinner table last night.

"Diazepam, Percodan?" Charlie said. "Quaaludes?"

"No, no, no! Those don't sound right. I'm sure not. Anyway, it's just too bad that older child didn't say something at the time. Of course, older can't always look after younger."

Beside her Charlie fell silent. Good. She liked it that he could be made to take something seriously. "So there's poor Jeanne Fallon, one child deathly ill, another young one at home, a husband to see after, funeral arrangements to be thinking of—"

Charlie stopped again. "Wait," he said. "What funeral?"

"Well, for the child! If she doesn't live, there's things have to be thought of."

He stood there shaking his head. "I think it's weird, Ma."

She burst into a fury. "It is not weird! And who are you to start *thinking*, at this late date? What I've told you was told to me in confidence! Jeanne Fallon opened her sore heart to another mother and you wouldn't understand, Charlie Carmody. People must think how life is to go on, what has to be done. You weren't even here when we buried your father! How am I supposed to hold my head up in this town when I have a son who has been behind prison bars? What is it exactly that you expect me to say to people? Have you given one moment's thought to how miserable you've made your mother's life, or your brother's? Of course you haven't."

He had gone quiet again, eyebrows lifted in that way that made her want to break him in two. That was it about Charlie, so much like his father that she could find herself bristling at him over nothing at all—except this was not nothing. She made up her mind to say not one word more, but by the time they were out of the hospital doors and picking their way across the slush in the parking lot, one more thought had struck her. "That Voigt girl. There's someone who thinks ahead. She didn't invite herself along to keep you or me company, now that's clear as day even to you, isn't it, Charlie?"

17

LYING IN FRONT OF THE BIG BAY WINDOW in the dining room, Charlie stared up into the morning sky. At this early hour it showed the palest blue, tinged with gold. He was glad he'd moved his sleeping bag down. The view from his old room upstairs was a crosshatch of tree branches cut by power lines. His parents' room was a little better, but he could do without the sagging double bed. Also the wallpaper—green roses on a black background; a standoff between gaudy and gloomy. He felt better waking up to the egg-yellow or whatever it was the dining room walls were supposed to make you think of.

Yawning, he raised himself up on his elbows, feeling oddly at peace, although his muscles ached from bending over the sawhorses, measuring and cutting wood, and his hands were stiff. He'd spent yesterday afternoon tearing out the old kitchen cupboards with a crowbar, chopping and stacking the wood for kindling. Today he would frame in the new ones and take a look at the plumbing. The wood underneath the sink was warped. It worried him. He hoped it would turn out to be something minor, like a bad seal in the trap. Anything more complicated and Si would need to get a real plumber in here.

He sat up and watched a black squirrel scramble down the cedar tree near the corner of the house. The first black one he'd seen. Sleet had laid a heavy crust on top of the snow, and the little animal leapt across its hard surface as if it were solid ground.

He went out to the kitchen and searched through the bag of groceries he'd bought yesterday—instant coffee, peanut butter, crackers, potato chips, a loaf of white bread, and a can of tuna fish. He rummaged through the shoebox where he'd dumped the kitchen utensils. Yes, a can opener.

As he crossed the gray-spattered linoleum to the refrigerator, he realized he'd forgotten to buy mayonnaise. *Damn.* He crumbled the tuna thickly over the bread and washed it down with a Coke. Why did the food seem to taste better here? Maybe what they said about clean air was true; clean air and clean living. *Not all that clean, not really.*

He sat with his feet on the table, thinking about the work to be done. A week or so and he'd have the kitchen in good shape. Then he'd move to the upstairs. Si had talked of dividing the bedrooms into smaller units. Was he planning to turn the place into apartments?

"Prettiest grove in Sherburne County," the old man used to say. That gorgeous green tunnel of a driveway leading up to the house—in the summer the shade so deep the temperature dropped ten degrees when you turned in from the road. Now all of the elms were gone, and the few oaks that

were left, with their clumps of dried leaves clinging to them, looked about ready to give it up. If the
old man could see the place now. Well, then, he
shouldn't have kicked off, left all the caretaking to
Miss Nellie. She was never good at that sort of
thing.

His father dying while he was in jail—that had
been the worst. Although at the time he'd been so
numb it hadn't fully registered. His mother hadn't
written to tell him about it until after the funeral,
but that was all right. He wouldn't have been able
to come home anyway. And they'd never been
close, never even been *friends,* for Chrissake.
Maybe that was what was hitting him now. No
more chances; it was all over.

He wondered how Simon had handled it. Simon
and the old man were always such big buddies—all
those hunting and fishing trips that he was at first
too young to go on, and then wouldn't go on,
purely out of jealousy and spite. He had never
forgiven Mike Carmody for showing such pride in
everything his older son was doing. Well, he'd sure
fixed him good for that one, hadn't he? Fixed himself in the bargain.

A lot of people had held opinions then about his
future: the principal of the high school, the priest
at St. Mary's, Boz Voigt. Old Man Fallon, too, for
that matter. High school had been a wild time, and
he had skated through, barely making it. He
winced to think of that month-long binge he'd
been on before graduation.

And suddenly he was seeing Marty with her
hands on the glass of the nursery window, staring
in at the tiny figure of Boy Carmody—spelled out
on a card taped to the hospital isolette.

"Looks like Edward G. Robinson, doesn't he?" he had said. "All he needs is a big cigar."

"He's beautiful," Marty had whispered.

"That's what I meant."

"He looks so helpless. With all that machinery."

"No way. This guy is tough. He made it this far, didn't he?"

That won him a smile. The baby was awake and turning his head from side to side; for a moment he thought that tender look reserved for Boy Carmody might transfer to the uncle. If so, he would not be above using it.

And then she had looked away. "It's late," she said. "I should go. Your mother . . . would you mind taking her home, as long as you're here?"

"No, I don't mind. She giving you a hard time?"

"I've got class tonight. I should stop at the library."

"Sure." He had let his tone go ironic. What the hell, he was already looking at her back as she walked away.

Sitting now in the kitchen where he'd grown up, he felt a sudden longing for all the things that were missing in his life. *Homesick.* That was how he felt. Weird to be this lonely in your own house in your own hometown; how could you be homesick for something that never was? Well, he'd be gone by the end of January, just do the work and split. He was already sick of the snow, and he hadn't felt like skiing since his army days. Go someplace warm. Someplace where nobody knows anything about you and hasn't any goddamn *opinions* either.

•

He had the cupboards under the window framed in by three o'clock and decided to push ahead, trimming the rest of the boards to the lengths he needed and stacking them in the corner. He swept up the sawdust and put it in the wastebasket. *A good carpenter keeps the job clean.*

He was a good carpenter, no doubt about it—the one thing he'd been willing to learn from his father. Mike Carmody had been the best around, and the whole town had known it. He had never lacked for work, even though he wasn't always dependable. The whole town had known that too.

He checked again for the leak underneath the sink; found it was at the upper seal of the trap. He would pick up what he needed at Gopher Lumber and start on that job tomorrow.

He shaved and put on a clean pair of jeans and the plaid shirt he had found hanging in an upstairs closet. It didn't look like one of his, but it fit him all right. He pulled his navy crew-neck on over it.

Elizabeth's emerald Camaro was parked near the back door. He loved that little car, stylish, easy to drive. He'd have to clean out the garage soon so he could put it away.

He drove out the long driveway to the mailbox with M. CARMODY written in longhand across the side. His father had written the name in pencil and filled it in, using his mother's red nail polish. A testimony to Revlon—not a chip after all these years.

Mike Carmody, whose printing was as precise as a draftsman's. Why hadn't he printed their name on the box? One of those stupid things that would never make sense. Charlie could still hear the voices when he got off the school bus: "Hey, where'd your old man learn to write cursive?" One day he'd blown a fuse and decked somebody over that. It was the last time he ever had trouble with them. Of course he'd been kicked off the bus for a month, had to walk the two miles to school, but it had been worth it. He wondered what all those guys on bus number seven were doing these days.

He drove into town the long way, past the Longest Continuous Granite Structure in the World— had that phrase come out of some Minnesota guidebook? As if the thick gray wall around the reformatory were something to be proud of. *"Look at genuine mortared granite cubes hacked out of native rock by your local captive work force."* Beyond the farthest guard tower were the tops of the oaks that stood around the quarry. Somehow the idea of cons breaking rocks used to be a lot funnier, back on those summer nights when he and Nick would sneak off to the quarry for a cold swim. A whole lot funnier.

He parked behind the new Herberger's Department Store and walked down to the Loose Tie. Fandel's was gone, other stores had changed names and faces, but he had the distinct feeling it was the same old place. The yellow egg-carton dome of the courthouse told him that. But he had to admit, the new library looked impressive. Someday he would go in and take a look around.

Down the steps of the old bank building on the mall Charlie tried to peer in the windows of the bar, but the ferns were too thick. He pushed the glass door open and saw the place was nearly empty. Early yet. A few college kids sitting around drinking beer. He could tell they were students; the girls all dressed alike—long hair, big-shouldered sweaters, baggy pants tapered at the ankles. The boys looked alike too. They all looked too young.

He sat at the bar and ordered a beer. He liked to blend into the background and watch things happen. At the nearest table they were talking about exams and the coming semester break. One of the girls kept looking over at him. She had hair the color of wheat, worn in a loose braid down her back. That old-fashioned look must be in again— he'd seen a lot of it in town lately. This one had a well-scrubbed look, with a wide grin; she kept including him in it. Or else he was forcing her, with his own staring. He spun around to face the bar. It didn't take much to amuse him these days—a glass of beer and a good-looking girl to flirt with from a distance.

He had a meat loaf sandwich while he watched two guys set up mikes and tune their guitars. When they got going they weren't bad, or else he was in a good mood. A lot of Hank Williams stuff. They both had voices that made those whiskey lyrics sound sensible.

The girl with the braid caught his glance and held it, then slid her eyes away. He decided it was time to leave.

She looked up as he passed her table. "Sit down, why don't you?"

He shook his head and smiled. "Like your hair," he said. He left without looking back.

The temperature had dropped in the time he'd been inside. He zipped his jacket, pulling his gloves out of the pockets. Heading down the street to where he'd left Elizabeth's car, he thought about the thousands upon thousands of nights he'd spent sitting and drinking at bars, letting his life slip away, not even aware it was happening. Stupid, that's what he had been.

He parked in front of Coborn's on Fifth Street, left the motor running while he went inside. He bought a six-pack of beer, a bag of honey-roasted cashews, and a small jar of mayonnaise. Then he drove to Voigt's Family Store.

He got out and locked the car—you couldn't be too careful, he didn't want anybody stealing his mayonnaise. He went around back to the open stairs that led up to Marty's apartment.

He was still preparing the speech he figured he'd have to give through the door when it opened and she stood there in jeans and a bright red shirt with the sleeves rolled to the elbows.

"I read my horoscope," he said, handing her the cashews. "It said, 'You won't believe the nerve of some people today.' I figured that meant me."

To his relief she didn't close it in his face.

"What do you want, Charlie?"

"Some conversation," he said. "I brought my own snacks." He produced two cans of beer from his jacket pockets. She hesitated, then beckoned him inside.

The small living room had tan walls and rusty tweed carpeting. A Danish Modern couch, left over from the sixties, was pushed against one wall. A round table stood between two soft, high-backed chairs.

He offered her a beer. She shook her head.

"I take it you meant it about not drinking," he said. "Since when?"

"A while ago."

"I should quit drinking." He popped the top of the can, watched white foam bubble up through the hole. Tipping his head back, he drank.

"So." Marty took a breath. "What have you been doing with yourself?"

"Since yesterday?"

"Since high school."

"Not a lot. I got out of the army in seventy-nine. But I didn't come back to the States until eighty-one. Just hung around Europe for a while. Then I bummed around Mexico."

"Doing what you do best, huh?"

He smiled. "I took the liberty of reading your horoscope too. It said, 'Your outspoken opinions will get you into trouble.'"

"Sorry."

He leaned back in the chair. "You mad at me about something?"

"No. Why?"

"You haven't been too friendly."

She shrugged. "I haven't been friendly at all. You make me nervous."

"Why?"

"I don't know. You came back to town when I wasn't expecting it, I guess."

"Me either," he said. "It's funny. This very morning I was sitting at the kitchen table eating my tuna-fish sandwich and pondering the vicissitudes of life."

It took her by surprise, and she laughed. "The what?"

"How I screwed mine up."

"How did you, Charlie?"

She seemed more relaxed, now, settled back in

her chair, her hair tied loosely with a red scarf. It reminded him a little of the girl in the bar.

"I'll tell you about it sometime." He took another sip. "When did you come back here?" he asked. "Last I heard you were out on the Coast."

"What coast?"

"The West Coast. San Diego, I heard."

She shook her head. "I've been back for nine years. I moved back here from Chicago."

To cover his confusion he took another long pull on the beer, then set the can down next to his feet. "Jesus," he said at last, "he's such a fucking liar. I wonder why I'm always so surprised."

Marty's voice was clipped and flat. "I wonder too."

"He told me you two got divorced," Charlie said. "That you met some guy and moved out to California with him. I would have looked you up if I'd known."

No reply. She brushed at the sleeve of her blouse. If he strained his ears he could barely hear the ticking of the wall clock out in the kitchen. He bent to pick up the beer and leaned with his head resting against the back of the chair.

"He was always fun to be with. Right up until the minute he fucked you over, you were having a great time."

"Speak for yourself."

"I was." He lifted his head and looked at her. "What happened with you two, anyway?"

"I don't really want to trade war stories with you, Charlie. I'm not much interested in ancient history."

"Marty. It's me, Uncle Charlie, you're talking to."

She wouldn't look at him. "I got sick. I got divorced. Then I moved back here."

"Do you ever hear from him?"

"No. But I'm sure you could find him if you tried."

He let that go. "So, what classes are you taking this year?"

"You wouldn't be interested. They're not exactly your line of work."

"My line of work. What's that?"

"Nothing. I just meant . . . they're dry. Statistics. Theory. Everything you have to know so you can forget it all when you go out to do the job." She stood.

His time was up. He set the beer can on the table. "Guess I'd better go," he said. "Got a lot of work to do tomorrow."

She walked him to the door.

"Cold out there," he said. "Hope it warms up before I leave."

She didn't ask when that would be. Her hand was resting lightly on the door frame, about six inches from his face.

"Nice to see you," he said.

"Same here."

"What about tomorrow?"

She looked puzzled. "What about it?"

"I'd like to see you again." It came out in a rush, or he might have tried for something smoother.

Marty was already shaking her head. "Charlie. I don't date."

"Could we call it something else? Like, better than being by yourself?"

"I have class tomorrow."

"What time d'you get out?"

131

"Eight o'clock."

"Which building?"

"Stewart Hall. Near the Union."

"I'll pick you up."

"Charlie, wait." She hesitated. "I'm thirty years old. . . ."

He laughed. "Me too. So, how'd this happen to us, anyway?" At least now she was smiling. He left before she could think of an argument.

On the way home he smoked one of the joints he'd stashed under the maps in the glove compartment, feeling at peace again, driving through the clear, starry night back to the house he wasn't homesick for.

18

THE LOBBY OF THE GRANITEWAY MOTOR INN was deserted, and the girl behind the counter had her head down, didn't notice him, although he was standing directly under the registration sign. Well, what he wanted was to be invisible, right? But not yet. And not to the whole sweet world of women. Leaning toward her he drummed his fingers lightly on the countertop. *A busy man.*

The girl glanced up, then, and smiled. The rectangular label on her dark green jacket read LAURA.

"Hi. Can I help you?"

"I'll bet you can, Laura," he drawled.

The smile vanished. She straightened her shoulders, all business. *Moving way too fast today, Nicko. Slow it down.*

"Nick Uhler, Uhler Computer Personnel. I'm looking for a room."

"How many nights?"

"At least two. Good as you've got. I'll be doing some interviewing so make it the second floor, not too near the pool."

"Single?"

He leaned both elbows on the counter. "Definitely."

Her hands paused over the terminal, but she did not look up.

"Bad joke," he said. "I'm feeling single today. My dog just died. Had him for thirteen years."

That got her. "Oh, I'm sorry," she said, her face going all melty. A nice St. Cloud farm girl. He liked those arched eyebrows and the dark, shiny hair, parted low on the side. He shrugged and gave her a grim smile. *A busy and a brave man.*

She got up and went to the card file, and he noted the pleasant curve of her ass in the tight skirt; her short, muscular legs. He stood patiently by while she located a room key for him.

"Will you be paying with a credit card?"

"What's the rate?"

"Forty a day."

"Still a small town, isn't it?" He pulled his billfold out of his back pocket and laid the cash down on the counter.

She handed him his key. "The room's around the other side of the building," she said. "Near door three. There's parking over there."

"Thanks a lot, Laura." He glanced around the lobby. "Quiet around here today."

"It always is, this close to Christmas. It'll pick up right after the holidays."

"Christmas," he said, shaking his head. "I guess I won't be forgetting this one. The year I lost my best friend." He couldn't help it, the stuff just flowed out of him, even when he didn't need it, couldn't use it in fact. Still, it wouldn't hurt. She would be good for any favors he might need.

"You could get yourself a puppy," she suggested.

"Good idea. I'll think about it. Thanks."

134

He turned then and pushed through the sets of double doors to the parking lot. *The brave, busy man goes right to work.*

•

Behind the wheel of the rental Buick—a step up from last time—he thought about the load he was carrying in the trunk. He had definitely turned the corner, was on the way up. The five thousand had saved his ass, but he'd never be in that kettle of soup again; he'd finally learned his lesson—trust your own instincts, nobody else's. He had let himself rely on bad information that last time, and it had been a close one.

Even here, in the town where he grew up, the same rules applied: you had to know exactly how far you could push. For instance, Mace was like every new dealer he'd ever worked with—dying to prove his reliability. Therefore, you could relax for the first few rounds, because the kid would be careful for both of them. After that—hell, even twenty-year-olds get greedy and start to cheat. So the early deals were where you stood to make the money; later on, Mace would either be after his job, or else out of the business.

He glanced at his watch as he turned onto Division Street. Two fifteen: a couple of hours to kill.

•

Nick ran his eyes over the frame bungalows on the block. The sign, VOIGT'S FAMILY STORE, was still above the door of the second house from the corner. He let the Buick glide slowly to a stop.

The curb still had the notch in it that he used to ride his bike through. *It all comes back. I mean, it all comes back.* Turning the key he sat for a minute. If this was Hallowe'en, he could predict, down to the last candied apple and stick of Juicy Fruit, what would come out of every door on this street. He bet the same old ladies would still answer the doors.

He got out and leaned against the car, taking a look around. Mrs. Dale's place on the corner, Mr. Schlimmer's fussy garden with the bird statues— nothing he hadn't seen one hundred million times before. Well, that was a good thing, right? The world needed places like this, places where everything stayed locked down tight. No surprises. So when you got the hell out, you knew exactly what you were missing.

He pushed off, picking his way through the crusty snow just as the old man came out the door of the grocery and stood squinting at him.

"Well, well," Boz brayed in that voice like a bullhorn. "You can tell when the river's down. The rats come sneaking around. 'Course if I was a drinking man I'd say I was seeing things."

He didn't slow down. Just act like everything's the way you expect it to be; people will bend to that. Still, he stopped short of the spread of concrete around the foot of the steps.

"Thought I'd stop and see Marty," Nick said. "Old times, you know?"

"Old times is why you ain't welcome here."

Nick smiled. "I guess not. Just let me grab a pack of Marlboros."

"Get 'em at a gas station." Up on the top step the old man staggered, then hunched over as if he meant to block the door.

Nick sighed. He took out a pack of cigarettes and drew out the last one. He crushed the pack, turned, and tossed it into the big trash barrel beside the Coke machine. Good old Boz. Still the king of drama, still wearing that face like a dirty fist, wanting a fight so bad he could taste it. He liked acting the DA in those black-and-white flicks he watched on TV. *If I was a drinking man.* What a joke.

He lit his cigarette and calculated how many punches it would take. He snapped the lighter shut and held it in his hand. Damn, this wasn't what he came for.

"So, how's business?"

"Good enough without yours." Boz came down two steps and stuck his elbows out. He was in shirt-sleeves in the cold, and shaking. "Quite the coincidence, isn't it? You and Charlie both stopping by the same week."

"Charlie's in town?"

"Don't give me that shit. You know he's here, all right. Weasels travel in packs."

Nick grinned. " 'Weasels travel in packs.' Where'd you get that one, Boz? That's a new one on me."

"He says he came in for the funeral. What's your excuse?"

On second thought. Maybe it might be worth it to wipe that sneer off the old man's face. "Yeah, I heard about it." He tossed the half-smoked ciga-rette into the snow. "What do you hear about the baby?"

The old man stopped. "What baby?"

"The one Elizabeth had. I heard it was a boy. He still in the hospital?"

Boz stood rocking on the porch, fists clenched. "You want to talk about babies?" he snarled. "You got a goddamn nerve. I told you what I'd do if you ever showed your face again."

"Yeah, I believe you did." Nick smiled. Then he put up his hands. There wasn't going to be any fight. He'd pick his own time and place to settle scores. "Just tell her I stopped by."

•

Angling the Buick into a parking space stenciled in white RESTRICTED DOCTORS PARKING, he glanced in the rearview mirror. A little risky, but he didn't plan to be here long. He locked the car and walked up the curving driveway.

The wide front doors swung smartly inward. He approached the woman behind the information desk.

"Where do I find the nursery?"

"Fourth floor, sir."

He stepped inside the first elevator, then faced front and gave the woman a wave and a wide grin. *The happy father.*

When the doors closed on him, his face went blank. The moment he'd been avoiding ever since he'd heard, and it happens to him in a goddamned elevator. Well, people die—that's the given. The thing was, he could feature her getting old, getting fat, dragging her string of kids around to piano lessons and Little League and fucking Europe. She had wanted that so bad she could taste it. Sure as hell wasn't his scene. Still, he guessed the whole thing got to him. *Well, Nicko, cry about it, then, go ahead.*

But when the doors opened again, he was over it. He stepped out into the hallway, turned left, and walked past the nurses' station. He'd gotten this far; he could find the nursery without their help. But there was only room after room; just a quick glimpse of a window frame, the foot of a bed, a straight chair, a TV set mounted on the wall. Then he was at the end of the corridor. He turned around, retraced his steps.

"I'm looking for the babies," he said to a brunette in a nurse's uniform.

"The nursery? That's on four," she said. "This is the third floor."

He smiled. "Guess I got off the elevator too soon."

Down the hall a plump blonde in a blue suit was taking a drink from the fountain. This town was full of women he knew. He took a long look as she stood up. But no. He felt her eyes on him as he pressed the button and stood waiting for the next car.

On the fourth floor he turned left again out of the elevator and there were the nursery windows giving off bright light into the hallway. This would be easy. Standing before the glass he scanned the name cards on the dozen or so plastic boxes, all occupied with little melon heads bobbing up and down.

Nobody was around, except for one lone nurse who sat at the far end of the room with her back to him. Security around here was lax as hell; he could be through that glass door and out again in one minute.

He spotted BOY CARMODY in the back row and stared hard through the glass, willing the bed-on-wheels to come closer so he could get a good look. He just wanted to *see* the kid for now.

Twenty minutes later he was pulling into the motel parking lot across from door number three. Room 332 was on the west side of the hall. He unlocked the door, switched on the overhead light, and crossed to check the view. Facing the parking lot. Perfect. He could keep his eye on the Buick with its special delivery package in the trunk. He still had an hour before he had to meet Mace.

The brownish gloom that settled in these closed up places reminded him of the house over in Pan Town. Saturday afternoons listening to the ball game on the radio and his mother on the couch, nursing one of her famous migraines. Funny. He hadn't thought about that dump since she died and now, twice in one week.

He dialed room service, ordered a giant roast beef sandwich with horseradish and ketchup, and two Moosehead ales. Then he flipped open the St. Cloud phone book and began looking up the numbers he would be needing.

Old times, all right. Imagine Old Man Fallon thinking money was all that made the world go round. Nick Uhler was here to show him a shortcut.

19

JEANNE GLANCED OVER HER SHOULDER where
her daughter lay so very unnaturally quiet. *Only
believe.* She got up from her metal folding chair,
which she had placed just outside the door of Molly's room. With her arm she nudged the door
wider and, without Terry's noticing, slipped
through. She walked to the bed and laid her face
next to the child's soft cheek. She needed to feel
the warmth, needed to feel the light breath play
against her skin. She allowed herself a moment
only. It was dangerous to wear down the presence
of the child's guardian angels with all her mortal
neediness.

Outside the room her father-in-law was pacing
toward her again down the long waxed hall. Under
the round fluorescent discs, rings of light showed
where the buffer had moved along, making end-
less circles. He dragged his feet like careless erasers through the perfection.

"The head nurse has no more idea than the
pope what's going on here." The word *pope* had
come out of his lips like a small explosion. Underneath the raked iron-gray of his hair, even his scalp
showed pink. Jeanne looked at her father-in-law
with a customary and determined affection. Terry

Fallon's rages frightened Tom still; Jeanne had never found him a threatening man. His voice was deep and forceful, the monologues wearying, but he was so lacking in essential menace. That was what *she* thought, Tom would say. Of course, what frightened you was what you grew up with. These last few days she had grown up so far beyond anything she had ever guessed was possible; she felt incapable of being frightened now. Though it was unwise to boast. She tried to offer Terry a smile. She knew, underneath all his restlessness, he was in pain. So lost!

Turning his head he aimed a forefinger at the nurses' station down the polished corridor. It stood momentarily empty, untended. But this was a quiet ward.

"I stopped to inquire about staff rounds—I have never missed a board meeting, I happen to know we instituted specific regulations a year ago. Rounds are to be maintained by the ward staff under supervision of the head nurse. In twenty minutes we have seen exactly two orderlies and one candy-striper. I cannot think how they can call this responsible monitoring of patients."

He would not say Molly's name. He would not look at the form that made such a small ripple under the white sheets. He would inspect the bathrooms and the drinking fountain and he would time the rounds the staff made. This was his way. Fine. It was up to her to see after Molly. Let him keep thinking he was of some use. His comforts were few.

He was the reason she'd put her chair out here in the first place, so that his voice and his continual pacing would have range. In the room with the child Jeanne thought they would drive her mad. This was the solution, but at this distance from the tents created in the sheet by Molly's two small feet, her body strained backward to lie next to her child as she had done all those nights when Molly had been a baby. Nursing meant picking her up from the cradle beside the double bed where Tom lay snoring beside her, and letting the fussing, mewling infant mouth find her nipple. Often she herself drifted off to sleep, but no harm had ever come of that. Her babies were protected. She believed deeply, gladly, in a God who could keep essential things ordered and safe. She could sleep because He didn't; she had never come awake with so much as a shoulder pinning one of her babies in discomfort. Just as when one of the children walked into a room where she lay fully asleep, a sacred awareness intervened and caused her to snap awake. She felt her heart drawn like an invisible bowstring between her chair and Molly's bed. Half of what was real was forever unseen. She needed to concentrate, whether Terry was here or not; she had to stay prepared to receive the message.

"When was the last time Simon showed his face?" he demanded.

"He was here this morning at seven, and again just before you came." She would not be drawn into this.

The old man mumbled under his breath, then looked at her narrowly. "What about Vogel? Rice? What about the ward supervisor?"

She placed no hope in the doctors, or in regulations; what difference could it make who came or when? Molly's life hung by one thread, and Jeanne

143

believed in prayer. Every breath she took went out of her as prayer. She did not pray for her child's life, which would be arrogance; did you convince God of anything? No. You accepted. If you were shown that you had work to do, you received the sign and offered your labor with thanksgiving. That was all.

"And the doctors around here may think they're God; it confounds the layman but it does not impress the board. Not with evidence of outright incompetence—"

She watched this aged infant, stiff with the memory of weight and power. Oh, he had it all once. Tom said nobody ever recovered from that much power. Well, it depended on what you were willing to face, what you understood you could give up. She watched his cream-colored leather shoes make streaks as he made his circuit back and forth in front of her chair. *Accept.* That was the trial of spirit before her. She would offer up what she had pridefully thought hers. The funeral would be brief; that she knew. No orations. What is more eloquent than a child taken to God?

"My beloved wife died in this building under all those miraculous hands." He spread his long bent fingers. "That fact does not escape me, nor the fact that my only daughter died here. Married to a man not worthy of the trust."

"Now, Dad."

"My only daughter, sent off to specialists *to help her get pregnant*! I was a fool to allow it! Simon Carmody thought he had to have a son, and he used—"

She cut him off. "That's not fair to Simon and not

144

fair to Elizabeth. They went through a lot for this baby."

"Indeed. Indeed. And so, we have a baby. What we do not have is Elizabeth." His voice clutched on the name, and she watched his eyes fill and their surfaces tremble. He struggled and then turned the force of his feeling back to rage.

"She was almost thirty years old!" The red face bore down on her now. "I tell you, this is someone's fault. Jeanne! Why don't you get that child of yours out of this place? Don't count on God to intervene—is that what you're sitting there dreaming about?"

At that she sprang up from her chair, seized his arm, and said with a firmness that surprised her, "Dad, I'm just going down the hall for a drink of water. Will you stay with Molly? Just here in the hall?"

The look of confusion that passed over his face almost confused her too. Had he forgotten where they were and what had passed between them? She hadn't! She knew she was standing in the hospital corridor, so angry at her father-in-law that she had wanted to harm him. She found she had gathered his jacket sleeve under her fingers; now she let go.

"Watch over Molly, please," she prayed aloud.

The old man nodded dumbly.

Turning from him she crossed herself. She didn't care if he saw her do it. Fear was the enemy; it was what there was to know of evil. If you ran from fear you never stopped running. Jeanne determined to walk, and steadily, to the drinking fountain. The long corridor seemed to feed itself to her feet. She longed to make it feed faster—

longed to run, wasn't that why her thigh muscles suddenly felt like jelly, wasn't that the leaking of fear? She had not left it behind her. She had brought the evil with her and now she breathed deeply and held herself upright. Turning the corner she saw no one. She reached for the knob under the white porcelain bowl and bent to its clear curl of water. How good it felt in her mouth, and running cold over her cheeks, her forehead, her eyes. A surge of pain: could eyeballs freeze under their lids? *If you do everything right, Molly will be safe.* What voice was that? Was it a voice? She straightened and leaned against the hard tile wall and wiped her face with her hands. That was when the vision came, another visitation of evil: she saw a man standing near the elevator wearing the face—she would swear it—of Nicky Uhler.

20

"I DIDN'T KNOW YOU WERE A PLUMBER." Simon was smiling down at him from his full height, hands in the pockets of his overcoat. Charlie tightened the last fitting with the wrench and slid out from under the sink.

"What brings you out here?"

"Just wanted to see how things were going." Simon looked around the small kitchen. "I sure hope you know what you're doing, because I don't."

"That a criticism?"

"An observation. I wouldn't have the faintest idea where to start with this. I never did pay any attention when Dad was talking." His smile was easy, relaxed.

Charlie grinned back, picking up his tools from the floor. "Inside the house, you mean."

"Oh. Well. A man with a gun in his hand—you do tend to listen better. Never could figure out the stuff with sawdust and plumb lines, though. Come upstairs with me, will you?"

"Sure." Charlie stood up and followed his brother down the narrow hallway toward the front of the house. They passed the dining room, where his jeans were hung over the backs of the chairs and his underwear was piled at one end of the table.

"You're sleeping in the dining room?"

Charlie gave a curt nod. Never apologize, never explain. He meant to discourage any and all discussions of his personal habits.

On the way upstairs Simon asked, "Could we divide the master bedroom, do you think? Make two rooms out of it? That'd give us five . . . and the porch off the living room would make six. . . ."

"If you're looking to use that porch year round, you'll have to have heat out there."

"What do you think—electric? We can't hook it up to the furnace, can we? Not at this late date."

"I doubt it."

"I guess I've got to take the next step. Get some input from the state."

"For what?" Charlie asked.

Simon glanced at him. "For the home."

"What home?"

"I told you."

"No, you didn't. You haven't told me anything."

His brother smiled. "I never said what this was for? I want to make it into a home for families of patients from out of town." Simon walked to the window and stood, looking out. "I want to do it in her name. Tom's going to handle the licensing end for me."

Charlie was silent, staring at his back. "Sounds like a good idea," he said at last. He bent to retrieve a scrap of paper from the carpet. "How's the baby doing?"

"The baby? Fine. Why?"

"Just . . . I haven't talked to you for a couple of

days. Mom's sort of vague. You never know if she's getting it all."

His brother gave a dry laugh. "An understatement if I ever heard one." He turned from the window. "This place feels chilly to me."

"I like to keep it cool when I'm working."

"Got plenty of wood for the furnace?"

He nodded. Together they headed back down the stairs, Charlie shuffling in his work boots, keeping up with Simon's clean and graceful stride. He felt itchy with sweat, looking forward to getting into a hot shower.

"We'd probably have to put in another bathroom up there," Simon mused. "I was thinking of drawing up a plan, but I wouldn't know what I was doing. I guess I ought to get an architect."

They had reached the bottom of the staircase but Simon made no move to leave, just stood looking around at the tattered, faded wallpaper in the foyer. Charlie felt the weight of some unasked question hanging in the air.

"I thought maybe you and I could sketch out a plan. What do you think?"

"Yeah, sure," Charlie said. "Whatever you want."

"Tonight? We could have dinner somewhere . . . ?"

"Not tonight," he said quickly, feeling a wave of guilt wash over him. This was the unasked question, then: Can you help me? I need to fill up some of this time.

"All right." Now Simon was moving toward the door, buttoning his coat. His foot kicked a wrench lying on the floor, and he bent over to pick it up. "Just give me a call sometime when you're free."

149

"Si. Wait a minute."

His brother looked up.

"The Celtics are playing the Lakers tomorrow night," Charlie said. "I was going to catch the game over at the Press."

"I haven't been to the Press Bar since before I was in med school."

"It's the same old place," Charlie said. "You ought to try it."

Simon hesitated. "All right. What time?"

"Probably around eight. I'll call you. Maybe we can grab a sandwich before."

•

In the shower he stretched his muscles, noting exactly where the tension was—his shoulders and his neck. He was learning to pay attention; it was good practice, helped him to control his moods.

So Simon wanted to be friends, after all this time. His own desire had vanished long ago. Odd how you could want something so much, and then when it finally moved toward you and you had to choose it, your fears leapt to the line.

The memories he had about Simon were mostly bad ones—Simon dumping him out of the wagon and breaking his collarbone; Simon leaving him stranded on the raft in the middle of the river—to teach him how to swim; Simon in the driveway of the old house, giving him hell about beer cans and cigarette butts in the brand-new car he'd lent him for graduation night. There had to be other stuff to remember; where had it disappeared to?

This whole thing felt strange—Christmas back in the town where he grew up. And then not as strange as some of the places he'd been— Garmisch, Greece, Mexico. Not to mention the slammer. That place had taught him all he needed to know about hard times.

The phone was ringing as he stepped out of the shower. Automatically he started to answer; then decided against it. He started dressing, imagining himself already on the road. *Too late to back out now, Marty.* It had to be her; who else even knew he was here?

He came down the stairs, grabbed his jacket from the banister, and heard the sound of a car. At the window he saw Simon's taillights disappearing down the driveway. Had he been sitting out there, alone in his car, all this time? Doing what? Charlie stood in the hall, staring up the road. He didn't know his brother.

•

He was waiting outside Stewart Hall by seven forty-five, having hurried through a sandwich and glass of beer at the Loose Tie. He listened to a Wynton Marsalis tape he'd found in the glove compartment, drumming nervously on his thighs, watching a couple of college guys throw snowballs at each other. Hell, if that's all there was to going back to school, he could handle it.

He waited until quarter after the hour, tracing the progress of several camel-hair coats down the wide sidewalk—all false leads. So, she had decided to stand him up. His move. Should he take a look inside? Go back to the Loose Tie and finish his beer, maybe.

The door on the passenger side opened and she sank into the seat beside him. She was breathing hard, as if she'd been running. "Sorry I'm late."

"No problem."

The smile on his face felt fake. He turned his head to pull out of the parking space.

"Oh, God," she said. "It's Elizabeth's car, isn't it?"

"Yeah. Simon lent it to me."

She was loosening the scarf from her hair; an odd, almost frightened look on her face.

"What's the matter? Does it bother you?"

"No. It's all right. I keep being reminded, that's all."

"Yeah. I think maybe Si didn't want it around either."

They drove in silence for a moment. "Where are we going?" she asked.

"No plan. Want to take in a movie?"

"Not really. What happened to the conversation?"

"We could go back to my place," he said. "Light a fire, have some hot chocolate."

"All right."

"First I have to stop at Voigt's Family Store."

"What for?"

"The hot chocolate."

Marty laughed. "Make it the 7-Eleven," she said.

He parked as close to the house as he could. The wind had picked up again; it stung their cheeks as they made their way to the back door. Charlie pushed it open, switched on the overhead light. Taking the paper bag from her he dumped it out on the table.

"So. How do you make hot chocolate?"

Marty laughed. "Get me a pan," she said, opening the container of cocoa. He hunted through one of the cardboard cartons, handing her a small saucepan.

"The water's turned on, isn't it?"

"Hey, what d'you think this is? Some kind of dive? We got water here. Both kinds."

"How about sugar?"

"Right here in the cupboard," he said, rummaging through another cardboard box on the table.

"I'll find it. You go light the fire."

On the hearth he laid twigs and chips over crumpled newspaper; then the logs he'd brought in from the porch. He lit it and watched the flames swim with the air currents over and under the split logs. The fire crackled as the dry scrap-wood caught. He brought his sleeping bag and spread it before the fireplace.

Marty came into the room carrying two cups. "Why's it so cold?"

"I'll turn up the heat," he said, going to the thermostat, pushing the dial up to seventy-five.

She had set his hot chocolate on the end table and was sitting on the couch, hunched over, warming her hands around her cup.

"Social work," he mused. "I bet you'll be good at that. Remember the baby bird that fell out of its nest? How you nursed it with the eyedropper? You always were good at taking care of things."

She winced. "I don't much like that one. It's got a dreary sound. Marty taking care of things."

"Uh-uh. Dreary is working in a grocery store your whole life."

"What's wrong with working in a grocery store?"

He looked up at her. "Hey, I'm just making conversation, okay? First one person talks, then the other person."

"All right, then. Let's talk about you. What are your plans, Charlie?"

"Right at the moment I don't have any."

"That's pretty dreary, I'd say."

Her sweater was a shade of rose, blooming against the whiteness of her skin. One strand of dark hair was caught inside the collar.

"Something on your mind?" he asked.

"Not really. Just . . . thinking about your nephew. I stopped at the hospital today. He's put on another three ounces. He's almost four pounds. He'll be going home soon."

He got up to throw another log on the fire. "We going to talk about my nephew now?"

"Why not?"

"No reason. He'd be a good topic. Or how about the Celtics? You used to like talking sports with me."

She laughed. "You talked. I only listened."

"True?"

"True."

He picked up his cup from the floor, came and sat next to her on the couch. "How about olden times?"

"I don't think so."

"Senior prom? The night we went swimming in the quarry?"

She looked at him. "How would you remember? You were out of your mind."

"I remember. It was a great time."

He put his arm around her shoulders, felt the softness of her sweater, brushed his hand lightly over it.

"Not for Valerie Burns, as I recall," Marty said. "Valerie Burns."

"Your date." He stopped his hand, and she gave a little sigh. "Anyway, you promised never to talk about that night."

"I didn't promise not to talk about it with *you.*" He shifted position, turning toward her. "Okay. On to new times. Why didn't we stop at the store? Afraid to let Boz see me with you?"

"It was out of our way."

"Is that all?"

"That's all."

She set her cup down. The look on her face made him brave. He moved his hand to her waist.

"Charlie." She said it once, a warning; then, without another word she was in his arms. "We can't do this . . ." she said against his chest.

"Yeah, we can," he whispered. "We have. Remember?"

Her hands were unbuttoning his shirt, and as she slid her arms around him, touching his bare skin, he kissed her. Then he buried his face in that cloud of dark hair as she pressed against him length for length. He could feel the urgency in it, even as she whispered, "Charlie, Charlie, this is a bad idea. . . ."

"Shhh . . ." He eased them from the couch onto the sleeping bag. Twisting her body, Marty pulled the sweater over her head, then reached around to unzip her skirt. He couldn't seem to take control of his hands; they were fumbling at every turn. *Damn these boots!* He jerked at the laces, gave up, unbuttoned his jeans and slid them down below his hips.

She was waiting for him, all fullness and

warmth, and he was holding her so gently, sliding
his hand down between her legs, stroking slowly.
But he couldn't hang on to it, he was an explosion
of light inside of her, hearing himself cry out, as if
from someplace far away.

She lifted and lifted toward him. He felt her
give, felt a trembling in her thighs. Then, with a
deep sigh, she relaxed. He held her close, staring
up at the triangle of amber wallpaper over the
couch, at the oak framing of the archway. His
jacket was lying somewhere beside him in the
dark. He found it, slid it clumsily over her. Then
he unlaced his boots at last, pushed his pants off to
the floor. He should throw another log on the fire,
but he was too drugged to move. He reached out
to smooth her hair back from her forehead.

"Marty. You've got a beautiful body."

"Don't say that." Her voice suddenly sharp.

"Why not?"

"Because . . . what did that ever get me? All
the grief I've ever had all my life."

He couldn't help it; he laughed. He said, "Listen. Uncle Charlie—"

"Don't be Uncle Charlie! I don't want to be who
we were all over again, for God's sake!" She sat up
and twisted away from him. "You don't know me
anymore."

He lay back against the sleeping bag. "I know
you run full speed until you hit a brick wall and
then you pick yourself up and run just as hard in
the opposite direction. I wish for once you'd make
up your mind—"

"And do what? Rewrite history, Charlie? We're
not back at the quarry."

"Of course we aren't."

"So tell me something," she said. "What did we decide tonight about birth control?"

He was stunned. "Marty, I'm sorry."

"I don't know myself either. It's exactly what scares me."

Her hair fell forward, shielding her face from him. He watched helplessly as she pulled her sweater on, then the skirt, the gray knee socks.

"All right, then," he said. "Why did you come with me tonight?" He got to his feet, fumbling for his pants.

She had her coat on. "I'm walking home, Charlie."

"Don't be crazy. It's freezing out there."

"I don't want to be with you in that car." Her words came at him from across the room. "That baby bird," she said. "The one we found in the park. It died, don't you remember? You never get things right. Not the way they really happened."

He stayed where he was at the fireplace. Fuck it. Let her go. He heard the sound of a train whistling in the distance, then a rumbling rattle that carried for miles in the cold air. God, but he was stupid! He'd been through all this before.

And then he had a picture of her walking down the road by herself. He swore, slamming his hand against the mantelpiece. He bent and tied his boots, grabbed his keys off the kitchen table.

•

Her scarf was lying on the front seat. He backed the car around and put on the brights. Looking to the right and left he drove slowly down the narrow lane. Where the hell was she? How long had he stood in front of the fireplace? Minutes, he thought, but maybe it had been longer.

The cold bit through the fingers of his gloves. Freezing air blew over his feet. He made it all the way into town and there was no sign of her. No point in waiting for her at the store. He knew Marty, whether she did or not. He knew he wouldn't find her unless she wanted him to.

21

NICK KNEW BEFORE HIS HAND hit the light switch. Something was wrong inside the room—some shadow on the wall that hadn't been there before; a soft resistance meeting the door as he pushed against it. The lamps came on, shedding benign light on the wadded sheets, on his upturned suitcase with its contents scattered about.

On the floor under the desk was more bedding —blankets and pillows from both beds in a pile. He shut the door, swearing softly as he picked up the empty suitcase and set it on the luggage rack.

Drawers open, mattresses askew, drapes unhooked, cushions pulled from the chairs—they had to know he wouldn't hide anything of value here. *Just a reminder.*

He laughed; shook his head. Those assholes knew how to hold a grudge. He went to the telephone, dialed for room service; a female voice answered immediately.

He said, "Laura, this is room 332. I need some major service in here. Also the manager"—and then hung up before there could be a reply.

Reaching into his pocket he pulled out his list of telephone numbers. The top name was his best bet. He dialed it and the phone was answered on the first ring.

"Say, listen, Tommy. I got a problem over here."

Silence. After a moment Tom Fallon's voice came back at him: "I thought I told you not to call me again."

"I got bad maid service. My room's a mess. You'd better send somebody over to clean it up or I'm calling the cops."

"Call the cops. Maybe they can help. While you're at it, tell them what you're in town for."

Nick laughed. "Always the philosopher. Your old man was probably arranging this whole thing while I was cooling it outside his office, huh? Waiting to get in to see him."

"You're not going to see him," Tom said. "Forget that."

"Fine. I'll see *you*, then. I'm not fussy."

"There's no point. Nothing's changed, Nick."

"A lot's changed, Tommy. Believe me, it's a whole new deal."

A knock on the door then.

"Hang on a second," Nick said. He went to the door, opened it to a young kid dressed in khakis and a navy-blue sport coat.

"Who're you?" Nick asked.

"The night manager, sir."

The kid manager angled his head inside the room. "Wow. What happened here?"

Nick said dryly, "Looks like my room was broken into, doesn't it?"

"You leave it unlocked or what?"

"No."

"Guess we'd better call the cops."

"Forget the cops. Just give me a different room, will you? I'm on the phone."

But he wasn't. The line was dead. He dropped the phone onto its cradle.

"Sir, this has never happened before—"

"Yeah, I'm sure," he snapped. "So where's the closest bed? I've got a tough day tomorrow."

He gathered up his things. In the bathroom his toothpaste and shaving kit were lying in the sink. The tube was still full; they must have gotten tired of the game.

The room they gave him was three doors down. Lying on the bed he reached for the cable remote, flicking the channels in irritation. He gave Tom twenty minutes, then tried the number again. No answer this time. *Fucker. You'd better talk to me, or you'll be sorry.*

Birdman of Alcatraz was on the late movie. He'd seen it before, but that was okay. He could watch while things fell into place. They would too. Good old St. Cloud, the city of his birth, would come through for him. All he needed was one idea by morning.

•

Divide and conquer. Whoever said that knew his business. He could do that easy, given the deck he was dealing with. He grinned to himself. *Divide and hide* wasn't bad either. He really ought to patent some of this stuff. He felt confident this morning, driving out to Charlie's place.

He pulled up beside the sagging garage door. Nobody in sight. Perfect. Through the clear air he could hear hammering from the back part of the house. He waited to see if it would stop, then got out and pulled the garage door open just wide enough.

He stood for a moment, waiting for his eyes to adjust. The place was a pit, just the way it used to be. He had to laugh, it was all so predictable. No way was he going to get all the way back to the tool crib. He'd have to improvise. Looking above his head he decided one good jump-shot would do it. He took the envelope from his pocket and stood on the seat of a broken-down lawn chair to gauge the overhead shelf. One flick of the wrist and the envelope sailed like a square Frisbee, raising a little dust as it landed. The whole thing took about ten seconds.

That shelf had gotten more use than Mike Carmody had ever dreamed. He and Charlie made it their clubhouse, and they worked many a picture puzzle up there. Once in a while old Simon would butt his nose in. Well, this made them even.

Climbing down he nearly fell over the snowmobile parked at right angles to the door. It was draped in its shroud of black canvas. Arctic Cat didn't seem Mike Carmody's style, but then, you never knew.

Outside again, the sun was brilliant as it cleared the line of trees. He covered his eyes. Minnesota was the sunniest state in the Union, if you counted glare. The hammering continued as he left the garage, continued as he crossed the yard and climbed the steps to the porch. The back door opened easily.

Charlie got up fast from kneeling on the floor, holding the hammer loosely in his hand.

"Ah. You're here," Nick said. "Boz told me you

were back in town. Thought we might as well get this over with."

Charlie set the hammer down on the counter. And there he stood. Jesus, the guy could pout. "It's over with."

"Come on. How long have we known each other? Twenty years?"

"Twenty-five. If you count the last few. I don't."

"So it makes sense we don't piss it all away over a stupid mistake."

A laugh exploded from Charlie's throat. "What stupid mistake was that?"

"Okay. You got every right to hate me. Believe me, I felt like hell about it."

"I believe you," Charlie said. "I believe you do things and then feel like hell about them. I believe you're a goddamn schizophrenic." He picked up a paper sack full of finishing nails, folding the top over carefully, creasing the edge with his thumb.

Moving forward Nick rummaged through the kitchen cupboard. "Where's my blue cup? Your ma used to keep it ready just for me. Never mind, this one'll do." He went to the stove. When he turned around, Charlie had left the room. He heard his footsteps tramping down the hallway toward the living room. By the time he got there, Charlie was seated in the deep easy chair in front of the TV, resting his arms on its sides, his fists loosely clenched.

"Will it make you feel better if I let you punch me out?" Nick asked.

"No."

"Good." He held out his hand. "What d'you say? We enemies or friends?"

The pouter kept his arms flat on the chair. Well,

he was in no hurry. He took in the lumpy, crowded room. "Weird how things work out, isn't it? Who'd ever think you'd end up back here, a wood butcher like your old man. Remember how we swore we'd never do anything those guys did, no matter what?" No comment, so he moved in closer. "Yeah, we used to sit around talking about whose old man was the biggest asshole. Mine was a legend in his own time."

"You've outdone him," Charlie said, his eyes on the TV. "Look, I hold no grudges. That doesn't mean I want to talk to you."

Nick reached down and snapped off the TV. "Don't be hard on me. I've had a very crappy day."

Charlie's laugh came back harsh. "Jeez, I know what that's like. I've had a few myself."

"I said I was sorry. I did what I could."

"You did what you did. Go away, Nick. I want to watch the news." He reached over and turned the TV back on.

"Listen a minute. I've got a deal going here. College money, very easy money. I'll let you in on it."

Charlie shook his head. "I don't want to know. I don't want to be in the way, in case somebody decides to kill you."

He laughed. "Nobody wants to kill me. I can't make money for 'em if I'm dead, can I?" He went to stand by the window. "You still own that woods out there behind the house? I'll bet the value just keeps going up and up. Or did you sell out to Simon? How'd he get so lucky in this life, anyway?"

"Get out of here, Nick."

"In a minute. Got a question for you. Last night somebody trashed my motel room. Got any idea who that might be?"

Charlie merely looked at him.

"People around here think they play rough," Nick said. "But that's all it is, play."

He started for the door, then turned back. "I gotta say, Charlie. You think you got suckered in that deal. You oughta look at your own behavior. Talk about schizo. You let me do it to you, you know."

He left by the front door, even though it meant walking knee-deep in snow in his cowboy boots. In the car he pulled them off and emptied the slush out the door. He put the key into the ignition and revved the engine, then shifted gears. It felt good to push the Buick hard, slithering back down the driveway thirty miles an hour in reverse.

22

HE WORKED IN A FRENZY that afternoon, setting up tile on the counter, all the time feeling vaguely anxious; that's what the tightness in his chest was about. But where was the rage? It had been there in the past, nearly choking him at times. He knew how a normal person should feel. He just couldn't follow the trail back to his own reactions.

At five thirty he quit and went to the telephone, dialed his brother's office number. Simon's nurse answered. Doctor was with a patient, could he hold?

"Just ask him to call Charlie out at the house." He stood in the kitchen, surveying the day's work, trying to recapture the way he'd felt yesterday and the day before, but he couldn't get there. The house was a dismal hole and no amount of renovation was going to help.

Simon called him back in a few moments. "What's up?"

"Nothing," Charlie said. "Just wanted to check with you about the time."

"Time?"

"Yeah. The game starts at eight. D'you want to meet before and go over some plans?"

A pause. "Charlie, I'm really beat. I thought I'd go home and try to catch up on some sleep."

This was it, then; the thing that drove him crazy. The invitation extended, then withdrawn. Let's be buddies; on second thought, let's not. Two of a kind, Simon and Marty. Fuck them both. Fuck him for being the fool.

"My mistake," he said curtly. "I thought we had a date tonight."

Another pause. "Sorry. I haven't messed up your evening, have I?"

"Not at all. Makes no difference to me."

"You still going up to the Press? Maybe I'll try to meet you later."

"Yeah."

"Don't drink too much."

"How much is that?" He didn't wait for an answer, just hung up and studied his face in the hall mirror. Was this the face of a person who deserved to be suckered? The sudden change in his expression startled him; there was the anger at last. He forced a silly grin.

"Just making conversation," he said to the image in the glass.

He grabbed his jacket from the rack, closed the door behind him, rattling the knob to make sure it was locked. *Don't ask for trouble*. But this was merely the voice of reason making a last-ditch effort.

•

The Buick with its Value Rental sticker in the back window was parked in front of Voigt's. He saw it as soon as he turned the corner.

He pulled up behind it. He felt no surprise. Of course it was always possible Nick had come to her

168

place the same way he'd come to his—walking to the door wearing his big smile. Possible. Not probable. More likely that she'd invited him.

He reached for her scarf, got out of the car, and walked around to the back. Above him the storm door swung wide and Nick stood, propping it open with the toe of his boot.

"Hey. What a coincidence. We were just talking about you."

A burning in his stomach was spreading. It could torch these flimsy stairs if he wasn't careful. Smiling, Nick was coming down those steps, zipping his leather jacket. "I'd love to hang around and party, but I've got an appointment. Sorry."

"You get what you wanted?" He heard the rage in his voice.

"Buddy, you can always get what you want if people need to save face bad enough. And we got a friend who's a face-saver from way back, don't we?"

Charlie let him pass.

At the bottom of the stairs Nick turned to grin up at him. "As far as this goes, I hold no grudges," he said, indicating the apartment above. "My blessings." He disappeared around the corner of the house.

Charlie made his way to the top of the landing. He could see into the living room, the hallway beyond. He knocked on the storm door, waited a moment, then opened it wide.

"Anybody here?" His voice was behaving itself, sounding friendly and calm in his ears. Good, that was a good sign.

Marty came down the hallway toward the door. She had on jeans and a white turtleneck, with a long red sweater over it. Her hair was mussed, and she would not meet his eyes. "What are you doing?"

Charlie stepped inside, handing her the scarf. "Just making sure you made it home all right."

"You can see that I did, can't you?"

He felt another surge of rage. He had to be careful; he could blow this place apart. He glanced toward the window, where the last of the sunset was spreading color over ragged trees.

"What about him?" he asked. "What was he doing here?"

"Charlie, I'm not in the mood for questions."

"No? What are you in the mood for?"

"Did he tell you to come over here? Was that part of the plan?"

Plan? What plan was that? Somewhere in the back of his mind was the knowledge that he'd already made some fatal mistake. "I want to tell you something," he said. "About Chicago. I was there six years ago. I came to see you, but you were gone. And Nicky had a drug deal going. Only he never told me he suspected it might be a setup."

"You came to see me." She interrupted him, her voice flat.

"Yes. I wrote you when I was in the army. A ton of letters, only I never mailed any of them. Marty, Jesus, I love you. The dumbest thing I ever did was let him take over. I've loved you since junior high—"

"Stop it," she said. "Just stop." She turned and went down the hallway, and he followed, stood in the doorway of her bedroom with his hands braced against either side of the frame.

"Let me finish about Chicago," he said. "I went

along on the delivery with him. Just for the ride.
The cops were there, and he got thirty days for
fingering me as the supply man. I got two years in
Joliet."

No response from her. The room with its neatly
made bed and ruffled curtains at the windows
gave him nothing.

He said, "I meant to tell you that first night."

"Nicky already told me."

He pulled an icy breath. "He hasn't lost his
touch, has he?"

"He hasn't. Neither have you. Not one thing has
changed in twelve years."

"What does that mean?"

"It means if you're still talking to him, you deserve whatever you get."

"I see you're still talking to him."

"I'm not dealing."

"Neither am I," he said. She brushed past him
and he put out a hand. The burning was in action
again; he was sweating to stay even. "Why did you
let him in here tonight?"

She was headed down the hall and he was talking to her back. He caught up with her at the front
door, grabbed her arm. "I want to know what happened here before I showed up."

"That's my business."

"Marty, listen, I didn't come here to make trouble." Was this the truth? He had no idea anymore.
With an effort he took his hand away.

She looked up at him. "Get this," she said. "You
are trouble. I didn't invite you back into my life, I
don't want you here!"

He swung his arm in a wide arc, crashing his fist
into the closet door. The wood splintered and

gave, and he felt a jolt of pain in his wrist and shoulder, then a yawning dizziness. He pulled his arm free, steadied himself against the wall. She shrank back. He knew she was afraid of what else he might do. So was he. He turned and fled.

23

TOM RACED DOWN THE CORRIDOR to Pediatrics. When he got to Molly's room the door was shut, a DO NOT DISTURB tag looped around the knob. He pushed the door open. It would have slammed against the inside wall if he hadn't held on to it.

Inside the room Molly's form was resting slight and still on one bed. On the other was his wife— her face wearing that placid, unnatural calm.

"What the hell are you doing, Jeanne?" He held his voice to a whisper.

"I told you. I'm staying. I'm not leaving."

"You come home with me. You need some sleep. The night nurse will stay with Molly."

"Did you bring the things I asked you to bring?"

Tom looked at his hands as though they might have belonged to somebody else. They were empty. He crossed the small room and placed them on his wife's shoulders. "Jeanne, I just got into the car and came."

She shook her head and smiled in her knowing way. "Even when I tell you what I need."

"Jeanne, you're very organized. We both know that. This is not about being organized."

"It *is*." She shrugged his hands off, a small fierce contraction that left him grasping air. "It *is* about organization, it always is, and you will not understand. Who is with Erin while you are here with me? Who will be with her when you have to go home and come back again to bring me the things I need?"

"Let's talk about the things you need." Tom looked over at Molly's bed. He let himself down on the bed beside his wife. He made his fingers open and he made his voice lower, calmer as he ticked off the items. "Your toothbrush, you said, a nightgown and robe, a change of underwear—"

"No! No! I *have* a toothbrush. I *have* toiletries; what do you think I do here every day?"

"—a gun. A gun, Jeanne."

"Did you bring it?"

Tom grabbed her shoulders again. "No, I did not bring you a gun. What on earth—"

"You have not seen what I have seen."

He made himself take a breath. "I want you to come home with me."

"No."

"We'll talk about it at home."

Jeanne half turned away from him, stared at Molly's bed. "Thomas, Erin is alone in that house! She could wake up to—Tom, you are a fool."

"I called Dad. He's with Erin by now."

"I don't believe you." Jeanne folded her arms. "Call him. I want to hear his voice on the phone."

"He was tired. I told him to lie down in the room with Erin, on Molly's bed. There's no need to disturb him."

Jeanne eyed him as though he were transparent and she could read the lies written like a text behind his eyes. He hoped she could not.

"Jeannie, Jeannie," he whispered, looking for

the way in. "Listen, darling, you are right. I just didn't see it. You belong here with Molly."

She hesitated. "Her life is in danger."

"Yes."

"Nicky Uhler gave her drugs, and now he has come to steal her. He is here in this building, Tom. I saw him. I know his thoughts. He is here to steal a child."

Tom made his gaze keep on meeting hers. Then carefully he pinched his lip between his fingers while his own thoughts flew. "I don't think we'll need a gun, darling," he said. "What we need is a private nurse to stand guard. Someone who can let you get some rest."

"An armed guard, Tom."

He nodded. "All right. One of the security people. I can arrange that right now." He was already at the door before he turned and came back to her. He tilted her face and kissed her. She allowed this, but did not cling to him. Her body was tense; she had the readiness of a warrior. He could use some of that. "When the nurse comes I want you to let her give you something to help you rest. Will you do that? Molly will be safe. You can rest."

"All right," she said. "As I am guided."

"What?"

"As I am guided."

"I want you to lie down now." He spoke in the most soothing tones he could find. "I'll have a nurse here in thirty seconds, and a guard outside the door in two minutes. Everything will be all right. I promise you."

Out in the hall he sprinted for the nurses' station. Within seconds one uniformed nurse was scurrying down the hall with the sedatives left on order, and another was on the phone to Security. Every now and then it paid off, being the son of Terence Fallon.

At the pay phone Tom heard his father's low drawl come on the line at the first ring. "Dad!" His heart was bounding out of his chest. "Where the hell have you been?"

"What's the matter?"

"I'm at the hospital. I've been trying to reach you."

"Did something happen? Is it Molly?"

"No, no, I had to come and be with Jeanne. I need you to go over to the house and stay with Erin. Nothing's wrong. I just want you there, do you understand? Don't leave until I get home."

"Tom, I think you and I had better talk—"

"Not now. Later. When I get home. Jeanne's really had it, I'll probably be here all night." He slammed the receiver down and checked his watch. Seven thirty. He raced down the emergency stairway, figuring that would get him to the parking lot the fastest.

24

THE PRESS BAR WAS HOT. Noise came at him from the bandstand, from the loudspeakers, from the wall of people all around. Funny, the place had been nearly empty when he walked in, but was that hours ago? What time was it now? After eleven. The game was over at eleven—no, later than that—they had gone into overtime.

Christ, he had to get home, had to work tomorrow. The thought made him lower his head, laughing. Wouldn't be the first time he'd pounded nails with a hangover. He rested his cheek against the smooth surface of the table; it smelled of old wood and oil and beer.

Listening to the noise going on around him was like being a kid again, while his parents were partying downstairs. He and Simon would creep to the landing and peer down into the cigarette smoke. When he wanted to watch longer than Simon would let him, he'd sneak back and lean out over the banister. He never wanted the people to go home. *Party boy.* His mother's nickname for him. She would call to him: "There's my party boy, Charlie Dean, he knows a good time when he sees one!"

Good old Miss Nellie. Mike would stumble up

and shoo him back into bed, but not his mother. A party girl herself, she understood the pull of that magic. But over the years something had turned her into a sour old lady. A drunk, face it. Her secret drinking was a secret only to her.

His table bumped. Somebody steadied his beer bottle. He heard, "This guy's a goner," and raised his head.

"Not yet."

"Dream on, buddy." The man laughed, and returned to his dancing partner—a blonde dressed in jeans and a pink sweater that sparkled when the lights swam. Charlie was sure she was someone he knew. He stared at her and she winked at him over her shoulder.

Ellen Morrison. No. Helen. With her blond hair and the gold heart on a chain around her neck who worked at the A & W. But she hadn't gone to Apollo, she was at the Catholic girls school up near Sauk Rapids—Sauk Center—what was the name of it?

"Helen Murphy!" he shouted. A couple out on the floor looked over, but there was no sign from the pink-sweatered girl, not even when he shouted out, "St. Scholastica!" She and the guy she was dancing with were over by the bandstand, bobbing and rocking beside the drummer. He picked up his beer and headed toward them.

"Helen Murphy!" he yelled at the back of her head. When she turned around, it wasn't her at all, but another blond—this one wore a green cowboy shirt. Where had she disappeared to?

He threaded his way back through the dancers until he was beside his table again. Only, someone else was sitting there now, looking up at him with pig-squinted eyes.

"My table," he said, and set down his beer.

"Got a bill of sale?" The guy asked him, squinting his eyes even tighter.

He grinned and reached into his pocket just as a couple on the floor backed into him; he took an elbow in the side.

"Jesus, Mary, and Joseph," he mumbled. The blow had started up the pain again, the raked skin of his knuckles and the ache in his hand. He saw the hole in Marty's door. *Not too smart, Charlie. Not too winning.*

"Get off the floor, man," somebody said. "You're in the way."

He picked up his glass of beer and waved it at the man. "If that's the worst thing happens to you, count yourself lucky."

"Jerk!"

"Hey, I'm only a jerk," Charlie said. "You're an ugly jerk." Giving the guy a smile he waved the glass again, stepping back toward the bar. Then he felt himself being grabbed from behind and propelled toward the door. His beer was lifted from his hand.

"You've had enough, my friend. On your way."

He turned his head. The bartender. Not nearly so friendly as earlier, when they'd watched the game from the bar, when Charlie was telling him all about Arizona, those peaceful desert sunsets.

"We don't go for that rough stuff here, understand?"

What rough stuff? He was the one who had his table taken and was being shoved around. The blast of cold air hit him like a wall. And it was snowing again. God, but he was sick of this weather, sick of this whole goddamned town.

"I'm leaving!" he yelled into the spinning lights of the bar. In the parking lot he dodged a couple of newcomers, reached into his pocket for Elizabeth's car keys. He came up empty. What the hell? He searched again and again. They were gone.

"Fuck!" He stood for a moment, then turned his back on the lights and walked away down the street. He would go down by the river and cool off. The keys were somewhere and he would find them, but first he needed to clear his head.

The trees along the campus were dark, shadowy, bending under the weight of the snow. You couldn't trust what you saw, something that looked solid enough to sit on would collapse if you leaned against it. He started on a path down the hill. He kept tripping over things—roots or stumps, who knew? Maybe he should find someplace to sit for a minute, until things stopped whirling around.

He turned to face the direction he'd come. The bar behind him, the river on his right. Or was it on his left since he'd fallen over the downed pine? The wind whipped snow into his face as he stared hard into the whitening darkness. He was lost all right. Lost and drunk.

"It would not be a good idea to stop walking," he told himself. He had read enough stories about people lost in blizzards, sitting down to rest and never getting up again. So he kept on going forward, or what looked the most like it.

25

THE HOUSE WAS LIT UP, practically every light blazing. Tom got out of the little car and slammed the door. Two doors down, at the end of the street, his father's house was completely dark except for the porch light. So what did it mean? He was too beat to try and put it together. He had done all the dancing he could for one night. Now he just hoped the old man was still awake. They were going to get a couple of things straight. Then maybe he could sleep.

Under the porch light of his own house he searched through his key ring. Why did he carry them all? Four for the office, two for the house, two for Dad's house, three for the lake house, three for Jeanne's parents' place . . . an efficient man would arrange his life better. An efficient man would have been born into some other family, some other life. Tonight was prime. How could he have ever planned all the separate things he needed to do? Before he got to the key he was looking for, the front door swung open. He glared up, ready to let the old man have it, no preliminaries. But it was Jeanne.

For the tenth time that night Tom felt his stomach go to water. He stared at his wife.

"What are you doing here?" He could hardly recognize his own voice. It wavered and went thin. "Jeanne. What in God's name . . ."

Her face was bright, eager. "Come in, Tommy. You look so worried!" He let her slip his coat from his sleeves and put her arms around him. "Everything is going to be all right," she said.

"You were going to stay in the hospital."

Her laugh was a little hysterical trill. "Tommy, you were right. I understood as soon as you left. The night nurse came and the guard came, and I had no business there. They were doing their appointed tasks! It was guilt that made me blind, Tommy, and I saw what I had to do, what *my* job was. I thanked the Lord for the help you had provided, and I got my coat and I left."

"Stop," he broke in. He looked around the living room. "Where's Dad?"

Jeanne smiled radiantly. "He's asleep, he's in Molly's bed, just like you told me. Now where are you going? You don't mean to wake him, Tom, he's had quite enough for one night."

Her voice followed him down the hall to the girls' door. The door was open, and he pushed it wider. In the small wing chair beside Erin's bed, his father sat smoking in the dark.

"Good evening, Thomas."

"I thought you might be awake, Dad. Come on. I'll walk you home."

"Oh. I'm not to enjoy your hospitality?"

"Dad, you can stay," Jeanne offered from behind him. "But why don't you come on out and use the ashtray in the living room?"

"He's happier in his own house, you know that, Jeanne." Tom spoke formally, and he gave his father the narrowed look he had learned from that very face.

Terence Fallon put out his cigarette in the doll's teacup that he had been using. He stood up and addressed Jeanne. "He's quite right, my dear. An old man's habits. Besides, what if the housekeeper came at seven o'clock in the morning and found my bed empty? That's what you're thinking, aren't you, Tom?" He handed Jeanne the small rose-printed teacup. "My apologies to Erin." He kissed her cheek and strode toward the front door.

Out on the sidewalk Tom ignored his father's comments on the beauty of the evening. He waited until they were past the corner of his lot and cut across a stream of adjectives to say, "Dad, this is not 1964. You cannot have a man's room searched in collusion with his hotelkeeper."

"I recall that a hotelkeeper may exercise a right to—"

"You cannot act in such a stupid, high-handed way. You can't break the law and expect—"

"I expect the law to bend," his father said. "As in my experience it has always seemed to do."

"What you did was cause more trouble than you solved. Take my word for once. You don't begin to know what you are meddling with. Now, I want you to go to bed and please do not tell anyone you left the house tonight."

"Surely to stroll down the avenue to my son's home to baby-sit—"

"Don't cut corners with me, Dad. I mean the other time you were out. The time you didn't answer the phone." He watched his father search through his own ring of keys under the porch light.

"Many things can cause an old man not to answer his telephone."

"That's right, Dad. That's exactly what I wanted to hear you say. Keep saying it, and don't talk to anybody until I call you in the morning."

"You've turned into a rather brisk young man," his father said, glancing over his shoulder. "How that would grieve your dear mother."

Tom turned on his heel and left the old man fitting the key to the lock.

Back in his own house he shut the front door and locked it with the dead bolt. He found Jeanne in the kitchen making him a sandwich. "No, thanks," he said. "We have to talk."

"I don't understand you or your father."

"I know. Where did you go tonight, Jeanne?"

"I went to the cemetery."

"Why?"

"I told you."

"Tell me again."

"After you left, I knew what I had to do, and I went to Elizabeth's grave and prayed."

"For what?"

"Oh, Tommy. I don't want to hurt you. But you are blind where Elizabeth is concerned, you always have been—"

"For God's sake, Jeanne. She's dead now, isn't that good enough? What are you doing, disturbing her grave like some avenging spirit? How long will she have to pay for what she did when she was sixteen?"

Jeanne stared at him. "And you think that's the only mistake she ever made, or the last one? She needs our prayers, Tommy. Her baby needs our prayers. And our Molly—do you know how she got the drugs that hold her in thrall this very minute? Elizabeth could have killed our baby. Are you blind to that too?"

"If anybody's trying to put Molly in her grave, it's you! What on earth do you mean, arranging for her funeral? What do you mean, asking Kathleen Mathews to let Victor be an altar boy at Molly's funeral? Jeannie, this has got to stop. I need you to be all right! Too much is going on right now. You and I have to get our stories straight about tonight."

"I've told you where I was."

"No, darling, no." He smoothed the light wisps of hair from her forehead. "Listen to me, Jeannie. You were here, with Dad. And me. Nowhere else. You came straight from the hospital."

"I had another duty."

He folded her into his arms. "I know. You're tired. So am I. We had a lot to do tonight, but you're saying things that might confuse people. So let me tell you what to say. Please? You know there's danger. You were the very first to know."

"Tommy, the danger is past. My prayers—"

"I know. They were heard. All our prayers were heard."

26

DRIVING OUT TO THE OLD HOUSE Simon felt his heart slowly and steadily lifting. He'd slept hard last night; the sleep of the dead, as his mother would say. Amazing to have a sense of his own strength again. The world was already seeming a better place.

A field of diamonds sparkled off to his right as he made the turn onto the road, and he was momentarily blinded. The sun was streaming out of a cloudless sky so blue it almost looked fake. A beautiful Minnesota winter day. No matter where you were in your life the world kept on; sooner or later you had to regard it.

Elizabeth's car was nowhere in sight. No tracks either. So he wasn't around. *Damn.* Where would he be at this hour of the morning? Simon felt a flare of irritation, then let it go.

The garage door was closed, the latch at a weird angle, caught nearly horizontal. He stepped through the snow and adjusted it. Exactly the kind of detail he *would* notice. Too bad Charlie wasn't around to point that out.

The kitchen was shaping up nicely. The new tile on the counter had been grouted. The cupboards awaited a coat of varnish, their hardware sitting in boxes on the table.

He walked to the sink where dirty dishes were soaking. He tested the temperature of the water; still warm. A full cup of coffee on the drainboard; warm. The woodburner was radiating heat. He stood contemplating it, opened the hatch. The logs lay across one another, ridged and ashy; when he gave them a nudge with the poker they collapsed like old white bones.

He mounted the stairs and walked through the upper rooms slowly, raising partitions and knocking down walls in his mind, feeling his ideas beginning to take shape. The house would be perfect for this; the ten-minute drive out would give the families some relief from the hospital setting. In his parents' bedroom he looked out the window and across the bare fields. He'd forgotten that you could see all the way to the highway from up here. Now he watched the familiar car make its way up the drive. Charlie got out, and a moment later the kitchen door slammed. Simon headed downstairs.

"Where were you?" he called.

His brother's back was hunched over the stove. "I had an errand. You want coffee?"

"No, thanks. Kitchen looks great, Charlie."

"Yeah, well. This kind of work's rewarding in its menial way." He looked haggard, hair uncombed, eyes bloodshot.

Simon raised his hands. "Don't, okay?"

"Don't what?"

"Pick a fight with me."

"Okay, fine. How's the weather? We can talk about the weather, can't we?"

"What's the matter?"

"I'm hung over, is all."

Charlie dumped his coffee into the sink, shook out more instant.

"Any special reason?"

"Celtics lost. You don't think I'd get drunk just for the hell of it, do you?"

Simon crossed to the sink and took a cup down. "I guess I will have some," he said. "So, how drunk were you?"

To his relief Charlie smiled. "Poor Si. Got your hands full, don't you? With me and Mom."

"Her I can handle. I'm bigger than she is. You, you're a different story."

"Mr. C. for Catastrophe, Dad used to call me."

"More like Mr. M. for Melodrama. Were you at the Press?"

"To the best of my knowledge that's where it happened, yeah." His brother lowered himself into the kitchen chair, pressing a hand to his head.

"I had something I wanted to talk to you about," Simon began. "I'm thinking of asking Marty Voigt to move into the house with Mother and me."

Charlie seemed not to have heard him. Then he looked up. "What the hell for?"

"What do you think? To take care of the baby. Ma's not capable, and it's time for him to leave the hospital. I've got to have someone."

"Why don't you get a real nurse? If you want my opinion, I think it's a lousy idea."

"Is it? Why? She's taking a real interest, she's been there every day to see him. I trust her."

"Fine. So you move her in and let her get attached to him. Then kick her out when you find somebody with a degree in child raising. That's what you're looking for, isn't it?"

189

"What are you getting so upset about?"

"Do whatever you damn please. What did you ask me for?"

Simon lifted his hands. "Come to think of it, I don't know exactly. I guess I thought you knew her."

"Yeah, I knew her. But I don't *know* her. Hell, I don't even know myself these days."

Simon hesitated. "Then, I hope you're being careful."

"What does that mean?"

"Nothing. Only . . . you want to be sure you're protected when you're walking around, not knowing yourself."

"Make it plain," Charlie growled, "so I can understand you. I've got a headache."

"I'm saying you should think about having a vasectomy, Charlie. Then if you get drunk in a bar and get yourself laid without knowing why or who, you won't be hurting anybody. You won't end up getting some scheming little broad pregnant. Is that plain enough?"

Charlie was looking at him. "Exactly where are you coming from, Si?"

"I'm sorry. I see a lot of that here. It makes me crazy." He waited, stuffing his gloves into his coat pockets and straightening the flaps. Finally he said, "I've got to get to the hospital." He walked through the kitchen in the silence.

All right, he'd said his piece. Sometimes people were ready to hear it, sometimes not. He opened the back door and stepped outside into the clear and still beautiful day.

•

Pushing through the glass doors from the physicians' lounge, he stuffed a pen in his white lab coat and ducked into the stairwell. Time he looked in on Molly Fallon.

Outside her room he caught sight of Danny Schenk standing in the corridor in his brown Security uniform. "Dan. Anything wrong?"

"Nothin' I know of, Dr. Carmody, except my orders are to stand here. I'm standing."

"I'll just look in."

"Sure thing." Danny moved sideways.

The room lights were off, the shades still drawn. Jeanne Fallon sat in the padded straight chair beside Molly's bed, one of Molly's hands clasped within her own. It was impossible to tell if she was asleep or praying.

He moved closer and looked down at the child's face. He lifted the edge of the sheet and picked up the other small wrist, pressed his thumb on the interstice of bones. Tracking the red digits on his watch, he lifted Molly's eyelid.

"Simon," Jeanne said.

"Yes. How are you, Jeanne?"

She took a deep breath, as though she herself were waking from a long drift of unconsciousness. "I was having a dream. . . ."

Simon lifted the other eyelid. He touched his breast pocket, where a very long time ago, years ago this was, he had carried a small flashlight. "Jeanne," he said, "would you mind turning on that lamp?"

She reached under the circular shade, and the light came on. He held Molly's eyelid clear of the iris and pupil, he saw a minuscule alteration in the proportion of pale blue to black. Carefully, so as not to alarm her, he said, "Will you press the call button, please? I think we need to get hold of Dr. Vogel."

But her eyes went shocky and wide. "What's wrong?"

"Nothing. I'd just like Dr. Vogel to have a look."

She didn't move. Simon reached past her and stabbed the button beside the bed. "Have you been here all night?" he asked.

A stricken look on her face. "I went home," she whispered. "I went home last night. I thought it was the right thing. . . ."

A nurse appeared in the doorway. "Possible code four," Simon said crisply. "Call Dr. Vogel, will you?" To Jeanne he said, "It's all right. This could be good news. I thought I saw a response."

It could also be a false alarm. He bent over the child's bed and again lifted an eyelid. He *thought* he observed a response. "Have you noticed anything?"

Unwillingly she shook her head. "Nothing. What are you seeing?"

"Maybe nothing." He dropped his hands to his side, steadied his breathing, decided to check the pulse one more time. He touched the small hand that Jeanne kneaded between her own. That curious coolness, but it felt like responsive flesh.

Footsteps in the corridor, and the metallic rattle of wheels. Two nurses entered the room, an orderly stood by with the cart, and then Ed Vogel was at his side.

"Possible pupillary reflex and seventy on the pulse," he said, as Vogel slipped an otoscope from his pocket and began to confirm.

192

"Better than what I've been looking at." Vogel slid a stethoscope up his neck and placed the disc on the girl's chest.

The blunt veiny knob of nose was at Simon's elbow. He nearly laughed out loud. What was with him today? Everything was striking him as funny.

Ed said, "This could be it. Can you stick around?"

Before he could answer, Molly's blue eyes blinked open of their own accord. The child's expression slowly formed a deep scowl. She began to thrash her limbs. One flailing hand caught Vogel's stethoscope and sent it clattering across the room.

"Grab her!" Vogel barked.

Two nurses moved forward and one captured both wrists while the other trapped the kicking feet. Vogel pinned the child's shoulders. When a leg escaped the nurse's grasp, Simon moved to catch it. The four adults gripped the struggling child.

Vogel said over his shoulder to Jeanne: "Sometimes they do this. You never know."

Their job was simple, and so frightening, a physical struggle against a process with force and timing of its own. It was nothing like surgery; it more closely resembled what wrestlers did. Again he felt exhilarated.

"Few more minutes," Vogel puffed.

In six minutes, almost exactly, Simon stood back a mere witness. Molly was conscious, and Vogel was in charge, fidgeting and monitoring. He felt himself divide into the surgeon and the uncle: the surgeon stood back saying, *I could not bear being at the mercy of guesswork.* Meanwhile the uncle was saying, simply, *Thank God.*

Simon watched Jeanne as she sat on the bed, cradling her exhausted child, smoothing her hair and having to explain the world again.

"Where are we?" Molly wanted to know. "Who is this? Where's Daddy?" Unable to retain the answers, she asked the same questions again and again, her eyes roving the small room for clues. "Who is that bed for? What does that button do? Mom, why are you crying? Are you sad?"

Her mother answered and answered, tears streaming.

"Why is my dollhouse missing?"

"This is the way they come back sometimes," Vogel was explaining. "With coma patients you never know."

"A miracle of atonement," Jeanne said. "I know exactly."

Simon stepped forward. "I'll call Tom."

Molly struggled free of her mother's arms, her eyes on Simon's face. "Did Aunt Elizabeth have the baby yet?"

Years ago he had stood in a second-floor hospital room in Chicago during a thunderstorm. He had been intent on scribbling a routine order when the corner of the building had been struck by lightning. A popping noise, a sense of blue vapor in the room. This is what he thought of now.

"Sweetheart," said Jeanne. "Let me see, your lip is swollen right here—"

Molly's gaze found him again. "Did she have the baby yet?"

"Shhhhhh," Jeanne said.

"She did," Simon told her. "It's a boy."

"Can I see him?"

"In a little while," her mother said.

194

Again Molly looked around the room. "Is that bed for Erin?"

"What a good idea. Erin's been lonesome for you."

"Is Erin lonesome?" she demanded of her mother.

Simon edged to the door and made his way down the hall to the bank of telephones. The bearer of good news, he spoke to Tom only briefly —Tom who surely wanted to be out of the house with Erin before the phone hit the hook. Simon hung up rather more slowly, feeling an unwelcome weight return.

On the way up the stairs to the surgical wing, he confined his thoughts to the last hour's sequence of events—his observations, his conclusions, his actions. Nothing out of line, and only one offbeat surprise. He ran his hand along the pressure points under his jawline. During the struggle with the little girl, he had thought spontaneously of Elizabeth. How unprepared he was for both the strength and the softness! Holding Molly's small foot and leg, he'd felt something close to horror— at the vulnerability, at the softness peculiar to children.

27

"HEY. PRINCE OF DARKNESS. Merry Christmas."

Bill Hessel lifted his head to his wife's warm kiss; tasted maple syrup on her mouth. "Mmm, gimme more," he said, reaching from under the covers, but she was too quick for him.

"Billy Boy, come on, now. The kids are *waiting*. It's after eleven."

"Christmas Day. My first day off in three weeks."

Val kissed him again. "Pancakes are on the table. You want 'em hot, you eat 'em now."

Meekly he got up, struggled into his robe, and followed her down the hall to the kitchen. At the table his thirteen-year-old munched on bacon that dripped with maple syrup. A thick puddle of it filled the center of Jim's plate. "That," Bill said, "is a disgusting habit."

Across the room Nan looked up from her book. *"Finally*. Now can we open presents, Mom?"

"In five minutes," Val said. "Let your dad eat first."

"Five minutes. Great. Forget digestion, I'll do that in my spare time, working on Nanny's doll-house, or maybe while I'm fixing the snowmobile, so you kids can take it for another joyride over Cameron's fence."

"Dad, how many times you gonna bring that up?"

"Until he's bored with it." Jim sighed. "Dad, you're so *predictable.*"

"Billy, do you want these pancakes or not?" Val held the plate above his head. He nodded and she set them down. Reaching for the maple syrup he slopped it over his pancakes and bacon. Jim laughed.

"I mapped out the whole tree," Nan said. "I know where all my presents are."

Behind them on the counter the telephone rang.

"Probably Grandma Burns," Jim said hopefully, going to answer it. A moment later he handed the telephone to his father.

Bakke's voice on the other end. "Chief, we got a body washed up at Sportsman's Island. Arvid Hammerschlag found it about half an hour ago walking his dog."

"Man or woman?"

"Male. Caucasian. About thirty. Doesn't look like a drowning. Skull caved in."

"Send Brunsvold and Lommel out to seal the area. Keep the snowmobiles out. Did you call Dr. Cook?"

"Just going to do that."

"I'll get hold of MCIU. Meet you there in ten minutes."

He hung up. "What is it?" Val looked at him anxiously.

"Somebody went in the river."

"Oh, please, not a kid."

198

"No. Not a kid."

He dialed the tricounty coordinator's office, gave the information and location to the clerk, made a request for a major-crime investigating unit. When he hung up, the kids were looking at him with long faces.

"Sorry," he said. He swallowed the last few bites of his breakfast and headed back down the hall.

Val followed him to the bedroom, sat down on the bed as he dressed. "MCIU," she said. "Then it wasn't an accident."

"Doesn't look like it."

"What else did Bakke say?"

"Not much. Male Caucasian washed up from under the ice. Suspicious head injuries. Have I got any clean wool socks?"

She went to the bureau, fished around in his drawer, tossed him the socks.

"Let the kids go ahead and open the presents," he said as he rummaged for his hiking boots in the back of the closet.

"Do they know if it was a student? Somebody from St. Cloud State?"

"Honey, I don't know."

She rubbed her arms with her hands. "Sorry. Just the idea of it. And on Christmas. Awful."

He bent over and kissed her. "I'll call if it looks like an all-day deal."

•

He guided the unmarked Plymouth Reliant around the icy ruts of the road. In spite of the new snow, here was one of those days when every surface stayed hard with cold—the plastic seat covers, the steering wheel. The grease in the door had frozen overnight, the hinge had creaked and

Killing Time in St. Cloud

groaned like an old man when he opened it, and
that was in the garage! How had he and Val managed, those winters they drove the VW bug with
the air-cooled engine? They were younger, for
one thing, but it had been insanity.

Through the steering wheel and chassis he felt
the hard ride the Reliant's tires were giving him
over the frozen ground. No flex in the tires, none
in the ice, and it was going to stay that way.

He pulled up just past the wooded area already
sectioned off with red surveyor's tape. SHERIFF'S
DEPT. KEEP OUT. Three patrol cars were parked at
the edge of the field—one each from Benton,
Sherburne, and Stearns counties—along with several other unmarked cars. He recognized Dr.
Cook's dark-blue Ford. Nearby he saw Arvid Hammerschlag, hands shoved in the pockets of his navy
peacoat, talking with a patrolman. Arvid's black
Lab sat, biting ice from between his paws.

Bill ducked under the tape and walked the flat
expanse toward the bank of the river, hearing the
snow squeak in protest under his boots. Behind
the cloud bank the sun was a bluish glow in the air.

Bakke was waiting for him at the top of the hill.
Behind him he recognized the assistant deputy
sheriffs from Sherburne and Benton and several
detectives from St. Cloud PD.

"Let's go have a look," Bill said.

Together they scrambled down the steep bank.

"Guy wasn't exactly dressed for the weather,"
Bakke said. "Leather jacket, no shoes."

"What about ID?" Bill asked.

"Uh-uh. No wallet, not even a wristwatch."

They made it down to the river, where several
patrolmen were already searching the area,

fanned out from the section where the body lay, facedown, on the crusted snow. Dr. Cook was on his knees beside it with the photographer. He glanced up with a grim smile. "Merry Christmas."

"Couldn't be an accident, huh?" Bill asked. "Wouldn't see that kind of battering under the ice?"

"No way. Skull's flattened. Back of his head caved in."

"How many blows, can you tell?"

The coroner shrugged his shoulders. "More than was needed. They killed him dead, all right."

The camera clicked and clicked. It always gave him a peculiar feeling, this taking pictures of the dead.

"How long you think he's been in the water?"

Cook sat back on his haunches. "Hard to tell. Not much deterioration. Water's too cold. Could be a week. Could be less."

"Call the Ramsey County medical examiner," Bill said. "Tell them we've got a body coming in."

"You want me to go along?" Bakke asked.

"Yeah." Bill turned to the deputies behind him. "Something tells me we're not going to find much here. We may have to go higher up for open water. Near Heim's Mill or the dam."

Hammerschlag came laboring down the pathway, his face red with the cold. The dog was on a leash now, held tight by his side. "Saw you drive up, Bill. Felt pretty sick this mornin' when I found him."

"Appreciate the call, Arvid."

"Yeah, people got no idea how dangerous that is. Fooling around by this river, get theirselves in all kinda trouble." He was looking for news, his eyes going everywhere, always sliding back to the still form lying face-down on the ground.

Bill began edging him back toward the path. "They get a statement from you?" he asked.

Arvid nodded. "Ain't seen no reporters, though. Guess nobody knows but us, huh?"

"So far," Bill said.

"Think he went in up by the dam?"

"Could have."

"Ambulance is here," a patrolman yelled from the top of the hill.

"Send 'em down," Bill called back.

To Arvid he said, "You look like you could use a cup of coffee. Why don't you head into town? We'll call you at the Dan Marsh if we need anything more." He turned back to Dr. Cook. "How much longer?"

"Just about finished."

Dr. Cook rolled the body carefully onto its back. Bill felt Arvid's curiosity as the old man took a step toward the body. *What the hell.* Together they walked over and Bill looked down into the pale face, the sightless blue eyes that seemed to stare off into the darkness.

"Christ," he said quietly. "I know this guy."

"You're kidding," Dr. Cook said.

Bill shook his head. "Haven't seen him for ten years or more." He gave a sharp whistle between his teeth.

Bakke walked over and stood beside him. "Who is he, Chief?"

He almost didn't hear the question, his mind was pulled in so many directions—back to high school chemistry class, screwing around with experiments in the back of the room, a wonder they didn't blow themselves up—forward again to the funeral, and the strange thrill of seeing Charlie Carmody there, knowing these guys were still around in the world, you couldn't change that just by not seeing somebody, could you?

"I went to high school with him," Bill said.

"High school." Dr. Cook's voice was skeptical. "What is that? Fifteen years? You could be wrong."

"I never saw this guy before," Bakke said. "He live around here?"

"No. He left town. I'm not wrong, though. He was my chem lab partner. Nick Uhler."

28

TUESDAY MORNING AT SEVEN thirty Bill Hessel
turned at the mailbox labeled in red. The rows of
windbreak spruce followed the fence line. He
could count on one hand the number of times he'd
been out this way since high school. As far as that
went, he could count on one hand the number of
times he'd been there *during* high school.

This first touch was supposed to seem like a
courtesy call. He could think of people in this town
who deserved the courtesy—Terry Fallon, Tom,
Jeanne, Simon Carmody. Bottom of the list was
Charlie Carmody, sharing that spot with his old
buddy Nick—quite the pair. Well. Courtesy was
also method, good sound method.

He prided himself on his memory. What he had
been taught in high school art class was, it takes a
lot of history to produce art. What he learned in
detective school was, it takes a little history before
you get homicide. He thought about Charlie—
thicker in the body now, and, as he pointed out to
Val, going bald. A history of a very short temper,
and very bad luck. You'd think a grown man would
figure things out better.

He followed the twin ruts into the yard, and
pulled up close behind Elizabeth Carmody's

Camaro, an easy car to keep track of in this town. Almost too easy. As far as instinct went, he'd just as soon be running the lights and flashing the bubble, just tear hell out of this winter morning. Let the neighbors see the show. Ah, well, he had a feeling that moment would come. Just a feeling, but he didn't discount it. Among themselves Bakke and the other deputies called him "the nose," thinking it was a private joke they got away with—thinking if he didn't let on, he didn't know. With his middle finger Bill adjusted his glasses on the bridge of his nose. Amazing thing about people. They never believed anybody else could figure anything out! As though what ran through their minds didn't show up in their mouths—hesitating on one word or punching up another, a change of subject, nervous laugh, sudden gesture, the places their eyes went. The game was giveaway; mostly all you had to provide was opportunity.

He got out of the car, and took a sweeping look around. He could see only his own tracks in last night's dusting of snow. If Charlie was supposed to be improving this place, it didn't show from the outside. On the garage and the house, same old pale-yellow siding and weathered trim. Starting up the front-porch steps he saw they had been swept this morning. Who could tell? Maybe Charlie had developed a talent for housekeeping. A sharp whacking came from around the house—then the sound of splitting wood. Bill stopped, turned, and jumped down off the steps to the shoveled path that led off to the north side. He landed lightly, and this small show of athletic grace cheered him; he pushed his glasses back into place.

Around the corner he walked through the bluish shadow of the house toward the plaid-shirted figure who stood facing away from him. He watched Charlie Carmody take a stance and hoist the ax, then bring it down; pieces of wood flew. The sound rang between the house and the woodshed.

"Merry Christmas!"

Charlie turned as Bill came on forward. He squinted and set the ax head firmly into the stump he was using as a block. "Morning," he said. Without a smile.

"Still got that old woodburner in the kitchen, huh?"

"Still got it."

"You need a splitter, don't you, or at least a wedge, if you're doing enough wood to last the winter?"

"If that's what I was doing."

Bill said, still amiably, "Know what I was thinking about when I drove into the yard? Art class. Remember Old Man Hofstadter? Flunking me on my papier-mâché balloon with two cracks in it and passing you with one? Remember him explaining, 'You got to draw the line somewhere'—remember that?"

Charlie rubbed sweat from his forehead. "What brings you out this way?"

Pointed enough, but he was still trying to lay the courtesy groundwork. "Looks like it might be the start of a bad week for me. Up late last night, up early again this morning. It tells on you. At our age we can't get away with what we used to. You know?"

"It's crossed my mind."

"I don't mind the piddly small-town stuff, a Sno-Pup missing from a garage in Pan Town, windows broken at the vo-tech. That's your basic ten-hour cop day. You'd think you'd get a break on Christmas, though."

Charlie bent over and began to gather the split wood that had fallen around the block.

"I should be able to spend the day opening presents with my family. Instead I'm out on the job."

"That's too bad." With his arms loaded Charlie reached inside the woodshed for his jacket, slung it on top of the pile.

"You didn't have such a good one, either, I expect."

"It was all right. Dinner at Searles', Simon had to work."

"Yeah, I don't know if this business of mine concerns you or not, but I thought I should ask."

"So ask."

"I want to know if you've been in touch with Nick Uhler."

"You asked me that two weeks ago."

"I guess I did. What did you tell me?"

"I said, 'What's it to you?' "

Bill hunched his shoulders against the cold. "You know, I always wondered: you and Nick, did you ever patch up that falling-out you had a few years back?"

Now Charlie showed him his eyes, level and hard. "Who wants to know? Bill from art class or Bill the sheriff? What are you getting at, Hessel?"

"We know he was in town and he saw a lot of people. Why not give it to me straight?"

Charlie stared at him. "Straight. I saw him once. At Marty Voigt's. For two minutes."

Bill's heart pumped. "When was that?"

"Friday night."

"You have a fight with him, by any chance?"

Charlie laughed. "A fight? No. We don't have that much in common anymore."

He shoved his hands in his jacket pockets. "I'd like to hear more about it if you want to tell me."

"Why would I want to tell you? Are you my best friend?" He shifted the load in his arms, and the jacket slipped sideways.

"You want me to grab that jacket for you?"

"Don't do me any favors."

"That wasn't what I had in mind. I just thought I should come out here and tell you to stick around for a while. Could be a bad week for you too."

"Is there a point to this?" Charlie asked. "If so, why don't you fuckin' get to it?"

"The point is, Nick's dead."

He watched the features wash clean of expression. Then a spasm of reaction as Charlie tightened his arms around the load of wood and fixed him with a look. Fear could do that, turns faces extra fierce. Sometimes it made them quiver around the edges. Fear of death? Fear of being found out? The look coming off this face didn't wobble.

"You son of a bitch," Charlie said.

"So the only time you saw him was for two minutes on Friday night. At Marty Voigt's."

"What happened to him?"

"Found him in the river yesterday. Up by Sportsman's Island." End of courtesy interview. "I'm going to need longer answers sometime soon,

209

Charlie. You see the problem here. I'll want you downtown in the next day or two to sign a statement, so drop in."

A pause. "Like we were old friends?"

"Yeah." He tried to give it a beat, but too late. "Like you and Nick."

Charlie wheeled toward the house carrying his load of wood.

Still feeling the goad of temper and still regretting it, Bill followed him. When the jacket slid off and fell into the snow, he picked it up, brushed it off—*a talent for housekeeping*.

Charlie went up the back steps, elbowed the door wide, and kept on going into the house.

Bill waited with a determined patience for him to reappear. An innocent man would have questions, would want to know more details. A man dead, after all. A man he knew, an old friend.

When Charlie didn't come back out, for one blazing moment he saw himself charging after him through the back door. *What's the matter with you?* He had screwed this job, put Charlie on too short a leash. But the son of a bitch gave him nothing, no room to be a nice guy.

He dropped the jacket, a quilted down number, on the back steps. It was brown, a dark khaki color, with a large attached hood. He followed the path back around front to his car. He climbed in and started the motor, gave it a few minutes to warm. No sign of Charlie. Sometimes, he made himself consider, it was the guilty ones who came up with all the questions and then had all the answers too.

He revved the accelerator. On the way out to the road he decided he'd learned a few things after all. One was, Charlie Carmody worked at being hard to read, and that was no accident. That was history speaking loud and clear, and history could be looked into. Another was, his crew could start asking about a man, medium build, six foot one or two, seen around town in a dark khaki jacket, possibly with the face obscured.

29

MARTY GRIPPED THE COUNTER while she watched the large man in the overcoat and the heavy black frame glasses say things to her. Every time he stopped talking and pushed the nosepiece up with his thumb and finger, it was her turn to talk. She had the answers, she had all of them. She could tell him anything he wanted to know, but that wasn't what she wanted to do. She wanted him to stop talking and leave. He kept saying, "I know this is going to be really hard on you, Marty." Now he had his notebook out, a little pad of paper.

"So he was at your apartment Friday night. Around six. And Charlie was there. Six fifteen. Right?"

"Right."

"Then they left."

She nodded.

"They leave together?"

"No. First Nick"—could it be true, Nicky dead at last? Why didn't she feel the relief? Nicky in the river, under the ice? Handsome, handsome boy, the face she had wanted—was it only Friday night?—to punch in. Forever dead. A gangster's death, he would've liked that. No. Nick wasn't a gangster. Yes, he was. Bill Hessel was staring at her. Bill Hessel was a sophomore, on the swim team. The sheriff. He was staring. Her turn. "I'm sorry?" she asked him.

"They leave here together?"

She got the thread back. "First Nick. Charlie a little later. I don't know. Five minutes."

"Five minutes?"

"I think so."

"So they were here together how long?"

"They passed on the stairs."

"Amicably?"

For some reason she wanted to laugh. "They argued, a little. I went inside."

"Recall any of it? Anything?"

"No. Just—they were kidding around. Like always. It didn't last long."

"Do you know if they were planning something together, Marty, putting together a deal?"

"I don't know." She did know. "Nick said"—there it was, she still had the instinct where he was concerned: Clam up. Cover. "Maybe," she said. She was out of practice. She wanted to be out of practice. She crossed her arms over the empty feeling in her belly. "I think so."

"Why do you think so?"

"He mentioned a deal. Nick always mentioned a deal."

"But with Charlie?"

She was so tired. "I don't think so. No." She looked out the window. Outside in the snow Mrs. Finch was taking her tottery steps on the shoveled sidewalk. "I've got a customer," she said.

A look passed over Bill Hessel's face. She knew that look. He wasn't nearly through, he wanted more.

Folding his notebook he said. "Why don't you hand me some of those pistachios, and the sunflower seeds."

Mrs. Finch was up the steps and trudging against the door to open it. The bell jangled, and she stepped in on the mat and stamped her feet. The little old frizzy head bobbed up from watching the clear galoshes meet the floor, and there was a smile pressed into the leathery wrinkles. "Hello, Marty."

"Hello, Mrs. Finch."

"Cold this morning," the old lady insisted.

"Yes."

"The ones with the shells still on," Bill Hessel said. "I'm giving up smoking, it keeps my hands busy to do the shells."

"My dear husband smoked, it was a torment," Mrs. Finch said.

Marty dropped the cellophane packages into a brown sack and made change from the five he had laid on the counter.

Mrs. Finch crept on by to the meat case.

Marty put his change on the counter and pushed the sack forward. The receipt went fluttering to the floor. She stooped to pick it up. She just wanted him to leave, and this kept going on and on. "I don't need the slip," he said. "Take it easy, Marty."

She dropped the piece of paper into the wastebasket and made herself smile back. Yes. All right. She understood everything. Handsome is as handsome does. Bill Hessel wanted what she could tell him. She would go to the police station and answer questions, sign a statement for him. Not for him, not for anybody, get that straight, but just to get this over with. A statement. Good-bye to Nicky. How tired it made her to think of it. Anything she'd ever signed before made her want to die.

•

She helped Mrs. Finch down the steps.

"I want to thank you again for inviting me to tea yesterday. It made Christmas so festive!"

"We were glad you could come." Marty handed her the bag with one wrapped pork chop in it. "Be careful, now."

Mrs. Finch said, "I will," and kept her eyes glued to her feet on the sidewalk.

Marty ran across the street and pounded up the back steps of the house. "Dad," she called. "Can you take over? I've got to go!"

He came around the corner from the hall with his flannel shirt unbuttoned and the undershirt showing white underneath. He was moving fast, for Boz. "What is it, what's the matter?"

She was stopped. "Bill Hessel was just in the store."

"Saw 'im out the window. His Reliant. What's got you so upset? Come sit down—"

"Dad, Nick's dead. They found him in the river."

"Jesus." He put out one of his big hands to take her by the shoulder.

"When?"

"Yesterday. Christmas morning."

"Huh. Best present *you* ever got from him."

She shrank against the kitchen wall. "I've got to go."

"Where do you gotta go?"

"To the police station. I have to sign a statement."

"Not this minute you don't. You sit down with your old man and we'll talk this over. This has been a long time coming, Marty, this ain't a big surprise in your life or mine. You sit down."

But she turned and ran out the door. By the time she got to the curb, Boz was bellowing at her from the doorway of the house. "You get a coat on. You calm yourself before you get into that car. You hear me, Marty? This ain't your worry this time!"

•

In the car her teeth still chattered. She pulled her coat together. She took the river road underneath the downtown bridge and drove straight past the caramel-corn place and the grade school before she thought to start turning corners. She drifted slowly around the neighborhood streets, hers the only car on the move on this bleak day, until she knew where she wanted to go. When she pulled into the visitors' lot at the hospital, she realized that the engine had warmed up and she could have turned on the heat long ago.

The fourth floor seemed empty as she approached the nursery. Ellen Maccobbee appeared on the other side of the glass. On her shoulder she carried a pink-blanketed baby; she patted its little back and Marty felt a riptide of pure longing. Ellen turned and caught sight of her then, and walked to the Carmody bassinet. With one hand she wheeled it to the front of the glass. She grinned at Marty, and for what seemed the first time, Marty took a full-sized breath.

Patrick Simon Carmody was sleeping peacefully. He was doing without the tubes and tapes, and he looked so *complete*—she was wiping tears without understanding exactly what they were for. God, they were for everything. All the sadness in this barren world. But what a release to be in the presence of this healthy life!

This was what she needed, this freshness. A clean slate! You couldn't have that at thirty, could you? Not the way she had got there. *Nicky! Look what it all cost!* No, this was not news, not even a surprise; she had seen him go in far worse ways in her imagination. Oh, but it hadn't started out to be that way, it had started with such a giddy sweetness—all of which was long gone. Face it. Face it. And that left her in the same old place: she would have to settle for what she could rake from around the ruins.

"What do you think?" She addressed this to the baby, sending her thoughts to him. "Do I look like a survivor to you?" She willed him to open his blue Carmody eyes. Her heart raced and raced until she thought she would be sick.

Simon came through the double doors. He saw her and looked at his watch, clearly surprised to find her there.

"I have the day off," she offered. "I just stopped in."

"I've been meaning to call you," he said. "I should have. I've been thinking about asking you —did Charlie already mention this?"

"Mention what?"

"Let me start over. I had planned—Elizabeth and I had planned to have my mother help her with the baby at home. But now, of course . . . Listen, I know you have commitments, Marty, please set me straight if I'm out of line, will you? Only, I see what an interest you take in him."

She wasn't following. Or if she was, it was making her dizzy with fright.

"Would you be willing to . . . I wonder if you'd consider taking charge of the baby. Moving in with us for maybe a few months. You'd have your own room, a car if you need one. I'd pay you the going rate—I'd pay you whatever you want."

She stared at him.

"You must think I'm out of my mind." He sighed. "The baby's ready to go home and my mother expects to do it alone, but that will never work. She's not up to it. It's her age, Marty."

"Of course."

"Would you want to think it over for a couple of days?"

He was waiting for her answer. Suddenly all those other questions waiting for her flooded back and the morning dissolved. "I need to tell you something." She held on to the rail. "I appreciate this so much, that you would ask me. But something has happened, Nick Uhler"—her voice grew very faint—"I was married to him. I don't know if you remember. His body was found last night."

"I know."

"You know?"

"Charlie got hold of me an hour ago." Simon turned red. "Marty, you have to forgive me. I'm awkward about these things. Charlie had to remind me you'd been married to Nick, and—I probably should have said something right away. I don't know how you're handling this, it's just in my own case, I hate for people to mention it." He bit his lower lip. "Anyhow. I want to express condolences, that is, if—"

She broke in. "I don't know *how* I feel."

"The only thing to do is get on with life. Take the next step," he said firmly.

"The next step is, there's going to be an investigation."

He nodded. "Charlie said Bill Hessel's been making the rounds."

His unspoken sympathy affected her, made her want to explain everything—explain what? "I hadn't seen him since I left Chicago." She stared at the floor. "And that's the way I wanted it."

"They'll talk to everyone who ever knew him, Marty. I hope you're not taking this too much to heart."

"What is going on, Simon? Everything's so strange." She locked her arms against her chest. "First Elizabeth, then little Molly Fallon, now Nick . . ."

"Molly Fallon's all right, didn't you hear? She's out of the coma."

She could only look at him.

"As of Saturday," he said. "She leaves the hospital today."

Marty shut her eyes and leaned her face against the glass. "You know, I heard somebody say her name after church. I didn't want to hear. I was afraid it was bad news."

The trouble was, everything was happening way too fast. She needed some way to cushion what each separate thing did to her. She used to understand how to steel herself, shut down. What undid her lately was the effort it took keeping the door open just that little space, trying to open up —not too wide, not to offer too broad a target—to hope again.

She kept her eyes shut. "Simon. Are you seriously offering me a job?"

"I wish I could say I was doing you a favor." His voice sounded tired. "The truth is, my mother won't be a blessing in your life. She won't be gracious about any arrangement I make."

She opened her eyes. "Neither will my dad. But it's time he got someone else in the store."

"You wouldn't have to be with the baby around the clock. Mother can help out some. But I've got to have someone I can rely on."

Beyond the glass Patrick stirred in his sleep, and they turned to watch as he lifted one fist and slowly opened it, extending five perfect little fingers.

Marty spoke first. "I would love to do this, Simon. I could get everything set with my dad by next week." She watched his face fall.

"A week is a long time in a baby's life. He goes home tomorrow."

"Tomorrow!"

"I ought not to pressure you. It isn't fair."

What was stopping her? Was she still trying to take care of Boz when she could be touching this baby, holding him—

"I ought to have come to you sooner," Simon went on. "But—Marty, there's one other thing, something I can't very well tell anybody else. Listen to me. The baby really does need someone." He looked toward the double doors. "Because it's not a wanted child. Not by me."

She looked into his set face.

"I know what you must think. I can't help it."

"Simon, you are being so hard on yourself. You loved Elizabeth very much and you've lost her. No

221

one can expect . . ." To her astonishment she talked to him easily, this man she had always felt uncomfortable with, going over the familiar ground, saying the things she had told herself a million times. "Don't think you're the only one ever to feel the way you feel."

Simon stared somewhere above her head.

"And if you need me, I've made up my mind: I'll come. Tomorrow."

His eyes shifted tentatively to hers. He moved his jaw and neck as though he were breaking up a vise hold. "Well. We'll be talking, then." He was in motion, walking away from her. Three strides and he stopped, turned. He stared at the baby in the window, and then down at Marty's feet. "Thanks for not treating me like Monster Man. Even if I am."

She gave him a grim smile. "You're not him," she said. "Him they found in the river."

30

WITH HIS APPOINTMENT BOOK OPEN to Friday, Simon sat in his leather office chair with his knees spread, a hand cupped over each kneecap. He didn't realize that he was staring vacantly at the door of his office until Kathy's gray head appeared in the narrow opening.

"Your brother's here." She waited.

"Sure." He'd make it plain: "Anytime."

She gave him the once-over. "You look like Abraham Lincoln," she said, and disappeared.

Abraham Lincoln. He thought about closing the appointment book and decided against it. No use hiding this from Charlie or anybody else. The whole thing was beginning to unfold, and he was in it whether he liked it or not. Charlie. Christ. Someday he'd manage to drag them both under.

Ever since his brother had set foot in St. Cloud, Simon had understood it was his job—hadn't it always been?—to keep him occupied and out of trouble. Under the circumstances he'd done what he could. Charlie would get fed up and leave; the best he'd hoped for was a clean exit. Well, kiss that one off. Lately Simon saw his life as a patched-over inner tube, and people kept coming out of the depths and stabbing more holes in it. Dead or alive, Nick Uhler had a talent for turning up where he was least wanted. That was simply the fact. And the other fact was, so did Charlie. Did Abraham Lincoln have a brother? He wondered.

Charlie pushed the office door open. "Simon. Kathy was telling me about Molly Fallon," he said. "Congratulations."

"Wasn't anything I did. She snapped out of it as if somebody had called her name. I happened to be at the right place at the right time."

"Good trick to know."

"Wish we both knew it." Simon slid a paperweight across the desk blotter, then glanced up. "I wish I could have put that better. Come in and sit down, would you?"

Charlie pushed the door closed with the back of his head. Warily he said, "I just came to tell you two things."

"I've got a few things to tell you too." He got up and came around the desk.

Charlie unhooked his fingers from his belt loops and walked to the farthest chair. Slid deep down into it.

"You want to start?" Simon asked.

"Nah. Go ahead."

"Hessel was just here."

Charlie shut his eyes.

"He got my phone number from Nick's motel room. Nick called here Thursday afternoon and made an appointment to see me Friday at five thirty."

"Why?"

Simon reached behind him and slid the logbook to the front of the desk. With a finger he tapped the lined space under the heading FRIDAY P.M.

"He never showed. I waited till six, then went home and made it through one show with Ma and went to bed." Simon blew his cheeks full of air and let it go. "Charlie. Let's talk straight. Do you know what Uhler was doing in town?"

"Having surgery, is my latest guess."

Simon shut the appointment book. "He asked me for an appointment. That's all I know."

"How come you didn't mention this Saturday when you came by the house?"

Simon shook his head. "Medical ethics."

"Jesus, they must come in handy. You don't even have to tell what he wanted the appointment for, is that right?"

"I don't have to, but the fact is, I don't know. What he said on the phone was 'How about putting me down for some of your valuable time?' You guys still remind me of one another, you know that?"

"Except he's dead."

"So what? You didn't kill him, right?"

"Hessel doesn't know that."

"No, Hessel doesn't know that you're too damned stupid! He doesn't know you'd rather get drugged up and go to jail for the son of a bitch. You're even dumb enough to go to Marty Voigt's and try to pick a fight with him Friday night, dumb enough to get boozed up at the Press so you could pick another one. I think you stay too fried to find your fly, Charlie, let alone kill somebody."

His brother stood up. "Well, I guess that covers it." He started that stiff amble toward the office door. "Looks like you already know the two things I came to tell you." He turned. "But here's one for free, Si, something else Hessel might not know: the only damage I did that night was to a door."

"What door?" He couldn't wait for the answer. "Christ. Why do you keep making trouble for yourself? Isn't life hard enough?"

Charlie stopped. Without turning around he said, "It is. It sure is."

"So, what's next?"

"I don't know." His voice was flat. "Maybe hop a bus to Guatemala."

"Leave town? You need a better idea than that. Hessel will send out the troops, Jesus!"

Charlie faced him. "Si, I was kidding."

"Seriously, have you ever thought about going into treatment?"

His brother looked stunned.

"I wish you'd let me sponsor you. You do this kind of stunt too often, and this time you could be in real trouble. You need somebody on your side."

"Well, when is that going to turn out to be you, Si? If this is you offering to be a great guy, I don't like wading through shit to get to it! You've been on the shit-giving side as long as I can remember."

Simon sat back on the edge of his desk. He rubbed his face with his hands. "Damn. You know who you sound like? Elizabeth. She never could understand that I was working for her best interests, she thought I was just crowding her. Jesus, if she'd taken care of herself—"

"Si, you couldn't have done anything to keep her from dying."

"You know what's hard, Charlie? Not getting any more chances." He looked at the shine of his black shoes against the gray carpet. "Look. You don't have to think of me as a great guy, okay? If it makes more sense, you can just assume I want your name clear because it's the same as mine."

A long silence dropped between them. Another three inches of snow had fallen early in the morning hours, and from beyond the windows came the whining diesel sound, snowplows clearing the streets. A rapid yellow flashing passed left to right on the wall beside Charlie's head.

"What is Hessel trying to do, Si?"

"I don't know. He didn't mention your record. He for sure knows how to work a data bank, though."

"Forget it. He knows."

In the parking lot the snowplow driver hoisted his shovel and threw the truck into reverse; a rapid ringing came up from the big tires.

"Hessel say anything else of interest?" Charlie asked.

"He had a few questions about Marty."

"What the fuck kind of questions?"

"Come on, Nick went to her place to see her." Simon lifted his shoulders. "She went through some rough scrapes with him, Charlie."

"Haven't we all. What did you say to Hessel? Or is that one covered by medical ethics too?"

Simon looked hard at his brother. "What do you think I said? You're my brother."

Charlie slid his eyes toward the window, and Simon followed suit. Outside of the medical complex two bundled-up women walking to their cars stopped and scooped up handfuls of snow. Laughing, they took their shots. The softly formed snowballs crumbled in midair and landed short.

"I'm glad to have you on my side," Charlie said at last.

31

FROM HIS OFFICE Tom heard Chris's cheery greet-
ing go forth. He had started keeping his door
open, depending on that musical evenhanded-
ness, the way she always sounded glad—actually,
she sounded delighted—to see you. As if she just
couldn't *be* disappointed. God, he needed some of
that in his life. This was why he needed an office,
not to conduct business, really, but to keep on top
of the checks and balances of living, just like gov-
ernment.

He heard, "He's expecting you, Sheriff. Just go
on back."

Hessel. He was expecting him all right. There
was nothing he wasn't expecting. The lining of his
stomach was tired of the clench of expectation,
and this was the time when things ought to be
better, wasn't it? Molly was home, Molly was fine
—they were all fine again.

"Bill!" He said it cheerfully, trying to match
Chris's no-fault tone. He pushed himself up out of
the chair, a little late, just a beat late, and leaned
over the desk to shake his old friend's hand. "Good
to see you."

"Thanks for making the time," Bill said formally.

That cleared things up. This was not a social call. Tom said, "No trouble at all. Cup of coffee?"

"Yeah, I could use one."

They walked to the window, and he shuffled a cup from the stack for Bill. It seemed to take forever to get one cup separated from the rest.

"This is decaf," he explained as he poured for both of them. "Chris still keeps the hard stuff out there. She's younger than we are."

"I noticed."

He glanced up. "She's a sweet one," he said. And didn't like the way Bill was studying him. "What's on your mind?"

Bill took the cup and tilted his head at the upholstered chairs. "Okay if we sit down? I'm putting in some long days lately."

"I'll bet."

They sat down.

"What a load off your mind, getting Molly back safe and sound. Jeanne must be real happy to have things back to normal."

Real happy? Normal? "Sure is," he answered. "Sure is."

"Now, if I could just get the Nick Uhler business wrapped up, Val would be real happy."

"How is Val? Haven't seen her since the party, I guess."

"Oh, you know how Val is. Just wasn't her idea of Christmas day, to have me trekking out to Sportsman's Island. But I do have to go around and keep asking questions till all the blanks get filled in."

"You know the cause of death yet?"

"Don't know much more than what you read in the papers."

230

Tom knew better. "You must have the autopsy report by now."

"Doesn't tell us much. Cause of death a blow to the head, some fragments of bark embedded in the tissue of the wounds."

"Maybe a log he struck when he was already in the river?"

"Doubt it. He was on cocaine. Not enough to kill him, though. Looks like murder."

"Murder." Tom tried out the word.

"We can't pinpoint the time of death—with the water so cold, you know; nothing deteriorates. Probably late Friday, early Saturday."

Bill paused, and Tom said, "I see."

"We're trying to get a picture. Don't have enough specifics to narrow the investigation, so we have to go wide."

The next long pause wasn't going to take care of itself either. "So," he said. "What do you need from me?"

Bill uncrossed his legs and put his elbows on his knees. "I'll have to be a bother for a while. Chasing down everybody Uhler had contact with—for any reason."

"Okay." All this indirect stuff made him want to grind his teeth. Maybe it was just Hessel in his plainclothes. The guy belonged in a uniform, with his yellow embroidery and holsters where you could see them.

"We have to get the fine-tooth comb out, and I guess we have to drag the history books down too."

"Meaning what?"

Bill lifted his eyebrows. "Uhler didn't live here quietly, is what I mean."

"When he lived here," Tom said. "That was a long time ago. So what is it you're after?"

"I'd like a statement on your whereabouts, as precise as you can make it, for Friday night and Saturday."

"Fine. That's easy enough. I was at home with Erin, then at the hospital with Jeanne, probably until ten or eleven o'clock. After that, home." He watched Bill pull out a pad and make notes.

"Was it ten or eleven?"

Tom shrugged. "Closer to eleven. We left in separate cars, she was in the side lot and I was on the ramp. I think she beat me home. Dad had stayed with Erin and I walked him home—yes, around eleven thirty. And let's see: Jeanne went back to the hospital Saturday morning early—six thirty—while I stayed with Erin, until Simon called us with the news about Molly. Around ten."

"And then you stayed there."

"All Saturday and Saturday evening, with Molly under observation." He smiled. "None of us wanted to let her out of our sight."

Bill smiled back. He sat with the notebook in his hand, making a series of dots. "I guess that takes care of the present."

"Good. It's practically my whole life story for the last couple of weeks."

"The part of your life story we haven't covered concerns Elizabeth."

"Right, right, I knew it." Tom got up out of the chair and started to pace. "Even though the *one* thing you know for sure, the *one* person who could not have been involved in whatever happened to Uhler was Elizabeth!"

"Elizabeth had drugs in her possession that may

232

have come from Uhler. The fact that she died in childbirth doesn't bring everything to a halt, Tom. You know how cases are built, you're a lawyer."

"Don't use that stuff on me, don't expect me to be reasonable about this. This is Elizabeth, this is my sister! Maybe Simon gave her those pills, did you ask him?"

"We asked," Bill said. "He says he didn't."

"I can think of plenty of people in this town a lot more directly involved with Nick Uhler than Elizabeth. You want history? Try Charlie Carmody, try Marty Voigt. And while you're at it, try Marty's dad."

"Thanks for the tips. I'm also talking to you. And I'm talking to *your* dad."

"Shit, Bill, my dad? Who is seventy-three years old, one stroke on his chart already?"

"And I mean to have a talk with Jeanne, at some time or other."

"Jeanne." He stood still. "Do you still have a heart beating inside that shirt, Bill, or is it just a clock? Jeannie has been through hell these last weeks."

"Look, I came here because I need your cooperation. I want you to understand it's nothing personal."

"It's personal to me, if you're going to involve my family. Why's my dad even on your list? He didn't talk to Uhler. He wouldn't give him the time of day! *I* talked to Uhler. Anything you want to know, you can ask me. Jesus God, Bill!"

"I do need to know exactly what Uhler said to you on the phone Thursday evening."

"Said he was back in town, and wanted to talk to my dad. Had been trying to get in to see him. I told

233

him what he'd already found out: no way. And I hung up on him."

"Did you get any specifics on what he wanted?"

"None."

"Had he contacted you or your dad previously? Anytime in the last ten years, say?"

"No. Of course not."

"What about Elizabeth?"

"Why should he?" This was getting under his skin. "I have no reason to think he would, do you?"

"When he spoke to you, did he appear to know Elizabeth was dead?"

"He didn't mention it," Tom said flatly.

"All right," Bill said. "Now I have to ask you about a story. Did Terry make a bargain with Uhler twelve years ago?"

"Twelve years ago."

"When Elizabeth was in high school. Hearsay, Tom, but I have to check it out."

He forced a laugh. "That's hearsay, all right."

"I figured if you knew, you could tell me about it. If you don't, the only person left to ask is Terry Fallon."

Tom pulled a sharp sigh. "Christ. Okay. You're right, Dad told Uhler to clear out of St. Cloud. He paid him five thousand dollars. Made it very clear he was to stay away from Elizabeth, made it clear there would be no more money, and he was not to come back here."

"Or else what?"

"My father was sixty years old. He hadn't had a stroke. He might have said a lot of things he'd be unprepared to act on twelve years later." He lifted his eyes to Hessel's. "He didn't take Uhler's call. He didn't speak to him, didn't see him."

"Okay. I've got that. Now I'm going to ask this again. When you talked to Uhler, did he know Elizabeth was dead?"

He hesitated. "I don't know. *If* he was after money, it seems to make more sense that he didn't know. I hadn't thought of that. Have you checked whether he tried to call Simon's house?"

"The phone company shows no record of a call from Chicago, or any other source we can't identify. Not for six months. So that leads nowhere."

"Look. I gave you precise information. You don't have to take this part of your investigation anywhere else. I'm asking you."

"What I have to have is the straight story. If that's what I've got, okay. If I come across something different . . ."

"You won't. I'd like to know how you found out about Uhler and Elizabeth. In all these years I never told anyone."

Bill sighed. "We both grew up here, Tom. This is a small town, that's all." He folded his notebook and slipped it back into his jacket.

Tom kneaded his hands together to try and make them warmer. "Look, I know you've got a job to do. But I wish you wouldn't involve Jeanne. She's been though a rocky time, I'm not kidding you. More than I like to let on."

"She knew your sister."

"So did you. So did I." He pressed on. "Anything Jeanne knows, I can tell you. Things are fragile with her, and I promise you, you can have whatever you need from me. All you've got to do is ask."

Hessel stood up. "If I don't get what I need, if I run across some pieces that don't match, I'll do my job as I see it. I'm not talking about brutalizing anybody. Accusing anybody."

"Sure. I know that. But I want one favor: I was straight with you. You think of some new question, something we haven't covered, you come to me first."

He watched Hessel consider. He didn't like the time it took.

32

HE PUSHED OPEN THE DOOR lettered with Hessel's name. You had to hand it to the guy; he'd carved out quite a spot for himself here.

"Sheriff Hessel around?"

"Charles Carmody?"

Charlie nodded. It had taken him five minutes to park the car. He ended up over past St. Mary's, walking the six blocks to the brand-new brick building that housed both the Stearns County Sheriff's Department and the St. Cloud police. The least they could do when they hauled you in was provide you with a damned parking space.

The girl bent her head, repeated his name softly into a black box, and, like magic, Bill Hessel appeared from around the partition.

"Come on in, Charlie."

The office was large and plush; a big oak desk, thick carpeting, miniblinds covering the wide windows. Charlie gave a whistle of appreciation.

Bill looked embarrassed. "You should've seen the one I had before we moved in here."

Good. So he could be caught off balance too.

"Sit down." Hessel crossed to his desk, easing into the rolling chair. He leaned back in it—all very friendly and relaxed. "I'm glad you decided to come in and talk," he said.

"You mean as in 'give myself up'?"

"It's nothing like that, Charlie. We need all the information we can get."

"Okay. I'll start by saying I didn't kill him."

Hessel reached into the bottom drawer of his desk and pulled out a small, slim-line tape recorder. "You don't mind saying it on tape, do you?"

"No. Why should I?"

He slipped a fresh cartridge into the machine; pressed the switch. "You're on," he said.

"I didn't kill him."

"Didn't kill who?" Hessel asked.

"Nick Uhler."

"You had some reason to, though."

"Everybody who knew him had a reason."

"Like who? Give me some examples."

"Like some of the suppliers he worked for. He had sticky fingers. Not a good trait in a dealer."

Hessel sat back in the chair. "Tell me something I don't know."

Charlie laughed. "Starting where?"

He knew it wouldn't set well, but Hessel was so obvious. *You had some reason to.* Smarmier than any priest he'd ever come up against. "You want me to tell you about Joliet? I was there two years. On drug charges."

"How'd that happen?"

"Come on, Bill. You know all about it. You know he set me up."

"So how come you're so cheerful, getting screwed like that by an old buddy? How come you're not mad?"

Something funny going on here, something about the tone. He raised his hands. "Guess I'm just an easygoing guy."

"Guess you didn't seem too easygoing Friday night at the Press Bar."

And then he got it. *This guy hates my guts.* He could be in real danger here. Always it made him reckless.

"You were pretty visible that night," Hessel said. "I didn't even have to ask around."

"Yeah, well, I was pretty drunk."

"That your alibi?"

"My alibi?"

"Nobody saw Nick after that night, Charlie."

"I didn't see him either. I was watching the Lakers beat the Celtics."

"Where'd you go after they booted you out?"

"For a walk. I walked home from there. I got in around midnight. That's the truth, Bill." He could have bitten his tongue. He tried to settle back more comfortably in the chair.

"Somebody said your car was still in the parking lot the next morning."

"Right. I couldn't find the keys. They were in the lining of my coat."

"Maybe. Or maybe you got picked up by your friend in the big Buick, and drove around for a while, and got in a fight."

"Then I'd be the one in the river, wouldn't I?" Charlie stood up. "I never saw Nick after I left Marty's apartment. I don't know what happened to him. That's the end of my statement."

"One more item," Hessel said. "Neighbors noticed a red Buick sedan backing down the drive out at your place on Friday morning."

Charlie sat down again. "Man, you're everywhere, aren't you? Checking with the neighbors, asking around at the lumberyard and the hardware—been through my garbage yet?"

"Not yet."

"Okay, he stopped by the house that morning. I didn't think of it, because I saw him later on."

"What'd he want?"

"I couldn't tell you. I watched TV the whole time he was there."

"He try to put together another drug deal with you?"

"He was always dealing, it was his job."

"What was this one about?"

He shook his head. "No idea. I didn't ask. I told him I wasn't interested."

"How long was he there?"

"Ten, maybe fifteen minutes."

"Did he say where he was going?"

"No."

Bill fussed with the volume control on the machine. "Funny he'd come all the way out there. I mean, knowing you might not be in a forgiving mood. Makes you wonder."

"About what?"

"I don't know. I'm just trying to get something to jell here." Hessel clicked the machine off. "I did ask you to stick around, didn't I? Until we get this cleared up?"

"How long will that be?"

He shrugged.

Again Charlie stood. "Well, this isn't getting my work done."

"I guess every con in Joliet thinks he gets a raw deal, huh?"

Charlie stared him down. "I guess."

•

He walked the long blocks over to St. Mary's and got into the car. Sitting behind the wheel he thought about Hessel's comment: *Funny he'd come all the way out there.* The surprise visit, Nick walking in on him. Looking for his goddamn blue cup. Making small talk about the old man. Asking about the woods behind the house.

Small talk, that's all it was. Even the offer of a deal had seemed halfhearted, just a way to hang around a little longer—to do what? Take what?

The way he had stood by the window, with his face half in shadow: *"You think you got suckered in that deal. You oughta look at your own behavior. Talk about schizo."*

Was that right? Had he set himself up, and was he doing it again? No. Nick was the schizo, the joker in the deck. Nick asked for this, had been asking for it for years. And he was wrong about this town, about people not knowing what rough was. *Nicko. Somebody played it very rough.*

What had he said about his motel room being searched? Somebody looking for a package. Some kind of stash. Whatever it was, something that didn't get found, or he would have heard a different Nick talking. *It didn't get found.* Jesus God, was that it? Not to take something away. He came over to hide something.

He pulled up beside the house. He had three good places to look. The hollow bottom post of the banister—that had been their favorite spot to hide things years ago. Then the edge of the windowsill where he'd stood alone for five goddamn minutes at least. Then, the back of the kitchen cupboard. After that he'd turn the fucking first floor upside down until he found it—whatever it was.

He had a moment of elation that lasted as long as it took him to bound up the back steps. The feeling settled back to a grim fury—the way he'd felt as a kid running last in the pack, after he'd vowed he wouldn't quit, even if he knew for a fact it was already too late.

33

THE DOOR CHIMED and Marty hurried over the black-and-white tiles. The baby was napping, and so was Mrs. Carmody; if this was Jeanne Fallon, she was an hour early. Marty frowned. She didn't want to have to disappoint Jeanne, who'd naturally want to hold little Pat; on the other hand . . . she put on a smile as she swung the door open. Charlie.

"I came to ask a favor."

"What?"

"I need to look around your apartment. Do a search."

As she started to protest, he quickly lifted one hand and she flinched. The hand went to the door frame for Charlie to lean on. He leaned, but his eyes rested on her. "Are you afraid of me?"

"I don't know what to expect from you."

"I'm still the guy you know, Marty."

She folded her arms. "You're such a kid sometimes. It scares me."

"Scares me too," he said. "But I didn't kill him."

This jarred her, and she gripped her arms harder. "Charlie, I don't want to talk about this."

"I don't either. But I have to, because Hessel is

on my case, Marty. He's going to drop this one on
me."

"How can he if you didn't do it?"

He pulled his hand down, and straightened. "Do
you think I killed Nick?"

"I know you didn't."

He took a breath and let it out. "Nick mentioned
something. I can't make it come back straight.
Sounded like he had something with him that he
figured would make him some bucks. Did he say
that to you?"

"No."

"He could have been lying to me. But I had the
feeling . . ." He brought his eyes back to her face.
"Look, Marty. You know how we used to hide
things, all those secret places we had. I've
searched my place. Somebody else already ran-
sacked his motel room, that leaves your apartment."

"How do you know—"

"I don't."

The whole idea repelled her. She wanted
Nicky's shadow gone from her life. "I don't think
there's anything. And if there is, I'll find it, I'll
search my own apartment. I know as much about
his tricks as you do."

"Can you come right now?"

"No."

"That's the problem. Time is not on my side. If
you want to help me out, Marty, all I need is your
key."

"I'll call my dad," she said, feeling small and
stubborn. "He can let you in."

"Boz is going to give me nothing but hassle. I

know this is a lot to ask, Marty, a personal thing. I
don't know how to make it right with you."

That stopped her. Always, just when she wasn't
expecting it, he backed off and gave her plenty of
rope. And she already knew she would do what
she always did with extra rope: hang herself, probably.

"All right." She went and got her purse. When
she returned, he was standing at the edge of the
porch, looking out at the fog-wrapped trees. The
morning's heavy mist had retreated that far, leaving the front yard looking clear. The sun was thinning the milkiness over their heads, but it was slow
work. Where the lawn faded into the trees, fog still
hung in wreaths.

"He never did anything by accident," Charlie
said. "He came to you for a reason, the same way
he did to me. Did he ask you for money?"

"No."

"So, what was he after?"

"I don't know." When he turned and walked
back to her, she dropped the key into his cold
hand.

"Little Pat doing okay today?" he asked.

"Doing great." She smiled in spite of herself.
"He's sleeping, though."

Charlie returned the smile. "Tell him I said
sweet dreams. And Nellie—same to her."

Marty laughed as he went down the steps.

Over his shoulder he said, "Hell, let's not forget
Pearl. This place is beginning to be like Sleeping
Beauty's castle."

"Pearl?"

"The cat. Pearl."

"There is no cat."

He stopped. "There used to be a cat. Gray, with yellow eyes." He searched her face. "Forget it."

Watching him move toward the car, she said, "Charlie. I know what it is with Bill Hessel."

"Tell me."

"He's still mad about Valerie."

"Valerie."

"Burns. Bill Hessel married Val Burns. Remember?"

He looked pained.

"You've been away too long, Charlie. I'll tell you something. There is no life after high school. Not in this town. The grown-up world is just high school with money."

"This can't be that," he said.

"All right. It can't be that."

She shut the front door and made herself walk away from the cut-glass panels so that she would not watch Elizabeth's car disappear into the mist. She went to the nursery and looked in.

He was sleeping with such concentration, the little chin sculpted like marble. What a miracle, this sense she had of belonging here with him! Who could resist this absolute certainty of what your purpose in the world was? She sat down in the white bentwood rocker. Someday Simon, too, would have to let himself feel it.

A dream of a nursery—could she have ever put together such a room? Papered in pale yellows, a suffused geometric pattern that was simple and sweet. She felt in these touches how Elizabeth would have wanted her child to be cared for, with a tenderness that still had some quality of restraint. She wondered at this. Was Elizabeth's idea that a child could grow up in this room and have these soft little bears and plush kittens on low shelves right in reach, and dignity too—was that it? In some odd way she felt she was being gently taught by Elizabeth, and at the same time there was something very like jealousy over the draw-string layettes already chosen and unwrapped and stacked, cotton balls and baby oil ready at hand, the soft little blankets. What absolute assurance! Or innocence—did Elizabeth never once think anything could go wrong?

Jealous of Elizabeth? Unwelcome thought. That went a long way back, so far buried that the re-membering made her tired. She'd been jealous of Elizabeth in high school, because that was easier than blaming Nick. She'd fought for some precari-ous balance along what she knew and didn't know, fought against Nicky's lies and ended up working hard to make them be true—so she could go on believing them. Did Nick know anything about Elizabeth Fallon's hush-hush disappearance to convent school? No. Of course not. And she be-lieved him, working very hard on that one. Oh, God: when had he finally admitted the money that got them to Chicago had come from Terry Fallon? After it was gone. A child born and sent off for adoption—Elizabeth had been a child herself. Six-teen? Not old enough to keep clear of Nicky Uhler. Not by half. So how about thirty? *Was thirty old enough, Marty?* Yes. Because Nick Uhler was dead.

But so was Elizabeth. In the last nine years she and Elizabeth had easily avoided each other. Out of a sense of contamination. The difference be-tween them was, Elizabeth had gotten clear— maybe her father's money did that much for her. Simon's love had done the rest. He had given her a beautiful home, this beautiful baby—even so, even desiring these things for herself, she welcomed Elizabeth's presence in her own child's life. Once again they would share.

She tugged the woven blanket over Patrick's shoulders. Her touch was clumsy and his small body quivered. He gave a little hitch of breath but slept wonderfully on.

Her bedside reading these days was Dr. Spock, who said that babies did very well at tuning out disturbing stimuli—telephones ringing, touch, adult voices—in order to have the rest and peace they needed. All right. She would do likewise and not let anything get her rattled. Silently she promised this to the sleeping infant, adding *Don't worry about your father either.*

And really, she wasn't worried about Simon. He would come around, the baby would win him easily if Mrs. Carmody would stop pressuring him at every turn to hold Patrick. How miserable it made him! How miserable it made Patrick! And Grandma herself—every time she grabbed him up, Pat protested with everything he had: little red feet kicking, a fussy whickering that eventually grew lusty-loud. Which Grandma deemed "spoiled," and Marty's fault. Having Dr. Spock on her side cut no ice with Mrs. Carmody. A little stab of fear: would Simon someday side with his mother? Would he be forced to, just to keep the peace?

When the telephone rang, she lurched out of the rocker and hurried across the hall into Simon's study to get it. Merely the dentist's office, confirming Mrs. Carmody's appointment. Marty slid the center desk drawer open and found a fountain pen; she jotted the date and time.

She hung up and screwed the cap back on the barrel of Simon's black pen. *Pelikan,* it said. Suddenly her presence in this study of his felt like an act of invasion. Maybe it was the smiling black-and-white portrait of Elizabeth in a frame. Anyhow, it brought to mind Charlie in her own apartment, and *that* she firmly resolved not to think about. She returned Simon's black fountain pen to its slot in the drawer, and glanced down to see, beyond the shallow partition, another gleaming black barrel.

She slid the drawer wider. A revolver lay resting on a stack of papers. She put her hand out, then drew it back. A gun! What was it doing here? The rush of adrenaline made her head light. This was nothing to do with her. She closed the drawer and left the room.

In the kitchen she rinsed the pacifiers and put bottles into the dishwasher; she ran it to sterilize them. She opened the cupboard and gazed at the cans of formula on the shelf. *How long would this last?* She was still standing there when she heard the door chime and realized it was not the first chime.

"I'm a little early," Jeanne Fallon said.

Marty hung Jeanne's black wool coat in the foyer closet. "Patrick isn't awake yet," she said, "but come in the kitchen and I'll make tea."

Jeanne walked in, hesitating at the hall. "Can we just take a look?"

"Of course." Marty turned and followed her lead upstairs to the nursery. She watched as

Jeanne leaned over the crib and took a deep breath.

"Don't you love that smell?" Jeanne said. "There's nothing in the world like it." She reached into the cradle for the pacifier that had slipped partway out of Patrick's mouth.

The gesture rang wrong. Marty's possessive instincts rose—or was it the influence of what Mrs. Finch had hinted the other day: that Molly Fallon's crisis in the hospital had unhinged Jeanne?

Smiling, Jeanne handed the small object to Marty. "He looks like his mother, don't you think?"

"I guess I hadn't thought," Marty said. "I just kind of assumed he looked like his father."

"With that dark complexion?" Jeanne hesitated, then added, "Of course, sometimes it's hard to tell."

Marty looked down at the yellowish-pink cast the baby's small face made against the white of the cradle sheet. She was not going to argue with Jeanne about Fallon complexion and Carmody complexion. But what did she mean, dark? Patrick had his own look. It was his own. "I could look at that little face all day," she said.

"I'm sure."

She looked up.

Jeanne's face did not explain the tone. "You can do that with one," she said more evenly. "With two it's different. Of course, if you have your own someday you'll find that out."

She felt a little down-spiral of dread. Why did this woman make her doubt everything she knew?

"You were so good to come and help Simon. How long will you be filling in?"

"We didn't really discuss it."

"Well, surely he—"

"I said I was available. As long as he needed me."

"Patrick."

"Yes."

"I wonder," Jeanne mused, "if he's mentioned finding a full-time housekeeper?"

Where was this leading? Marty didn't like the tenor of it, of anything that was going on. "He hasn't."

Jeanne nodded. "Poor Simon, he ought not have the burden of all this. I'll have to help him get organized. In the meantime, Marty, let me apologize for this—these vague arrangements," she finished. "The whole family has been so taken up."

"I'm so glad little Molly has recovered," Marty said in a rush. She should have mentioned Molly earlier.

"She's absolutely whole again. Restored to us." Jeanne smiled up at the nursery windows where, beyond the eyelet curtains and storm glass, snow rimmed the sills. "We're overjoyed."

"I know how much time you spent with her in the hospital. That is, I heard."

"The whole experience was not ordinary and not easy for people to understand. I'm glad I did what I did." She looked at Marty, and away. "Of course, nothing has been simple. I'm sorry about your ex-husband."

At this Marty, too, squinted at the window. The sun had burned through after all; shadows were back, reaching toward the house from the trees. "Thank you," she said. "Would you like to come and have tea now? Mrs. Carmody should be up any minute."

"Oh, why don't you go ahead and start the water?" Jeanne said. "I'll stay here with little Patrick."

Marty felt the blockage of Jeanne's body between her and the baby. It made her so uneasy. She gazed at the doorway as though she had never considered it as an opening before. "Actually, I think I'll just scoop him up and take him along. I have the roller-crib set up in the den."

"Oh, let the poor lamb sleep!"

Marty hesitated just long enough to let her unwillingness imprint itself upon the atmosphere. "I'd feel better if you came with me," she said.

"I'll come." Jeanne smiled. "We need to have a talk anyway. And we can hear him from the kitchen if he cries."

In the kitchen while Jeanne watched, she filled the kettle and warmed the teapot. *A talk about what?* Her hands began to shake as she measured the tea.

"He's gained weight," Jeanne offered.

"Nine ounces. I tell Simon he's getting stronger every day."

"And how does Simon respond?"

Marty raised her eyes to Jeanne's.

Jeanne said, "Perhaps I ought to be more direct. This is why we needed to talk, Marty. We both know having a child without a mother to care for it would be a difficult adjustment. But for Simon, perhaps it's especially difficult. Tom and I have offered to take Patrick and raise him with our girls. We believe it's best, though Simon needs reassurance, I think, that he'd be doing the right thing. In the meantime I'll be taking a strong interest, and it seemed only courteous to let you know what we expect to happen."

"You expect?" These were the first words Marty could hang on to. "Why? Why would caring for his own child be especially difficult for Simon?"

"It's been so lovely of you to do this interim caring, Marty, while we sort things out. I gather he hasn't mentioned this to you. Men can draw such blanks where babies are concerned; Tom didn't really get interested in the girls until they could walk and talk. But in this case, to speak frankly, it was never Simon's idea to have children."

Not a wanted child, not by me. At the time Simon had seemed to think it was his secret.

"Because Elizabeth was the one. I can't sit here in her kitchen without thinking of her. All those talks we had! She had to convince Simon, then the tests, she couldn't seem to get pregnant for so long —then bang, she was. You don't know what trouble she went to, how far she went! I wish I didn't." Jeanne smiled at Marty. "I'm old-fashioned about many things, and so is Tom, but not Elizabeth. She was always crazy about our girls but it's not quite the same, is it? Do you mean to have children of your own someday, Marty?"

Confusion made the blood rush into Marty's face. "I don't think that's a concern here."

"I'm so sorry." Jeanne looked contrite. "You're right, what a thoughtless remark for me to make, especially to you. Forgive me if I touched a sensitive area."

"It's okay." Although it wasn't.

"Once I got Molly home and safe, my concern

has been for the baby's welfare, and to tell the truth, Simon's. Do you think he's all right?"

"All right?"

"Not letting himself get too low, I mean, with his grief. Though of course he's not much of one for letting things show. I just thought you might have noticed something."

"No." Using a spoon handle she pressed the lid of the tea canister on securely. Was this real, was Simon really considering giving Patrick up? She *had* been noticing things, of course, waiting for him to soften toward the baby. It hadn't happened. Simon wasn't ready yet. *But ready to use that gun? Give up Patrick and kill himself?* The logic fit and gripped like pincers. Marty said carefully, "I don't think he's ready to make a decision like this." She turned. "He can get past this grief. I think he needs his child."

Jeanne pursed her lips. "Perhaps you're judging from your own loss." She smoothed her blond hair and didn't look at Marty's face. "I hope you're not standing over this baby's cradle thinking, *Nick Uhler, Nick Uhler.* Your thoughts are your prayers, Marty, a thought is a summons."

Marty set down the canister she was still holding. These infuriating half-hints—how much did this crazy woman know about her life? Had Boz told things? Had Simon? Had she been living in this town thinking no one knew while *everyone* did? She said, "Jeanne, if Simon is considering this plan, it affects me. I don't want to discuss it until I talk to him myself."

"I'm sorry I've upset you," Jeanne said in a soothing voice. "Simon ought to have told you, but with all this tragedy, he's hardly himself. None of us is. You'll have to forgive us."

Marty stared her down right through the "forgive" part. *Tragedy is no excuse.* For once Boz had said it all.

Jeanne rose from the chair. "Please tell Mrs. Carmody how sorry I am that I couldn't stay for tea. My sitter is expecting me."

In the brittle silence of the foyer Jeanne slipped her black coat over her shoulders. She said, "You know the verse about the sins of the fathers."

"I don't understand what you're talking about."

"No, neither did Elizabeth."

This time after the door was shut, Marty watched through the glass until the car disappeared. Then ran up the stairs to the little yellow room.

Patrick Simon Carmody had his eyes open. He was frowning into the bright daylight, blinking and making halfhearted fussing noises.

Marty lifted him gently to her shoulder, felt the active, organized resilience of his small body. "I'm here," she whispered. *And you are alive. This is not like before.*

34

CHARLIE PULLED UP OUTSIDE the circle of street-light in front of the store and waited several minutes. Across the street Boz's house had lights on, but no activity that he could see. He got out of the car. Around back he climbed the stairs to Marty's apartment and let himself in with the key.

Switching on the overhead light he saw the closet door, still with its splintered panel. He ran a hand over the ragged edges of the break. He'd pick up some wood and take care of this for her. It wouldn't take long, and it would make him feel better. He'd do it tomorrow, before he returned the key.

If he could ever understand why these things came over him. The part of himself that he couldn't control—it seemed that Marty was destined to know only that side. *What did we decide about birth control, Charlie?*

Enough. He had work to do here, but where to begin? Four small rooms—not a big task, but it would help if he knew what he was looking for.

Something small enough could be stashed almost anywhere. Nick would have to be certain it wouldn't be discovered in the normal course of events. Therefore, coat pockets were out. Dresser drawers were out. And there hadn't been a lot of time. Between the pages of a book? Inside a chair cushion?

All right, he'd seen this stuff done on TV. Pushing aside the coats in the hall closet, he got down on his hands and knees to examine the baseboards. Sealed tight to the wall with paint. He stood up and looked at the shelf. Nothing but a few scarves, gloves, and hats. He passed a hand over it, came up empty.

He went slowly and thoroughly around the living room, checking baseboards, cushions, seams. He lifted each picture from the wall, looking for loose backing, for any odd crack or space where a flat packet or a strip of film, anything could be pushed in. *Good idea, Charlie. Good idea, but no cigar.*

He headed down the narrow hallway. No place to hide anything here, no picture frames or mirrors, only bare walls. Like the corridor outside Sister Agatha's office, where he used to sit by the hour in grade school, waiting to be called in. God, when was the last time he'd thought about the nuns at St. Dunstan's?

Inside Marty's bedroom the white bedspread was folded across the foot of the bed. A dresser, a desk, and a chair. A row of stiff white ruffles across the top of the window frame, and a rag rug on the floor. That was all. As chaste as any nun's quarters.

He walked to her dresser and opened the top drawer. What for? He'd already decided there was no point in looking where she touched things daily. He saw the jewelry in a flat cardboard box— bracelets, necklaces, earrings. Next to it a straw purse with a leather-trimmed flap. He picked it up and looked inside, rimmed the inner pockets with his fingers. Nothing. A stack of embroidered white handkerchiefs caught his eye. *JSV.* Her mother's name was Josephine, he remembered. Josie Voigt. Had she kept this memory of her mother all these years?

He shoved the drawer closed. Goddamn you, Nick, why didn't you kick off in Chicago?

What had he said? *Nobody wants to kill me. I can't make money for 'em if I'm dead.* Did that mean he was working for somebody in town? Who? That line about the face-saver—what did it mean? A face-saver from way back. Christ! Terry Fallon.

Terry Fallon used to play rough, but that was when he was part of that crowd of black Irishmen in the construction business. Terry Fallon was an old man now. Not too old to mess up hotel rooms maybe, but too old to kill somebody. Too old to have somebody killed? True, he had told Nick never to come back to St. Cloud, but what else would he do after some kid from Pan Town had gotten his only daughter pregnant? That was years ago, a lifetime ago. *You can always get what you want if people need to save face bad enough.* Did it mean Nick was on his way to see Terry Fallon that night?

He sat down on the edge of the bed. Nicky was a hider, always had been. He loved a secret like it was alive and he could pinch it in his fingers. And he was a tease. That whole conversation at the house had been a tease. *Face-saver.*

Shit, this was getting him nowhere. He took a quick look under the mattress. No luck. Too corny,

anyway. He crossed the hall to the bathroom and
turned on the light.

*Nick, if I were you, I'd hide whatever it is in
here. The one room where you could lock the door.*

Leaning forward he felt around the bottom and
two sides of the medicine cabinet. He couldn't see
the top edge, but he could feel the crack between
the cabinet and the wall.

He brought a straight-backed chair from the
kitchen, stood on it, staring down at the top edge
of the medicine cabinet. Goddamn. Could it really
be this easy? He could see what looked like a piece
of paper stuffed down there. Probably a bill for the
cabinet, or directions on how to install it. But his
heart was tripping, all the same. The screwdriver
in his pocket was too wide. He needed something
smaller.

In the bedroom he opened the top drawer.
There among the combs and other toiletries was a
metal file.

He went back to the bathroom and slipped the
file down behind the box. Two sheets of folded
paper came cleanly up. He held them both under
the harsh bathroom light: a photocopy of a check
for five thousand dollars dated December fourth.
Made out to Elizabeth Carmody, signed by
Thomas Fallon. The second page was a copy of
the back of the check, endorsed by Elizabeth
Carmody to Nicholas Uhler, second endorsement,
Nicholas Uhler. Tom! Why hadn't he thought
about her brother?

Tom gave Elizabeth five thousand dollars. Then
she gave it to Nick. And then she died. When did
she die? He thought back to the Sunday before the
funeral, the day he had flown in from Arizona.

Sunday the tenth. Elizabeth had died on Saturday the ninth. So sometime after the fourth and before the ninth, he got the money, and—

Without warning the blow landed against his left shoulder and he was thrown into the tub. Arms out, he grabbed at the towel bar as another blow caught him square in the back. His head hit the tiled wall as the light went off. He scrambled and slid as a figure came at him, landing another blow to his ribs. Crouching, shielding his head with one arm, he tried to get to his feet. His hand hit the faucet and cold water came gushing out of the shower head.

Heaving himself up and over the edge of the tub, he landed on his hands and knees. He rolled hard into somebody's legs.

"What the fuck—!"

The man's knees buckled. He staggered backward, and Charlie was on his feet and past him.

"You son of a bitch—"

He knew who it was now. "Boz, it's me, Charlie!"

The old man had regained his balance. Before he could plow after him again, Charlie grabbed the doorknob and slammed the door closed in his face. Boz hit the door like an elephant, then banged on it with both fists.

His skull pounding, Charlie searched the empty hallway for something to hold the small knob, something to give him leverage. The knob slipped out of his grasp, and Boz jerked the door open. He came charging out of the bathroom.

"You get out of here! Goddamn if she can't stay away from losers!"

Charlie leaned against the wall, feeling suddenly dizzy. "I've got a key. She gave me a key."

"I don't give a damn about no key, you ain't movin' in here!"

Boz's face was next to his, but he couldn't see him clearly. "I got to sit down," he said. He made his way to the bedroom and sat on the bed. His ears were ringing.

"I swear, every time you guys come around, her life goes to pieces!"

Charlie shut his eyes. "Get it straight, will you? I'm Charlie Carmody. One guy. And what are you talking about, moving in?"

"What are you doin' over here?"

"I'm looking for something."

"You don't touch her things!" Boz thundered. "You put every goddamn thing back, you hear me?"

"Everybody hears you, even the fucking guards over at the reformatory. Quit yelling. My head hurts."

"I hope to God it does! I hope sometime you hurt as much as you've hurt her! Can't you see the way things are?"

"Boz, I love her, dammit! I've loved her my whole life."

"Yeah, tell me about it! So where were you when she marries that asshole and then that baby dies. . . . I shoulda gone to Chicago and killed the son of a bitch with my bare hands!"

"What baby?"

A silence. Cautiously he raised his head and stared into Boz's face. The old man looked bewildered. Charlie stood and took him by the arm. "Boz, what baby died?"

Boz cleared his throat, stared down at the floor.

"Did Marty have a baby, Boz? Did she? Tell me."

Boz shook his head. "Long time ago."

"What happened?"

"Born on drugs—too sick to make it." He was mumbling to himself. "It broke her heart. My little girl. . . ."

"God," Charlie said. "My God."

He let go of Boz's arm and leaned against the door. His head cleared, and he went across the hall to the bathroom. Switching on the light he saw the sheets of paper lying on the floor. He bent down and stuffed them inside his jacket, then got up and shut off the shower. Boz was in the doorway when he turned around.

"He got just what was coming to him," the old man said softly. "He got what he deserved."

Charlie couldn't look into the old man's face. He moved toward the door and Boz let him pass. He walked the length of the hallway and let himself out into the cold night.

35

TIRED OF LISTENING TO THE SILENCES between clusters of largely unhelpful words uttered by Mrs. Finch, Bill Hessel pulled the earphones from his ears. He stared at the sticker on the file cabinet in the outer office: STEARNS COUNTY SHERIFF'S OFFICE: TO PROTECT AND TO SERVE. With the earpieces dangling from his hand, he let the tinny little voice go on, insectlike in its fits and starts, before he punched the stop button on the recorder. He tossed the headset on the desk. Yeah, yeah, Mrs. Finch had seen Nick Uhler's car twice: once parked in front of Voigt's, and once parked in the alley. She had precise information on just how long Uhler had stayed at Marty Voigt's apartment, also how long Charlie Carmody had stayed—information which was not too hard to get if you didn't mind standing in your bathtub and craning your neck out the little window to watch somebody's back stairs. And the upshot was, everything checked out. Everything just like everybody said.

He paged through his notes one more time. He had taken every scrap of useful data from his notebook and recorder and transferred it to more formal data sheets. He was a great believer in organization; the right peg in the right slot.

He had no trouble making certain connections: Nick Uhler, Charlie Carmody, Marty Voigt. Easy. Add Simon Carmody, Tom Fallon, Terry Fallon: phone numbers found in Uhler's room. Add Boz Voigt, who according to Mrs. Finch was out on his front stoop, waving a fist at Uhler the day before Uhler was last seen. Then add Jeanne Fallon, who had mentioned Uhler's name to various people around the hospital that same day. Funny how a detail like that kept coming back. Didn't seem to fit, but sometimes it was the wild card you might be looking for.

He shuffled pages. He found the schedule of alibis for the night of Friday, December twenty-second. He pushed the button on the intercom. "Hey. Bakke."

No answer.

The door opened and Bakke stuck his head inside. "Got the report on the rental car, Chief. Trunk's clean, glove compartment's clean. No prints other than Uhler's on the steering wheel, door handles, or dash."

"That's it?"

"That's it. Except for this."

He came forward and dropped a small plastic bag on the desk. Through the bag Bill saw a flat black disc about the size of a fifty-cent piece.

"Found on the floor in the back," Bakke said. "No prints on it, no identifying marks."

Bill opened the bag, let the disc fall into his hand. Made of molded plastic, smooth and flat on one side and slightly convex on the other, with sharp little bumps at intervals. A hole through the center with what looked like rust around the edges.

"Looks like a hole for a screw," Bakke said, "but what you screw it onto . . ."

"I know what this is," Bill said. "It's a heel plate for a cross-country ski."

"You sure? I got skis. I don't recall ever seeing anything like this."

"My daughter has them. This one was found in the back?"

"Up under the passenger seat. Could have been there a while. Could have been overlooked by the cleaners the time before."

"Somehow I don't think Uhler was the type to come to St. Cloud and rent skis, but check that out. We still don't know how his body got to the river. Either his car never left the lot that night, or whoever killed him drove it back after the murder."

"And walked from there?" Bakke asked.

"Depends. Had a room in the motel, got a ride from someone, or maybe"—he dropped the disc back into its plastic bag—"cross-country skied. Anything else on that khaki jacket the night of the twenty-second?"

"Just what I told you. College kid saw a man in a khaki jacket walking by the river between Division and Tenth, campus side, about eleven thirty."

"Nothing else?"

A long pause. Bakke paged through some printouts in a folder. "Nothing else on a khaki jacket. One snowmobile suit walking toward Talahi Woods below the dam. One skier on the river around ten."

"One snowmobile suit. One skier. Great. Any

267

other Friday night, and we'd have a dozen leads here."

"Yeah, you'd think the town rolled up the sidewalks."

"It does," Bill said, "over quarter break."

Bakke left the office and Bill reached to pull down the laminated map. He found the juncture where the Sauk River angled into the Mississippi. A body could have gone in at Heim's Mill. Water's always open, nobody around to see. Hell, that body could have done a backflip over the concrete breakers at Tenth Street Dam, right under a thousand empty dormitory rooms, and nobody there to see either.

Of course, the corpse would have shown more battering if it had gone in above the dam. Say it went in below: the water stays open through the Beaver Islands. Groaning aloud, Bill leaned back and stared at the map. The river made its crooked wrist and fingers just below the center of town. He had *X*'s on the locations of all the principal suspects according to alibi—eight of those. Circled *X*'s for verified alibis—about half. And some of the verifications—husband-wife, parent-child. He shook his head. Too many of those for comfort.

Some of the *X*'s stood without circles. And as usual some would have a fudge factor, ten minutes here, half an hour . . .

"Bakke," he said, his finger on the button.

"Yeah."

"Get over to the hospital. Find out who saw Tom Fallon leave the night of the twenty-second. Also Mrs. Fallon."

"I thought we had that stuff."

He could hear Bakke rustling papers on that shredder-heap of a desk he kept.

"What about Fallon's neighbors? Want me to check them out?"

Glancing at the map Bill pictured the old college area, the way Hightower Place curved down from Third Avenue toward the river, dead-ending at Terry Fallon's tennis court. "Wait on that one. See what you get at the hospital."

He heard Bakke's sigh. "You're the boss."

He took his finger off the button. Right. He was the boss. He shifted his gaze to the map and fixed on the unshielded *X* downtown. *Look for the wild card, Hessel.*

Marjorie tapped on the glass window of the office door, and he stared at her through the gold lettering that spelled his name backward. He let the ill will he was feeling stream full force to her face. She blinked, and tapped again. He was losing his touch.

She opened the door a crack, put her head in. "Charles Carmody to see you, Sheriff."

He pushed his glasses up. Whatever it was, this was more like it. "What does he look like to you? Like he's got a lot on his mind?"

She shrugged.

"When I buzz you, send him in. And not before."

When Charlie's face appeared behind the lettered glass twenty minutes later, Bill leaned back in his chair. He spread his knees and let his hands dangle off the chair arms.

"Charlie," he said. "What can I do for you?"

"I don't know." He was wearing the khaki jacket, jeans, no gloves, hands empty. He kept coming forward with that slow walk until he stood directly in front of the desk. Bill kept his expression neutral, but he felt his fists gather of their own accord.

"You got a nice clean desk there," Charlie said. "File folders nice and neat."

"Thanks."

"Takes you twenty minutes, I bet, to make your desk neat?"

"Takes me all day, sometimes. Got something on your mind?"

"Yeah. I do. I'm wondering if you know about Nick's business with the Fallons."

Bill looked at him steadily. "I know Uhler called Tom Fallon from his motel room. He says it was a nuisance call. He hung up on him after a minute or so; the telephone records verify that. What do you know?"

"More than that."

"I never doubted it."

Charlie reached inside his jacket and pulled out a folded sheet, dropped it on his desk. "Maybe it's time to make a whole new file folder, Sheriff."

Bill slowly picked up the sheet and slowly opened it. A photocopy of a personal check, five thousand dollars drawn on Tom Fallon's account, made out to Elizabeth Carmody. "So?"

"You see the date?"

"I see it."

"December fourth." Charlie reached into his jacket again and pulled out another sheet. "Let me do this for you, Bill, save you half a day." He shook out the second sheet and placed it open on the desk. "A copy of the back of the check."

"I see it's a copy of some check, not necessarily this one."

"Oh, come on, Bill. Elizabeth's endorsement, pay to Nick Uhler. Which check do you think it is?"

He raised his eyes to meet Charlie's. "Sit down, why don't you?"

"I got these from Marty's apartment. Nick slipped them up behind the medicine cabinet when he was there."

"And you found them." He gave a little twist to the *found,* and watched that cocksure face draw.

"Hessel, you are so full of shit you wouldn't know which part of the outhouse your ass belonged in. Yeah, I found them. I found out that Tom and Elizabeth paid Nicky five thousand dollars almost two weeks before he died, which was one day before Elizabeth died. This is one trail that does not lead back to me. Now, what are *you* going to do?"

Bill shifted in his chair. "What does Marty Voigt know about these?"

"Nothing."

"I'll have to verify that."

"Goddammit, how about asking Tom Fallon some questions? Ask him about blackmail."

"I'll take care of it."

"Good. 'Cause I thought for a minute this town might still be Terry Fallon's little pocket-game of marbles."

Bill stared him down. "You don't have to worry about that."

"I would like to see a house call paid to Tom Fallon. It's a Saturday, maybe if he's home he could lay hands on a certain canceled check, right then and there. How about if I go along, so I can see what it is I don't have to worry about?"

Bill said quietly, "Terry Fallon's line of work these days is more in the area of grandpa. He does not run the sheriff's department. You want to worry about somebody, Charlie, worry about me."

"I'm worried. Was it your guys searched Nicky's motel room? If it was, these copies of Tom Fallon's check are what they were looking for. They didn't find anything, according to Nick. So this was the stash."

"Grow up. I didn't order a search."

"Well, somebody did. Somebody who cared about a check with the names Fallon, Carmody, and Uhler on it. What's the matter, didn't the motel staff report a break-in?"

"Not yet."

"And are you going to sit there and tell me this isn't Terry Fallon's work? It's got his name written all over it. Illegal, quiet, and wired from the top."

"Let me tell you something," he said, following the tension like it was a rope. "Your Xeroxes—that's interesting. Your motel story—that's hearsay, also known around here as horseshit, till proved otherwise. I will check it. Meanwhile, you are still a suspect, everybody is a suspect. You brought in something that may turn out to be important. Maybe not. I don't owe you anything, except thanks." He picked up the two sheets on his desk. "Did you make copies of these?"

Charlie nodded. "You bet."

"Good. Protect yourself, that's your right." He gave Charlie a sideward glance. "I imagine that's what Nick was trying to do."

"I imagine. Who are *you* trying to protect?"

"Me. You. Everybody. It's in the job description."

"I've heard that job described before."

"Charlie, you turned in your evidence. Now, you get in my way, you go to Tom's and make a scene, I'll get you for assault. I'll ride your ass to the ground."

Charlie flipped the cover of a file folder open on the desk. "Wouldn't be a very long ride, would it?"

36

SHE HAD HAD JUST ABOUT ENOUGH. She stood in the dark of the garage and clutched her fur collar to her throat. It was time for Simon to arrive. He had called from the hospital to say he was leaving, and that was fully twenty minutes ago. She stamped her feet in their rubber-soled shoes. The cold was creeping in, making her toes numb. It was not like him to be late; but when she had seized her coat and wool scarf and come out here to catch him, she should have taken her cozy lamb's-wool boots. She'd been in a hurry then, and she would have a sore throat tomorrow to show for it. But she was not going back into that house until her son set things right.

Suddenly over her head a switch clicked and a light went on as the big jointed doors rumbled and jerked and crawled up their tracks. Nellie stepped forward into Simon's headlights and waved, waved. He put on the brakes so hard the car died. Then he was out of the Lincoln and running to her. She met him and he seized her forearms.

"What is it?"

"Nothing. Just get back in the car," she snapped.

He crossed behind her to open her door. Well, his precious good manners wouldn't get him out of this fix they were in. Why couldn't he do as he was told, for once in his life? "Just get in." She pulled her door shut. The car was warm. She stamped her poor feet to get the circulation back.

Simon climbed in the driver's side and shut his own door. He looked at her.

"Pull in, pull in!" She waggled a hand toward his regular space in the garage.

"Delighted."

"Don't you talk to me like that, Simon Michael Carmody. You came home from medical school with that voice. What did they teach you there? To ignore everything that's going on in your own household under your very nose?"

He reached across her to the glove box. "Excuse me." He opened it and punched the contraption to make the doors come wiggling down. The overhead light went off. That left the headlights, shining point-blank on the garage wall.

"Do you want me to keep the car running?" he asked.

"And asphyxiate us both? Don't you have any sense?"

He turned the key off. "The headlights will stay on for five minutes," he told her. "And that's about how long the heat will last. Wouldn't you like to discuss whatever it is indoors?"

"If I had any privacy *indoors!* It's a fine state when a mother has to go sneaking off to the garage to have a word with her own son in his own house!"

"Seems to me we've had these garage chats before, Ma."

"That was different, and you know it. That was

me trying to keep you boys out of trouble with your father."

"Okay. What is it that's so urgent?"

"Don't you know? Don't you have a ghost of an idea, Simon?"

He rubbed both hands over his face the way he used to do, waking up from a long sleep. "Just tell me, Ma. I'm too tired to guess."

"The Voigt girl! Haven't you noticed? Simon, she won't let anybody near Patrick except herself! If I so much as touch him, she says, 'Oh, Mrs. Carmody, I'll do that.' " Imitating the voice Nellie made a sour face. "Heavens, if I want to feed him a little sugar with his water, if I want to carry him down the hall to my own room to watch television with me—why, you'd think—you'd think—"

He wouldn't help her.

"You'd think I hadn't raised two of my own, that's what. You'd think I'd forgotten how. Simon, I won't be treated this way. It isn't as though there aren't other things she could do. The living-room floor could use a good waxing, and I don't know when a hand has been turned to the windows in the den. 'Here's a case for you,' I was saying to her this morning, 'look at those streaks!' I might as well have been talking to that post."

"Ma. I didn't hire Marty to clean the house. Her job is to look after the baby."

"Hah. That woman fancies looking after *you*, and well you know it."

"Sorry. We're not going into this again. I hired Marty to look after the baby, and that's all."

"Then who do you think will do what needs doing? Your own mother? Down on her hands and knees waxing floors! Just because I did it when you were small, is that how you see me, Simon?"

He reached over and patted her hand. She jerked away from his touch.

"Ma. I see you sitting down with your feet up, knitting up a storm and enjoying life, enjoying being a grandmother. Mrs. Noonan comes in on Fridays, same as always. She'll wax the floors, and I expect she'll use the electric buffer. Tell *her* about the streaks. Marty is here for the baby."

"Spoiling him so nobody else—"

"She's the one getting up for night feedings, she's the one responsible for his schedule. I want you to enjoy yourself."

"How can I enjoy Miss Snip saying, 'Patrick can't have this, Patrick can't have that.' That boy has got to grow! It's past time for him to start taking cereal, I told her that. Three times this week I told her."

He sighed. "And Ken Rice's orders are formula only."

"Yes, well, whose orders tell her to send your only sister-in-law packing when she comes to call? You didn't know that, did you? And whose orders tell Marty Voigt to wholesale move a cot into the baby's room and sleep there nights? Tell me that's not peculiar."

"When did she start doing that?"

"You see? You see?"

The headlights clicked off, leaving them in the dark.

Simon opened his door, flooding the interior with light. "Let's go in. I'll have a talk with her."

Nellie could not recall when she'd enjoyed a meal so much. Not that Marty Voigt's meat loaf was anything to brag about. The Germans just didn't have the touch for meat loaf. She didn't say a word tonight, though, merely asked for ketchup and then, as soon as they were finished, said, "I'll do the dishes." She smiled meaningfully at Simon.

"I'll give you a hand," Marty Voigt put in.

Her son scratched the back of his neck, three or four quick scrapes at the base of his hairline. His one nervous gesture, and somehow it gave her more satisfaction than dessert would have.

"Marty, I'd like to talk to you," he said. "In my study."

"If little Patrick wakes, I'll take care of him," Nellie said.

"Oh, I'll hear him up at that end," said Marty Voigt.

Nellie turned her back as they left the room, making a great clatter of the dishes, rinsing them off and putting them into the dishwasher. She worked quickly, leaving the few pans to soak. Then with her hands still damp in the drying towel, she crept upstairs and through the hall nearly to the open door their voices came from. She stopped there and pressed against the wall, steadying her breath. The only voice she could hear clearly was Simon's.

". . . has been under a lot of stress. I've met with Jeanne at the hospital and I can guess what you were up against. Of course I won't give the baby up. It's just—you need to use some tact."

Nellie couldn't make out the reply.

"This is quite different." Simon again. "Your

baby died. You didn't give it up; it failed to thrive.
You were addicted to several drugs and malnourished."

"I wanted to be a good mother, Simon."

"The point is, there was no chance. You were
virtually starving, and so was your baby. None of
that is happening now."

To hell and damn that girl for mumbling! What
was she asking now?

Simon's voice carried clear. "No one knows unless you've told them."

This made a picture as definite as the one across
the hall from where Nellie stood wide-eyed. She
pressed the drying towel to her mouth to keep
from making a sound, and edged closer to the
door.

". . . true I've made every mistake there is. But
I am responsible, I can take care of a child."

"I know that. I never thought otherwise. That's
why I chose you."

". . . want children of my own someday."

"Many things are possible, Marty."

At that she almost fled, but the voices went on.
She had to lean tight into the wall to hear the little
bits and pieces.

". . . worried and then when I opened the desk
drawer . . . scared me so much, I didn't know
what to think. . . ."

"That's nothing for you to worry about. It's
there for protection, that's all."

"But, Simon, a gun in a house where there's a
baby. . . . I don't know. It doesn't seem right."

Nellie gripped the door facing. What was this
sniveling about? Her boys had been raised with

guns, Mike had made a great point of it. Who did Miss Mumble think she was?

". . . thought you seemed so low, I just wanted to be sure you wouldn't—you wouldn't think of doing anything to yourself. . . ."

No sound that she could hear! Nellie's heart beat wildly until Simon's voice came again: "Please don't worry. That's not my way, not at all." His voice continued, stronger now, more confident. "I know how to steer myself out of low moods, Marty, believe me. And I don't project my violent feelings onto others either."

A silence. "Is that what you think I'm doing, then?"

"Maybe. Yes, I guess I do."

Breathing hard, Nellie crept back down the stairs. She reached for the kitchen counter and leaned her weight against it, then went all the way and sank into the wooden chair beside the telephone. What did Simon mean, bringing in this—! She opened and shut her mouth, then set it firmly. Bringing such a woman here was his idea of charity, she supposed. It wasn't only his heart that was soft, her fine son, he had gone soft in the brain. She fumbled with her knitting bag and took a long draught from the bottle, capped it, and stuffed it into the bag again. A starved baby! Violence, drugs! And now this snooping-around business about the gun—she picked up the telephone. There was plenty here that somebody ought to know about, somebody whose brains hadn't gone to mush.

37

"BILL." The door was opened by Tom, who looked pleased to see him. "Had a feeling you might stop by."

"Why is that?" Bill stepped inside, took off his jacket to Tom's outstretched hand.

"Saturday afternoon. Game of the Week. Bucks and the Pistons."

"Tell you the truth, I forgot all about it. I've been busy."

"Come on. Nobody's that busy." Tom steered him toward the den.

Was it all an act—the easy smile, the friendly hand on his back? For the moment, anyway, he welcomed it. Normal, everything normal here. "Got a couple of things to clear up with you," he said.

"How about a beer?" Tom asked.

"Can't do it. You go ahead, though."

Tom left the room and, a moment later, a small blond whirlwind blew in, red ribbons flying.

"I left my monkey in here!" Molly said, looking around. "Where is he?"

Bill reached into the depths of the leather chair and came up with a small windup chimp with tiny cymbals clapped to his hands. "This what you're looking for, Molly?"

"Yes!"

Tom returned to the room. Bill saw the look of love he fastened on his daughter. No wonder things were normal around here.

She grabbed her father's hand. "Daddy, you promised we'd go to the mall!"

"We will, honey. Soon as the game's over, you and me and Erin."

"Erin always gets to go. I wanna go just with *you*."

"Mommy's not home. We don't want to leave Erin all by herself, do we?"

"Yes."

Laughing, Tom looked at Bill over her head. "Let me talk to Mr. Hessel and in a while we'll go. Will that make you happy?"

Evidently so, for she left smiling.

Tom sat on the corner of the desk and popped the top of the beer can. "So. What can I do for you?"

"Got something to show you." Bill drew out the two photocopied sheets and handed them over.

Tom studied them side by side. At last he looked up. "You went into my bank account?"

"No. These belonged to Nick."

"What do you want to make of this, Bill?"

"I don't want to make anything of it. You tell me."

"All right. Elizabeth came to my office. She needed money, she didn't tell me why. I wrote her the check."

"End of story?"

"Right."

284

"You didn't know she'd endorsed the check over to Nick?"

"I didn't know she'd cashed it. I asked her to think it over. Wait until the following Monday."

"You haven't seen your bank statement?"

"No. It comes after the first of the month."

So far, so good. "You have a copy of the stub?"

"At my office. But I can tell you right now the date's been changed. She came to see me on the eighth. Look at this. I know I postdated it to the eleventh."

"So you had no idea he'd gotten the money until now."

"That's right."

He let it sit there for a minute. Then: "Sorry, Tom. It won't wash."

"What d'you mean?"

"I mean Nick wanted you to know about it. He made a point of telling you."

"When was this?"

"The night you saw him."

"Bill, I didn't see him, I told you. I talked to him on the telephone and he never said a thing—"

"You saw him Friday night, the twenty-second, sometime between seven thirty and ten."

"What are you talking about?"

"You left the hospital long before Jeanne did. One of the security guards saw you pull out of the parking ramp around seven thirty."

Tom stood up, his face stern. "Bill, Jesus, do you honestly believe I could kill someone? You know me. You're a friend of mine."

"I know you lie to your friends, Tom."

"I was afraid. I knew it must have happened that night. I got worried. I saw him for ten lousy minutes, Bill! And when I left the motel, he was packing. He said he was leaving that night."

Tom was a liar, but there was some comfort in the fact that he wasn't a very good one. The bluff had worked; he'd broken and got flustered. The only time he was dangerous was in the mushy parts. Tom talking personally was Tom buying time to slide away. "What time was your meeting?" Bill asked.

"I think around eight."

"You *think*."

"Look, I was damned . . . I was upset. Jeanne had seen him at the hospital earlier and she sort of . . . she freaked. She had some idea he was after Molly. You don't know what we've been through, Bill. . . ."

"Did he tell you why Elizabeth gave him the money?"

"No."

"Did you ask?"

"No."

He said, "Tom, you're making this harder than it needs to be."

Tom lowered his head. "Ever since . . . he had a hold over her, you know? That scared her, I think. It sure as hell scared me."

"He was blackmailing her, then?"

"Look, I only know what he tried with me. He had a story about what happened in Chicago. When Elizabeth went to the fertility clinic."

"When was this?"

"She and Simon—they'd been trying for a long time, but she couldn't seem to get pregnant. Simon had himself checked out and everything was normal, so she went there to have the tests. It was sometime last April."

"Did she go alone?"

Tom nodded. He ran his hands through his hair.

"And Nick's story was that he'd seen her there?"

He grimaced. "Not just that he'd seen her, he'd *been* with her. Of course I don't believe it for a goddamn minute. She spent both days *and* nights at the clinic, she told Jeanne all about it."

Bill calculated. "April would have been about right."

"That was *his* angle. He was trying to stake claim on this baby, start a custody suit, if you can feature this. He kept calling him 'my kid.' 'Play fair with me, Tommy, and I won't take my kid away.' Then he said, 'I guess if you can't spare the dough, there's always Big Daddy.' I knew he'd already tried to hit Dad up. I wasn't about to let that happen."

"How long did you say you were with him?"

"Not long. Maybe it was ten minutes. Long enough to tell him he was a bluffer and a goddamn ghoul. For God's sake, she's dead! And what kind of custody suit? Simon's the legal father. End of story. He couldn't get a lawyer in his right mind to touch it."

"But he could get it into the papers, couldn't he?"

Tom flushed pink and shook his head. "I told him to go ahead to the papers, there wasn't going to be any money. And that was it. Money was all he wanted." He looked up. "You believe me, don't you?"

"Depends on what happened next."

"What do you mean?"

"I mean you left him at around eight and you didn't get home until after eleven. It's a ten-minute drive from the Graniteway, Tom."

"He was meeting someone. He wouldn't say who it was. So I waited in my car and when he came out I followed him. He lost me on the cutoff to Highway 152, behind Byerly's. I drove around looking for him but I knew I had screwed up. I don't know how you guys manage to tail anybody." He smiled faintly. "I had to turn around and come home."

Bill sat back in the chair. "That," he said, "is bullshit. You screwed up, all right. You're still doing it. You want to go to jail, my friend, or what?"

"Look, I'm trying—"

"Just tell me the truth, Tom. Cut the crap."

A long silence. At last Tom flung himself into the chair, stared out of the window. "All right," he said, his voice clipped. "I stopped at a friend's place."

"Who's that?"

Another hesitation. He wasn't anxious to let this one out. "My secretary. Chris Martin."

"From when to when?" Bill asked.

"From just after eight until about eleven, when I drove home. I was upset, Bill. I needed to talk to someone. You can call her. She'll tell you."

"That the building on the corner of Seventh and Kilian? Apartment number six?"

Tom's head jerked up.

"Your car was parked there from eight fifteen until eleven on Friday night. In the wrong parking spot, as I understand it. Somebody in the building reported it to the landlord."

"She's just a good friend, Bill."

"And on Thursday night after Rotary," Bill said. "And the following Monday."

Tom looked over. "Fuck you."

Another silence. Bill stood up. "Well. Seems like we've got you squared away, Tom. Now there's just Jeanne."

"Jeanne's had nothing to do with this! She's been at home or at the hospital the whole time. Leave her alone, can't you?"

Bill said, "I'll stop back tonight. Tell her it won't take long."

•

Stuff like this made him hate his job at times. Amazing, the way everybody looked so human at every single moment except the one when a murder was being committed. All he ever needed was the key to that moment. But sometimes getting it meant jerking people around. They didn't like it. Their privacy got lifted—a privilege of civilized life. But murder was uncivil, and all privileges were canceled. He'd jerked Tom Fallon maybe a little too hard, but only because Tom had been trying to do the same to him.

So where was he going to come down with the Fallons? He had liked both of them, had been friends with them for years. Close enough to be invited to the annual Christmas party. *And this would be the last year for it, you could bet on that one.*

He drove to the clinic and parked in the back, next to Simon's Lincoln Continental. One more task. He needed to find out a couple of things that only Elizabeth's husband could tell him.

There were always two kinds of evidence—the kind you stored in plastic bags, and the kind you

289

mulled over in the middle of the night. Personally he preferred the latter, but the kind in plastic bags could make you lose sleep too.

Item: a plastic heel plate from a cross-country ski.

Item: Uhler's departure. So far Tom's story fit with the night manager's. He saw the Buick leaving the parking lot of the Graniteway as he arrived for work at eight o'clock. He hadn't noticed whether Uhler was alone or with anyone at the time.

Somebody drove with Nick to the death scene in his own rental car, killed him, and then returned his car to the Graniteway. Or else Nick drove to meet his killer—in which case, two cars to be disposed of after the murder, requiring some planning. Depending upon where the body was put in, there could be some distance to cover. How good a skier would that take? Check the newspaper files for all the local ski champs; then check every cross-country ski in St. Cloud for a missing heel plate, and he'd have the case wrapped up. Just like they taught him in detective school, hah!

Well, some people collected garbage, some sold aluminum siding, some made those little crocheted things that went on the backs of chairs. *Consider yourself lucky.* As Val would say.

Bill shut off the motor and got out of the car, slamming the door behind him. In the waiting room he stood next to the window while the nurse let Doctor know he was here. At the last meeting had he called him Simon or Dr. Carmody? He couldn't remember. Somehow it was hard to imagine that he had addressed this formal, dignified man by his first name.

Inside the office Simon was waiting for him behind his desk. "What is it, Bill? Something important?"

That took care of one problem. As for the other, might as well get right to it. "Sorry about this, Simon," he said. "I have the rather unpleasant job this week of raking up old stories."

Simon merely smiled, raised his shoulders in a shrug.

"First. How well did you know Nick Uhler?"

"Scarcely at all. He was one of the kids who hung around with my brother."

"Did you know he was a friend of Elizabeth's?"

Simon's face was calm. "I knew she had a baby by him when they were in high school. Is that what you're getting at?"

Nicely done. He got the message: he'd been clumsy. Mentally he took a step back. "When did you find that out?"

"About eight years ago. On our second date, in fact. Why?"

"Just checking a theory. Our Nick was always looking for the quickest way to make a buck—"

"Your Nick? So you're in this one too?"

Score two. A sense of humor here, and a certain toughness of spirit. He had a quick flash of sympathy for Charlie Carmody. He would not want to be tangling with this guy every day of his life.

"He wasn't a very nice man," Bill said.

"My impression, also."

"From . . . ?"

"Just what I remember. And on visits home, when I was in college."

"Nothing more recent than that?"

"Didn't we go over this once?"

"What I'm wondering," Bill said, "is whether you knew that your wife had been in touch with Nick recently."

The eyes gazed levelly into his own. "How recently?"

"The day she died."

The gaze didn't waver. "No," he said. "I didn't know that."

"Did you know about the check she signed over to him for five thousand dollars?"

Simon sat down behind the desk. "Just tell me all of it, will you?"

"She borrowed five thousand from her brother on Friday afternoon, the eighth of December. She endorsed it over to Uhler and he cashed it that same day."

"Why? What for?"

"I was hoping you could help me with that."

"I can't. I don't know. Tom never told me."

"He says he didn't know about it either."

"Well, he sure as hell knew he gave her the money!" Simon's voice blazed with anger; his jaw was set. "As to why she might have signed it over to him, I have no idea."

"Maybe that's one of the things he wanted to talk about the day he made the appointment."

"Well, I was here. He wasn't. So I don't see how I can help you with that one."

"You can't think of anything else he might have had on his mind?"

Simon gave him a clenched smile. "Uhler's mind? Sorry, no." Abruptly he walked around behind the desk. Getting ready to dismiss him, Bill could sense it. He stepped nearer.

"You a skier, Simon?" he asked.

"Pardon me?"

"Downhill, cross-country? You do any of that?"

"Not since I was married. Why?"

"Just curious. I figured you probably didn't have a lot of time for that. How about Charlie? He do much?"

"We both used to, years ago. He did some in the army, I think." He glanced toward the door. "Bill, my patients are waiting."

Bill put out his hand. "Thank you, Doctor."

Simon hesitated, then took the hand that was offered. "Elizabeth was my wife," he said. "I loved her. I would have forgiven her anything. I would have understood anything."

A change of subject. Bill said nothing. A reply was not expected, he knew that.

38

OKAY, *he stopped by the house that morning. I didn't think of it, because I saw him later on.*

Bill leaned forward and pressed the button to fast-forward the tape, heard his own voice: . . . *pretty visible that night. I didn't even have to ask around.*

Yeah, well, I was pretty drunk.

That your alibi?

He was sitting in his den, in front of the fire Val had built for him. She had brought him coffee in his extra large cup with WORLD'S GREATEST DAD lettered on the side. Now she and the kids were doing New Year's resolutions at the dining room table. He could hear their laughter, hear them teasing each other over changes that would never happen. He got up to close the door.

. . . I walked home from there. I got in around midnight. That's the truth, Bill.

Was it, Charlie? He wondered. Last night on the way home from the movie, Val had started in asking if what the newspapers were saying was true—that Nick Uhler's death was drug related. Nick Uhler's whole life was drug related, he'd answered, so what was new?

"And what about Charlie?" she had asked.

"What about him?"

"I think Charlie would have settled that score with Nick a long time ago if he ever intended to, don't you?"

"I don't know. It does strike me as odd that a guy with Charlie's temper could be so philosophical about spending two years in Joliet on someone else's ticket."

"Not philosophical. Just used to it," she had said. "He was always getting blamed for stuff he didn't do. It goes way back, Billy, you know that."

In fact he knew nothing of the sort; so what made her so wise? He didn't say anything. Then she asked him straight out if he'd already made up his mind that Charlie was a murderer. He'd lost it then and there. "It's not about me making up my *mind*, for Chrissake, it's about the facts!"

Of course she'd forgiven him, as she always did. Happy New Year with champagne and chocolate walnut pie after the kids went to bed, and then today, all the comforts of home. Yes, he had a pretty good life, and it only made him wonder all the more. Because he *was* always looking on the darker side of things, at least always knowing it existed and needing to be convinced of a brighter aspect. Still, he hated the idea that Val could zero in on his own character in that same knowing way. *Billy? Oh, he's methodical, all right. But he misses the point. You have to watch him.*

He hadn't settled on Charlie Carmody, exactly; it was just his instinct. And of course there were other suspects. He wasn't completely convinced by Tom Fallon's bewildered-but-generous brother act. Tom had written Elizabeth that check on Friday the eighth without a murmur. Was he in the habit of writing checks to her for large sums of money without asking for explanations? No. That had been the reason for the postdating: to give her a chance to change her mind. Of course Nick had taken care of that, a quick little fix on the numbers. The bank's transaction date was Friday, December eighth. No doubt he had skipped out that afternoon with the cash. Fine and dandy. So what brought him back?

If Tom Fallon was not a clever liar, that didn't mean he wasn't clever in other ways. His story never came together. Bill had the distinct feeling there was no bottom here, that he could keep turning up Tom's lies and half lies forever.

What about the pills on the floor of the girls' bedroom? Tom could offer no explanation. Did he think the money he'd given Elizabeth might have gone for drugs? No, absolutely not. Elizabeth didn't take drugs; he had been adamant. The autopsy report seemed to bear this out. Other than a small amount of alcohol, no drugs had been found in her system. Tom's view was that Elizabeth was a soft touch for Nick. But something didn't compute. Why still so soft? Why, after all these years?

Everybody seemed to be playing it pretty dumb —Tom about where the money had gone and what it was for; Charlie about everything having to do with Nick, period; Marty Voigt, too, had switched gears on him a dozen times at the store. And the big question remained: what was Nick Uhler doing back in town? Nobody he'd talked to so far seemed to have the least notion.

He couldn't let go of a nagging suspicion that it had something to do with Terence Fallon. Why was Nick trying to see the old man? Did he think

Simon didn't know about that first baby? Did he
want to peddle the Chicago tale? But Tom was
right; it didn't make sense. Terry Fallon wouldn't
pay to protect Simon Carmody's feelings. And
who else mattered?

Tom was working overtime to keep his father
out of this. Well, he was in it—insofar as on Friday
the twenty-second Terry Fallon had spent the
early part of the evening with Ed Gunderson. The
link here was the motel room search at the Graniteway, which Gunderson flatly denied. His staff
was more helpful. According to Laura Moos, the
desk clerk, a college kid had been around, asking
for Uhler. That had checked out to be one Greg
Mason—or Mace, as he was known on campus.
They had nothing on Mace. Except his name kept
coming up in connection with campus drug traffic.
Could Tom Fallon have a drug habit? Could Chris
Martin?

On to Simon Carmody. Simon, for whom the
term *Big Daddy* could also apply. Nick made the
appointment with him and then didn't keep it.
Why? He saw Marty, saw Charlie, saw Tom. Why
skip the person most likely to suffer from the tale
of Elizabeth being with him in Chicago? There
was no doubt that he had ducked the meeting—
both the girl at the desk and Simon's nurse had
confirmed it. What was the reason? Theory one:
He made his score before he got to Simon. Theory
two: He couldn't prove anything. He had to have
known that.

But he had to keep reminding himself not to
give Nick too much credit. Somewhere down the
line a big miscalculation had been made.

This business of proof; medical proof. He himself had chosen this line of work, what was he going skittish about? He'd never forget that first autopsy, nobody ever did. You saw a surgeon's knife poised above a human chest, and you saw the plunge and rip—and you got over it. Going green the first time was a med-school cliché. Still, he had gone queasy at the sight of Nick's smashed head— *they killed him dead, all right.*

Simon Carmody was a surgeon, supposed to be a fine one. That didn't make him a ghoul. Maybe Nick was smart enough to figure out he wasn't a good target for blackmail. There were people in town who combed the papers daily for tidbits about their neighbors' drunk-driving arrests, court cases pending. Simon wasn't the type. But did that mean he would be immune to Nick's threat to go public? *Elizabeth was my wife. I would have forgiven her anything.*

A knock on the door. Val called to him: "Anyone for sledding?"

"Sure," he called back. "Give me a couple more minutes."

He popped Charlie Carmody out of the tape deck and slipped a new tape in. Nellie Carmody's whine began at once.

. . . the girl is dangerous, I've tried to tell Simon but he won't listen. . . .

Mrs. Carmody, could you be more specific? In contrast, his own voice sounded oily.

She's had a baby, don't you see? It died and was buried and nobody ever knew a thing about it, not for all these years!

That's not exactly illegal—

Unnatural is what it is! She could be taking drugs behind a closed door! You know she was married to that Uhler boy, don't you? Simon himself said she was violent and I've seen her at night, sneaking around the house—is that machine still on?

Yes, it is. Mrs. Carmody, I do appreciate—

Appreciation is not what I'm here for, Sheriff. Action is more what I had in mind.

I'll have to talk to Simon—

The tape clicked off.

And when he had called him, Simon had been all reassurance. He was aware of his mother's prejudice against Marty. He hoped Bill hadn't been inconvenienced. Period.

One last tape and he'd be finished. He heard Jeanne Fallon's high, sweet voice:

Feels strange to be talking to you this way. I suppose you'll play this back, won't you?

That breathy quality in her voice always made him nervous as hell.

Maybe we should start at the hospital on Friday morning. When you first saw Nick.

I only saw him the one time, the way you mean. But that was enough. I knew what that meant. Believe me, I knew. All the things Elizabeth told me, but I never hardened my heart, never. . . . God would forgive her, I told her that.

He fast-forwarded to the section he was looking for.

. . . never loved him, you know.

Never loved who?

Simon. She couldn't have and still have done those things. I tried to tell her, but nothing I ever said seemed to make a difference. She loved them both, she kept saying. Can you believe that?

What things, Jeanne?

Oh, please. You do live here, don't you?

Yeah, I live here. But I don't know what things you're talking about.

The baby, Bill. Nicky's baby.

But that was high school. Before she'd even met Simon—

Not having it. The voice was suddenly sharp with impatience. *Keeping it a secret from Simon. I told her that was foolish. Too many people knew.*

How many?

The curve of her slender, upturned palms. *You knew, didn't you?*

Right. And since it all kept going back to high school, he had his own memories to draw on, of at least one time when the three of them—Nick, Charlie, and himself—cruised Cathedral High looking for talent on the other side of town. How many girls besides Marty Voigt had there been in the backseat of Nick's old car? And one particular night when William Carl Hessel, lying drunk in that very backseat, had come awake to overhear a discussion about how Nick Uhler could do a lot worse than elope with Elizabeth Fallon; the old man was sure to come around as soon as the kid was born.

You'll never have to worry about money, Nicko. That had been Charlie's view. But something else had been worrying Nick. Down that road he could see a total loss of freedom; he would be tied to St. Cloud for life. Maybe the smart thing was to take the money and run, go to Chicago, where the action was.

He couldn't recall a decision that night. But he did know that he hadn't told a soul, and to his knowledge there had never been even a whisper

301

of rumor about it in town. He had not been straight with Tom about that the other day; St. Cloud was small, but not that small. So who, besides the Fallon clan, were all these people who supposedly knew? The doctor who delivered her, but he was somewhere in Iowa. Had Nick told anyone other than his best friend, Charlie? Had he told Marty?

Damn. He was getting lost here. Moreover, that wasn't the point. The point was, *who had lied?* Either Elizabeth had lied to Jeanne, or else Simon had lied—right in his face the other day.

I kept telling her over and over that Simon would understand, that he'd forgive, that he should be given the chance to forgive—

Bill stopped the tape. There it was, the forgiveness theme again. Jeanne and Simon were a perfect match on that one. It kept coming up and coming up. On his pad he scribbled the word, *Forgive.* Again he pressed the fast-forward button

. . . time did you go to the cemetery?

It was cold out there. . . . I knew when I left the hospital it was the one thing I had to do. I was afraid they'd close the gate, but it was wide open and I went right through. . . .

What time was that?

. . . I drove to her grave. I remembered where it was . . . and I went down on my knees to her, begged her, 'Elizabeth, don't do this, don't take Molly, it isn't fair, I'll do anything you ask, I'll take care of Patrick, and Simon will never know. . . .'

The telephone rang sharply at his elbow. He nearly jumped out of the chair.

"We got it, Chief!" Bakke's cheerful voice on the

other end. "Came through the computer from Chicago. Want me to read it to you, or should I bring it over?"

"I'll be right there."

"Wait a sec," Bakke said. "You asked where Garmisch was? Where Charlie Carmody served his army time? It's in the Alps."

"Don't tell me," Bill said.

"Yeah. He was in the ski troops."

His daughter burst through the door. "Come on, Dad, we get the big sled! Mom and I flipped for it, and she lost!"

"Nan, I'm sorry. I gotta go into work."

"Mom said we were all going sledding—"

"I know, but this can't wait. I'll be back in a while." Over her head he met Val's look of resignation. "I'm sorry," he said again.

•

"Boy, the old lady was right on the money with this one," Bakke said, handing him two sheets of paper. He took them and sat at his desk without removing his coat. Quickly he scanned the documents: a summary of medical procedures performed on Mrs. Nicholas Uhler, December 10, 1977, at Cook County Hospital, presiding resident physician, Dr. Simon Carmody. Caesarean section, resulting in the full-term birth of a five-pound, six-ounce Caucasian. Tubal ligation performed. The second sheet was the permission-to-operate document executed same date, signed by Dr. Simon Carmody and Martha Alice Uhler.

"The baby died in the delivery room," Bakke said, handing him the death certificate. "Fifteen minutes after birth."

Hessel picked up the phone.

He was at the Carmody house in River Haven at ten minutes of eleven, standing on the rubber mat outside the door. When she answered it, he smiled to reassure her.

"Hope I didn't make it sound too urgent. Just needed to clarify a couple of things."

"That's all right," Marty said. She stepped back to usher him inside, but she was not pleased to see him.

He was used to that by now. His job was not to let on that he noticed. "Cold out this afternoon."

"Yes."

All business. There would be no Happy New Year, no taking him into the living room and serving him tea. He pulled the sheets of paper from his pocket.

"These came today. From the Cook County Records Department."

Her face was expressionless. "Who told you?" she asked.

"I just need to know whether Nick knew."

"About the baby? He knew. He wasn't there, however. He made it a point to take a pass on the bad times."

"Were you separated by then?"

"Right."

"So, the baby must have—"

"The baby was born addicted and died immediately. It's all there on the paper, isn't it?"

He nodded.

"What do you need from me?"

"Verification," he lied.

She snatched the papers from his hands. "Fine. Let me read them. It's all a matter of record. His name was Nicholas Richard, see here on the death certificate? Nicholas Richard Uhler." Her hands shook. She shoved the sheet underneath and stood reading the next. After a moment she glanced up at him. "What's this?"

"The permission for surgery that you signed." She was staring down at it, as if it were written in a foreign language. He leaned over her shoulder. "That is your handwriting, isn't it?"

"I see," she murmured. She looked at her watch and then away, toward the stairs. "Is there more? I have to see the baby."

"No more," he said. "I appreciate your time, Marty." She handed him the sheets of paper, then stood stiffly by as he folded them into his back pocket. Before he could say another word, the door was opened and he found himself once again on the porch. It closed behind him so fast that it nearly caught his heel.

If he'd had time, he might have warned her about Patrick Simon's grandmother: that she had tried to get a writ served yesterday, barring Martha Alice Voigt from the door that had just been closed on him with such speed. He *could* have told her. And the fact that he held back on it didn't have much to do with a violation of procedure.

On the drive home, he thought: Marty and Nick Uhler, the parents of an infant son who lived only fifteen minutes. Marty alone during delivery, and alone ever since. And now, Marty living in the house in River Haven, caring for the infant son of the man who delivered her baby and sterilized her. *Forgiveness.* Who was the person in need of that here?

He put his foot on the brake so hard it made the shoulder harness snap his body back against the seat. He'd been working on the assumption there had been only one murder here. What if that wasn't the case? Lord, he had been slow in putting this together. Slow and clumsy.

His tires gave a sharp squeal of protest at the turn onto County Road 8. Time. He needed just a little more of it. Also he needed to get hold of Charlie, and fast.

39

CHARLIE GRABBED ONE DOOR HANDLE and yanked it. After it grated and stopped wide, he grabbed the second handle and did the same. This one had always been stickier; the squalling of wood on concrete was not a pretty sound. Too early in the morning for this shit. The door shuddered and stuck, then squawked as he forced it wider.

Sunlight filled the garage. He had figured this out last night, or sometime this morning, one of those times he was up. He had run out of coffee along the way; how many cups of hot chocolate could a grown man stand to drink on New Year's Eve? His stomach felt queasy from all that sugar. But here he was, because he'd decided that if he got out here by ten, the angle of the sun would give him all the light he needed to work, and some heat too. Though somewhere in all this rubble he knew there was a portable electric heater. Used to be one, anyhow. And in this garage, what used to be, was. With the toe of his work boot he kicked the edge of an old Three Musketeers box, under which he could see the broken rawhide laces of his old softball glove.

One softball glove, one hockey skate, an open

box of old sheet music—God, how long since that old upright had been hauled away? Broken wicker chairs, Rototiller, snowmobile. That was just what he could see in a two-foot radius. Beyond that old greasy boxes, stacks of newspapers, old wood cross-country skis, carpentry tools, fishing poles. Depressing. This kind of thing Simon would be good at. Dig in, tear out all the mess, know absolutely what to keep and what to toss. Cut back hard and make a nice clean job of it; no wonder his brother had turned pro.

That time they'd been out fishing on the river. Charlie had flubbed a cast and heard the scream behind him—he'd twisted in the boat to see his Rapala sunk into Simon's neck behind the collarbone. Christ. His stomach turned over just to remember. Simon wouldn't let him touch the thing, not that he really wanted to. Back at the house with the blood streaming down his shirt, Simon wouldn't let Miss Nellie touch it either, just went into the bathroom with that thing crouching on his neck like some weird pet with hooks for feet, and shut the door. Locked it, in fact, while he sterilized a razor and took care of himself. Came out looking a little white around the gills but wearing a nice clean Band-Aid.

Charlie squinted at the sun reflecting off the blank white snowfield. As he recalled, his brother had cleaned up the bathroom floor before he came out. He took in the dim skyline of junk against the far wall. Well, he wished his brother were the one looking at this job. It needed a guy with a solid-gold stomach. Not him. He was the weak one. He'd just as soon be looking at this prospect with some good rose-colored weed on his side.

However. He was playing this New Year business straight. And it wasn't a cleanup job that he
had in mind, just a bad feeling that all the pieces of
whatever puzzle this was had not been found. A
bad feeling, too, that he'd better not rely on Bill
Hessel to find them. "You have your lookers, and
you have your hiders," Nick used to say. Then
sometime in the night he had gotten the rest: "Divide and hide." Nick believed in spreading the
risk. Whether it was alibis or women: if he had one,
he had two. Two hiding places—he could've
sneaked out here before he came into the house.
Charlie surveyed the mountain of junk, feeling
shrewd and stupid at the same time. It was all so
fucking unlikely.

He began dragging the boxes nearest to hand
out on the concrete apron in front of the door.
First project: to make a path so he could get in and
take a look. Would Nick spend time out here with
all this stuff everywhere? What did he do, leap
from box to box like a mountain goat? Didn't
sound much like Nick. There was one guy for the
path of least resistance, all of it headed downhill.
So: whatever he was looking for would have to be
right up close. He pried open the flaps of the big
box he'd just dragged, labeled DISHES. Inside he
found old mildewed living room curtains. He recognized the pattern, great spiderlike splotches of
brown on yellow. Well, this was easy, this he could
get rid of. He kicked the box through the doorway
so that it skidded and fell backward in the snowbank. Now for the sheet music. Nick used to come
and beat hell on the old upright, how Nellie loved
him for it—but Nick couldn't read a note. That was
Simon's department. He thumbed through the

stack of crumbling printed sheets in the box. Of course Bonnie Prince Charlie couldn't take the pressure of practicing mistakes out in the living room. He'd always intended to get a guitar, which he could keep in his own room. But. He heaved the box out of his way. Guess the party girl would take her talent for the piano to the grave with her.

The Rototiller was new, the snowmobile was an old gas-guzzler, a Mike Carmody special about a million years old, and if he knew the way his dad did things, still brimful of gas. He walked over and unscrewed the lid of the tank. Empty. Or nearly empty, which was even stranger. If there was a leak in the tank or a way for the gasoline to evaporate, you'd think it'd all be gone by now. Not just most of it. He shook the tank, tapped on it, trying to make it be something besides nearly empty, trying to make it explain itself. *Christ, Charlie, waste some time, why don't you?* He slapped the lid back and screwed it on tight. He grabbed hold of the front end as if he were wrestling a steer, trying to drag a five-hundred-pound animal out of this junk pile. What was he doing? He let go and jumped onto the seat and twisted the key. The old motor started right up, as good as if it had been used yesterday. Charlie goosed the accelerator and made the skis throw sparks across the concrete until it zipped into the snow and glided in easy, easy circles around the snowy yard. Arctic Cat. Hell, this beast was ready to go, he wanted to take it out through the trees and streak up the river like the old days. If the tank had been full! He pulled up next to the garage, slammed the brake so hard he nearly threw himself off the thing. It just pissed him off, this one detail. The gas tank should have been full! He was truly nuts, was his problem.

Who are you to start thinking at this late date? Right on, Ma. The trouble was, nothing was adding up, nothing was staying in place. Marty with a baby! A baby that had died, and she hadn't told him! It had made him snap awake four dozen times during the night. And now every fucking thing Nick had said kept coming back, sounding like some stupid oracle. *We got a friend here who's a face-saver from way back.* Face-saver. Terry Fallon? Face-saver. Terry Fallon?

"Why don't you talk to me straight? Why don't you talk some goddamn *answers*?" His voice, sounding so strained, probably carried ten feet. He pounded the steering loop, beat and beat his fists on the black metal. *You let me take the rap last time. Are you going to do that again? Weren't we ever friends?*

You know we were.

I know. Friendly as you get.

Charlie boy, I'm out of this one. You got to run the combinations, all the faces in all the right places, just like those rainy-day puzzles we used to do.

Face-saver. Is that all you can give me?

I gave you everything, man. That's a promise.

He could almost believe it. He stood up on the footpads of the machine and swung off the saddle like an old man.

He walked back into the garage and picked up Mike Carmody's old snowmobile suit from where it had fallen behind two crushed-looking boxes. Keep it or not? Too much like having a ghost around. He leaned over and hooked the suit on a

nail on one of the joists. Directly above his head
was a platform his dad had built into the eave. A
small plywood square where he and Nick and now
and then Simon had gone up and played Chinese
checkers and sometimes, just like Nick said, jigsaw
puzzles on days it rained. They had to drag the
ladder over and climb up, then chain hand over
hand across the beams to land on the platform.
Crouched there under the peak of the garage roof,
eighteen inches from the rain beating down above
their heads, they would stay as long as nobody
missed them.

Not an easy climb up there now, but it was
worth a look. He put his foot on the wicker seat
and tried his weight gingerly; the back of the chair
was broken and the seat board squealed a little
under his weight. It held. He shucked off his gloves
and grabbed on to the two-by-four that supported
the platform, and pulled himself up. What did he
expect to see? Nothing. Rat pills, maybe. But instead there lay, in the thick curled dust, a piece of
paper. No, a small envelope. His arms trembled,
the muscles giving out on him. He gripped the
board with one hand, and with the other reached
and slapped at the envelope. It fluttered to the
floor as he came crashing down, knocking the
chair over. He stood up and looked around, shoved
boxes aside trying to see, frantic that the thing
would evaporate before he could get to it. He got
down on his hands and knees—there it was, at rest
in the grimy folds of an old badminton net. No
ghost of any kind, but a blue envelope, handwriting he didn't recognize, an address he'd never
heard of: *353 West Van Buren, Chicago.* He picked
up the envelope and wiped off the smudge marks

on his jeans. Postmarked in St. Cloud in May of last year, a letter addressed by hand to Nick Uhler.

The envelope had been ripped open raggedly along the top. Well, it was nobody's mail anymore. He shook out the blue sheets and read in the rounded female hand:

N,

    I have just come from the airport. I smile at the wrong times, Nicko. All the way down I-94 Simon would look at me and say, 'What are you smiling about?' I don't like to lie, you know that. I told him, 'I'm happy about the chance we'll have a baby. People at the clinic were so encouraging.' It's the truth, and not the truth. And pretty soon he asks me, 'Still the same thing?' And I say, 'Yes.'

    Do you tell me the truth? When I asked if you ever thought about our baby, growing up somewhere in the world, you said you didn't. I don't believe you. How can I?

    Nicky, this is the whole truth: I didn't know I could still feel this way. If you came for me tomorrow, I would go. Can that be wrong if I have always felt married to you? If it's what I always wanted?

    But I have found out how far wanting is from getting. If I don't see your face at my door I mean to forget you. If you won't come, Nicky, burn this letter and wish me some of your luck. I want a baby, and on the nights he tells me I'm fertile, I'll act as if I never imagined there could be anyone else.

Your E

Charlie folded the blue pages over his finger and shut his eyes. Some of your luck. Uhler, you total total rat-shit.

He came out the mouth of the garage and leaned against the door frame, let his eyes scan the line of pines with its eroded burden of snow. Marty. That baby, was it ours? Would you not tell me something that important? And if I even mentioned the things I'm afraid are happening, would you listen?

In a minute, he decided, his stomach would settle. In a minute he'd figure it all out, he'd work all the faces into all the right places, nail down the pieces if it killed him.

40

IN THE WHITE-CANED NURSERY ROCKER Marty sat
still with Patrick on her shoulder. She breathed in
the faint milky smell of his skin, her hand riding
the accordion rise and fall of his breathing. She let
herself soak up the peace, the connection. The
painful hollow just above her stomach didn't go
away. She knew by now it wasn't hunger, although
eating was a way to ease the feeling. The only
other thing that worked was to keep the baby
close.

She pressed him tight against her. In his sleep he
startled and whimpered, kicked his foot. She loos-
ened her grip. What she was doing was wrong,
unfair to him. She got up, shifting him gently in
her arms, and settled him with final reluctance
into his small barred bed. Was it true, thoughts
constituted prayers? That part still bothered her.
It meant the present, when she had been thinking
the past was the only danger. If she wasn't safe
with her own thoughts—did she actually project
violence? Consider the source. Consider the
source.

She sat down again in the white rocker. That
paper—how did it fit? It didn't. As soon as she tried
to make it fit, her brain reeled and she got this sick

feeling. Which stopped everything. And stopping now, she bent over to enfold the hurting place. Danger was present—which danger? She would have to wait to see. Until she could think again.

How had it gone? She had walked to the hospital, walked through the steel doors to the desk. That much she remembered clearly. *The desk under white lights, white-dressed nurses, white-shirted orderlies. They put her in a wheelchair and she tried to refuse, thinking how much extra they would have to charge for that. Rolling anyway down the long gleaming halls, a blank until—into the white lights again—Simon's face.*

She sat forward and checked the linchpins at the head and foot of the cradle to be sure it wouldn't swing free if Patrick suddenly made up his mind to turn over. He hadn't done that yet, but she had read it was possible. You never knew what to expect.

She gazed at the baby's small, precise features. Who did he look like? No matter. The face tore her heart. And she was not his mother, she wasn't anybody's mother and never would be. That was no projection, that had been the order for surgery, signed and executed, no projection. She closed her eyes against the spiraling that made her want to lie down on the soft yellow rug of the nursery and sob. She had to think clearly. Elizabeth was Patrick's mother, not she, yet she felt this overpowering connection. Maybe the fear and the wariness just went with it, this animal sense of anything that might break the bond. *Break?* She would not let that happen. Her voice the one Patrick quieted to, her arms the ones he sank into without squirming

316

or fussing. Who else was there to care for him? Not
Simon! She fought the spiraling.

He was not to be trusted, she knew that for
certain. But how long had she known? Since that
day in front of Patrick and the other babies in the
hospital nursery? Calling himself Monster Man.
That had been a daring move, knowing what effect it would have on her, and it had worked,
hadn't it? While he had only been telling the truth.

And always, something had been off in this
house, way off. Not Mrs. Carmody's troublemak-
ing—that was distraction, the thing to keep her
from attending to the heart and bone of it. No, his
deadness toward Patrick. The lack of curiosity, the
indifference—this wasn't normal, wasn't merely
grief. The night he'd found her up so late in the
nursery, rocking the baby to sleep, that look on his
face. She hadn't understood. Now she could place
it: a look of pure hatred. Why?

Stop trying to figure this out. What she knew for
sure was, there was a signed order for surgery in
her file. Signed by herself, signed by Dr. Simon
Carmody.

Who'd said to her, *Some people don't deserve to
have babies.* That was the time he'd talked about
child-murder. Was that who she was to him, one of
that army of careless, murderous women who
didn't deserve to have babies? *The permission for
surgery that you signed.* The source of this peculiar emptiness she'd been living with ever since
Chicago. Not just that her own infant had died, but
—that is your handwriting, isn't it?

Her handwriting. It had to be; there was too
much she could not remember from those last
shadowy months with Nicky that had all turned

317

out to be true—the drugs, the sex, the long poison-
ous blanks she could not recall, did not wish to
recall. But from the shadows came a glimpse of a
dark apartment in Chicago, a memory so lost to
her that it could have been nothing, no translation
into meaning. Yet she felt choked, wounded.
Sometimes you could stumble into furniture at
night in a dark room, then come awake on a day
that should have been brand-new, not knowing
how you got so bashed up and hurt. But you did
know. Somehow you knew.

This part about Simon she'd known all along.

She got up and closed the door of the baby's
room. Then stood there, hand on the knob. She
held herself still, the way animals do to protect
themselves, to blend into their surroundings
against danger. But what surrounded her was
Simon's house; the danger was from without.
Within was where her knowledge was. What
would happen to her if she gave in to it?

*The sudden, sharp pain making her draw
breath, the warm trickle of water down her leg; it
was time. Into the street, then. Never mind the old
men with their sacks and their newspapers and
their whispers and demands, never mind the
bright, bright lights, or the new clenching in the
center of her belly; never mind that the steel hospital doors shut her out because they move when
she pushes them. She herself moves to the desk
that is bathed in such brilliance. The nurses have
so many questions but she has answers, not the
right ones. No prenatal care, no insurance, no ad-
mitting doctor. Helping her, insisting on helping
her, into the wheelchair, taking her up the elevator
to the enema, the razor, the starchy white gown*

and steel cart and then that sweet relief, that shining miracle: Simon Carmody staring down at her.

"Marty? Marty Voigt? Is that you?"

Taking her hands in both of his, holding them firmly—the first time she has cried in all those months, the first time she has felt safe enough to let go and let anything break—there he was, with that steady voice, treating her as if she'd been his patient from the start. And when it was over, sending the nurses away, staying behind to share her grief. No, not share, because all the while, all the while—

She leaned her back against the door. That was the truth, what had really happened. She must not lose it now, must not get confused. If I don't deserve to have babies, then what am I doing here? There had to be a reason. She looked around the yellow room. Where, precisely, was the danger?

That look the other night. Not for me, but for Patrick.

She turned and began jerking drawers open, throwing shirts, nightgowns, and blankets into the diaper bag. She scooped up the open box of diapers and struggled through the door with her haul. Tossing it into the backseat of her car, along with the canned formula and baby bottles, she went back for the car seat. She retrieved her coat from the front closet.

Back upstairs Patrick squirmed as she slipped him into his yellow snowsuit. "No time to change you," she whispered, as though the words would explain all this to him. She clasped him to her and gave a final glance around.

In the hall she paused and closed the door to the nursery. The sun cast sawtooth patterns down the stairs. Carrying Patrick she carefully placed each foot, praying Mrs. Carmody would sleep for another thousand years. "I'm here, I won't leave you," she whispered to the baby, her cheek next to his. *Here's my voice against the strangeness.*

The car started up smoothly. She backed it out and closed the garage door again with the device Simon had given her. So very thorough—she rolled her window down and threw the thing out of her car, watched it fall into deep snow. She focused on the gas gauge, which showed nearly empty. The Clearwater exit station was in range; farther than going into St. Cloud, but safer, much safer.

The two-lane road was clear of ice, and she accelerated. Gusts of wind sent powder swirling, but the white lines on the blacktop showed plainly. Along the outside curve of County Road 8, where the river veered away from the road, a grove of young spruce trees squatted in rows. So, the world was still out there. Till then she hadn't stopped shaking long enough to notice.

A cloud cover was forming over the western half of the sky; for extra safety she put her headlights on. The rearview mirror showed her Patrick bundled up in his car seat, oddly businesslike, serious eyes peering out from the ring of yellow fur that rimmed his snowsuit hood. She laughed out loud from sheer relief. "We're on our way," she told him.

At the Amoco station a green-and-silver moving van blocked the self-serve pump. She waited, then pulled up and filled the Datsun's tank, reached for her purse. The attendant was in full view at the window, making change and talking to the driver of the van. Nobody could steal a baby from his car seat while she was paying for her gas. Still she was taking no chances. *None at all.* She opened the back door, unsnapped the straps, and lifted Patrick out.

Inside the warm enclosure she handed the attendant a twenty-dollar bill, then bought three candy bars with the change.

"Cute baby," he said with a grin. The drive bell sounded and he grabbed his jacket. "You need anything else?"

She shook her head. He shut the cash drawer and left. Did she need anything else? She had gotten this far without knowing what was to happen next, but the strength she'd felt in the car had drained away. Leaning against the glass counter she shifted Patrick to her other arm. His head flopped against her shoulder and he gave a small cry. She patted him while she stared at the painted cinder block above the pay phone. Her career of running into brick walls—was it over?

She walked to the phone, put in a quarter, and dialed. The number rang and rang. Could she have dialed it wrong? At last she heard a click, a voice.

"Charlie?"

"Is that you, Marty?"

At the sound of his voice saying her name, tears stung; she thought she would break down. She put Patrick on her other hip, clamped the phone in place with her chin. "Charlie. I need your help."

"Where are you? Are you at home?"

Was she really safe this time, could she ask for help that would not bring harm? "I don't know what to do next," she said.

321

41

FOUR FORTY-SIX. Simon checked his watch as he came in the back door. He was early for a change; the sun was setting under a coil of snow clouds. He hit the garage button and the light switches. No appointments to keep him at the office late, and he had beaten the slow traffic on East River Road. Two lanes, three significant curves, and you were stuck with what speed somebody four cars ahead of you wanted to drive. Tonight he had been the front car. Every now and then things worked out.

He walked quickly through the kitchen, happy not to see anybody. He had begun to dread this, his mother hanging around, waiting for him to come through the door and referee. What a relief to have a few minutes to himself. He needed time to think.

Upstairs the nursery door was closed. Another break. Marty would be in there with Patrick, doing whatever justified her constant smothering. He smiled; Nellie was right about that one. Marty stuck to the baby like glue, but he'd settled the matter of her sleeping in there—he needed that much leeway.

Working the knot of his tie he pulled it off. The house was silent. Nellie must be taking a nap; with luck she might sleep through dinner. He sat down on the bed and bent to unlace his shoes.

Something wasn't right. The garage, that was it. The garage had been empty when he'd pulled in. Marty's car was gone. He had seen that, and it hadn't fully registered. He'd entered the house and turned on the lights himself. At the door of his bedroom he turned off the switches to the hall and stairs. No light coming from under the nursery door. No lights anywhere.

He made his way down the hall, opened the door to the nursery. Empty. He looked in the closet: the diaper bag was gone. Also the little yellow snowsuit-thing. Where was his mother? He hurried down the hall to her room. He opened the door and found her stretched out on the bed, snoring in the bright flicker of the TV. He shook her.

"Ma. Where's the baby? Where's Marty?"

Nellie eyed him groggily. "What?"

"Where are they?"

She stared up at him. "I was resting my eyes, son."

He raised his voice as though she'd confessed to deafness. "Where are Marty and the baby?"

"Why, where are they? In the nursery? Did you look?"

He drew an exasperated breath. "They're gone. They're not here."

"Where are my glasses?" She groped for the cord at her neck.

He turned away, heading back down the hall. This didn't have to mean anything. She could be anywhere—at the store, at her father's—but then, why take the baby with her? And why was his own heart beating away like this?

Back in the nursery he opened dresser drawers —nothing. The closet nearly empty. *Bitch! She's done it, she has gone and done it!*

His mother stood behind him in the doorway. "Maybe they went to the clinic?"

"The baby isn't due for a checkup," he snapped.

"Call the police!" she said hoarsely, having understood it all at once. At last.

He turned. "That is what we will *not* do. Do you hear me? Not yet."

She looked stricken.

"She may be with Boz. I'll call him." He went quickly across the hall to his study.

On the line, the phone rang several times before it was picked up.

"Boz? It's Simon Carmody."

"Yeah?"

"I'm trying to locate Marty."

"She ain't at your place?"

"No. She's not. I've just come home—"

"Well, I been at the store all day. But I ain't seen her. She's not here."

"Have you talked to her lately?"

The front doorbell rang a sharp summons. Nellie gave a start.

"Sunday," Boz was saying. "After church—"

"Never mind," Simon stopped him. "I think I just heard her come in. Sorry to have bothered you. Thanks." He slapped the receiver into its cradle.

Behind him Nellie said, "I tried to tell you!"

He ducked past her. Downstairs at the front door he switched on the floodlights. A force of cold air entered as he pulled the door open. Charlie stood on the porch.

"What the hell—?"

"It's okay," Charlie said. "Everything's okay. Marty's got Patrick with her."

"Where is she? Has there been an accident? What is it?"

"No, no accident. I'll take you to her. Come on."

Nellie had tottered into the hall, holding on to her glasses. "What does he say?" she shrilled. "She's dangerous, that woman!"

"Shut up, Mother!" Simon put out his hand. "What's going on, Charlie?"

"I don't know. She called me up and said she couldn't stay here any longer. Said she needed to talk to you—"

"About what?"

"She wouldn't tell me. Just that I should get you and bring you out—"

"No need for that," Simon interrupted. "You can tell me where she is and I'll take care of it from here on."

"Fine. Great. Take care of it, then." His brother started down the steps.

Simon came out on the porch. "Damn you!"

Charlie turned. "Look, I didn't ask her to call me! I'm only trying to help! Get it?"

"I'm sorry. I'm upset."

"You and me both, Si."

"I'll get my jacket."

Nellie stood fussing at his sleeve. Simon took her arm and steered her back into the den. "Make yourself some tea, Ma. We'll be back soon. It'll all be fine."

"Call the police," she hissed. "Let them take care of it, that's my advice."

"There's no need. Charlie's going to help me. Just tell me you'll sit tight here and wait."

Her eyes narrowed.

"I mean, stay off the phone," he ordered. "I will call you as soon as I know anything. Will you?"

She lifted her chin and nodded at last.

As he turned back to the door, Simon hesitated. The trip-hammer beat was back. He turned and ran up the stairs, heading back toward his study and the top desk drawer.

•

Charlie was waiting for him in the car, leaning forward with his arms around the wheel. He was shivering. "Christ, it's cold."

Simon got in and slammed the door. "What's her reason for this?" he demanded. "What did she tell you?"

"She was upset." Charlie eased the car into gear. "Not making much sense. She just kept saying how the baby was in danger."

"What kind of danger?"

"I don't know."

"And that's it?" Simon eyed him. This brother of his: how much of an actor?

"What happened between you two?" Charlie came back.

"I might ask the same question. Are you going to come through for me, Charlie?"

"I'll get you there, if that's what you mean."

Simon stared out of the windshield. "It's not that I don't trust you. I just don't like having you involved."

"I'm involved. That's the way it is."

"Where are we going?"

"Boz's cabin. Out near Annandale."

"Why would she take him there? It's just a shack, isn't it?"

"A hunting cabin. It's got heat and electricity." Then he blurted, "She loves that baby, Si. She wouldn't do anything to hurt him."

"Charlie," he said firmly, "she's got a gun."

"What?"

"She took my revolver from my desk. I checked."

Charlie's head swung around. "What are you talking about? Si, what the fuck are you doing with a revolver?"

"It was in the drawer yesterday. Now it's missing."

"Are you sure? Why would she—?"

"Because she's unstable as hell, Charlie! Anybody but you could see that! You don't know half of it!"

They were headed south on County Road 8, nearing the intersection of 23, where the big blue barn stood under the yard light. Charlie barely touched the brakes at the stop sign. Turning right onto the highway he gunned the engine. They shot across the bridge high over the Mississippi and, a moment later, the Interstate.

"What don't I know?" Charlie demanded. "Tell me, Si. I want to hear it."

Simon slumped against the seat. Having to depend on Charlie in an emergency—he shook his head. "Ma was right, for once. I should have called the police."

"What don't I know?"

"What Marty Voigt has against me!" He pressed a hand to his forehead. "She was admitted to Cook County when I was in residency there. She had a baby. It died. She was on drugs, and the infant was born addicted. Didn't stand a chance."

"That's not your fault—"

"Of course it wasn't! She was malnourished, there was infection. . . . She hadn't seen a doctor through the entire pregnancy. Listen, you can't believe how people live."

"I believe it. She was a kid. Nineteen years old. She didn't know anything."

"No, it's worse than that, Charlie. People don't want to know. They make it a point not to know. They take stupid chances, they cut exactly the wrong corners—then keep on doing it unless something stops them cold. It's just as well that baby died. What would its future have been?"

Leaving the perimeter of the lake they cut across woods until they came to the end of a section of tall pines. Around a curve the car lights fanned a flat expanse of land, spiked here and there with cornstalks. The bleached leaves fluttered raggedly in the wind. "I haven't been out this way in years," Simon began. "Not since you and Dad and I spent that night hunting ducks in the rain. Remember? Ma sure does."

Charlie's head was turned away from him. "Was that it, then?"

"What do you mean?"

"The baby dying. Was that all of it?"

He didn't answer right away. He looked over at his brother's profile. Charlie, who supposedly knew what to pay attention to. "No," he said. "The infection was such that I had to perform a tubal ligation."

A long silence. "Why?"

"I told you, there was infection."

"It couldn't be treated?"

"Can you treat poor judgment? Lack of control? A suicidal personality?"

"Si. She's not suicidal, she never was suicidal."

"You weren't around then, were you?" A break in the snowbank revealed a plowed trail through the field, and without warning they took it at a long slide, the roadway bucking under them. He was flung against the passenger door. "Give me some warning, for Chrissake!" he snarled.

"Sorry. Didn't see it coming. Sorry."

The lights of the car were angled low, casting bluish shadows on the frozen ruts. Charlie switched to the high beams.

"How much farther?"

"Couple of miles, maybe."

"You're sure you know where you're going."

"I'm sure."

They drove on in silence, Charlie keeping the car to the center of the road, steering carefully. The road here was overgrown. Snow-laden branches slapped and sprayed the sides of the car.

Charlie shot him a look. "I'm just trying to understand what your thinking was then. How you explained it to her."

Simon stared straight ahead. "My thinking was that I didn't want her to mess up any more lives."

"Is that what you told her?"

"What are you asking? If you mean, does she know that she had the operation, of course she does. There are regulations, you know. She signed a form. Just like everybody else did."

"Everybody . . . ?"

"Watch out!"

Charlie jerked the wheel as the car slid around a

Killing Time in St. Cloud

fallen tree jutting halfway across the road. They hit a dip, bottomed out, and rose again around a curve. "There's her car."

The headlights picked up the white letters on the license plate of the Datsun. "Okay." Simon let out a long breath. He hadn't realized he'd been holding it.

Beyond the car a small log cabin stood at the edge of a clearing: lights in the left half, the curtains drawn. A blue haze hung in the air above the roof. Off to the right in the woods was a small shed, half buried.

Charlie cut the lights, shut off the engine. "How do you want to handle this?"

He put his hand on the door. "I want you to leave me here. Take the car and go call the Annandale police."

"Si, it'll take half an hour—"

"It'll take twenty minutes at the most. If you get going."

"Fine. Then I'll stand guard and you go. When you get back, we'll both go in."

"Charlie, didn't you just ask me how I wanted to handle this?"

"If you really believe she's unstable—"

"I'm not leaving here. That's that. It's my kid in there with her!"

His brother looked at him for a long moment. At last he nodded. Simon opened his door and got out. "Call Ma, too, will you? Tell her everything's okay. Tell her we found Patrick and it's okay." He walked around to the driver's side.

"Everything's not okay yet, Si." Charlie's face was tense.

"It will be. I promise."

331

He watched the car slide crazily as Charlie backed and turned it around, the red taillights jumping over the uneven ground. He watched until the red disappeared between the trees, then turned back toward the cabin with its windows glowing orange. Reaching into his jacket pocket he slipped his hand around the gun. What was going to happen here would have to happen fast. He was ready.

42

THE WIND MADE ITS WHOOSHING SOUND above his head and sent small loose showers of snow down from the cedars. He waited, willing the wind to hush. Then he moved from beneath the trees to the tire tracks behind the Datsun. He ran up the path her boots had made between the car and the front door. In what light there was, he could see she'd made several trips, carrying things in. He stopped at the porch and listened again. No sound.

It all came down to decision, and then a series of well-timed, unequivocal moves. That was his training, which served him well enough with Uhler—that grinning moron. Walking in the door like Santa Claus, making a gift of just the information he'd been waiting for. Here was the "real father," in the very flesh. Threatening a custody suit, headlines in the papers—in a way it was hilarious. Uhler, in fact, died laughing. But not before the fool understood—after all, one confession deserved another—how he'd known all along there wasn't one chance in hell that baby was his own.

Uhler was a creative son of a bitch; he'd switched to what he would tell Terry Fallon: that Elizabeth had hired him, paid him off with an emerald bracelet to fuck her the way she always liked it. That was as far as he'd gotten, dying in midsentence with Elizabeth's name burning above them like a thrown spark. *The beautiful Elizabeth,* Uhler had called her. So right, so right. He'd never in his life seen anything so beautiful, or wanted anything as much. Only her, all to himself. *The beautiful liar Elizabeth.* Living a lie all these months, forcing them both to live it.

No matter, he had worked everything out in his mind: so many little ones lost every year to Sudden Infant Death Syndrome, no way to predict it, no known cause. You put them down for a nap and suddenly, mysteriously, they stopped breathing.

It would have been hard on Elizabeth, of course, but what had these past months been for him? *Beautiful liar Elizabeth.* Going off to a fertility clinic in Chicago and coming back pregnant. Coming back without her bracelet.

He could have forgiven her everything and they could have gone on. But this last, cruel joke—nobody dies in childbirth anymore, for God's sake, it was like dying of pneumonia or appendicitis. He'd had a thought that it was some kind of punishment. But for whom? Who was the one being punished here? Him, only him! He'd vowed he would not be the only one to pay. And sure enough, there he was that night in the kitchen of the old house, routinely feeding the woodburner, and he was not the only one.

So easy to calculate the correct amount of force, the correct angle; afterward all he had to do was stick the piece of wood into the fire. The rest not quite as elegant, zipping him into Mike's old suit with the hood lined with plastic bags, riding double on the snowmobile through the white

woods and then along the riverbank until he found
a hole in the ice—always a hole in the shallow
channels around the islands, Uhler would have
known that much himself. He'd tossed in the
watch, the fat wallet, the cowboy boots, and
watched the current take them. It didn't have to
be so easy, but it was. The snow had been coming
down that night, covering his tracks as fast as he
made them, and he saw no one, not even a tilting
headlight through the trees across the river, and
Uhler fell out of the suit and into the water like a
peeled snake.

Simon glanced once more around the stilled setting of the cabin, trees silent in the yard, the dark
road. Tonight the logistics were simpler—no car to
move, no skiing back downriver in the dead of
night—but he needed margin in the way of timing. This might not be quite so tidy.

Gently he placed his gloved hand on the curve
of the door handle, tried the iron tongue-latch:
locked. He took a breath and rapped on the wood.

Behind the door careful footsteps approached.
"Who is it?"

"It's me. Simon."

He heard the bolt slide back, and then the door
swung open. Marty stood there in her red sweater
and dark skirt; on her face a wary defiance. He
pushed the door wider and took in the room. A
stone fireplace, bright fire licking up. To the left a
kitchen table, a brown couch. To the right closed
doors to bedrooms on either side of the hearth—
the dark windows he'd seen from outside. No baby
in the room. Beside the couch a bottle and a pile of
diapers heaped on a small table. Hanging from a
chairback the yellow snowsuit.

"Where's the baby?" he asked.

"Where's Charlie?"

"Were you counting on Charlie? He's gone to get the police."

"That wasn't the plan—"

"What was the plan, Marty?"

She took a step backward. "I asked him to bring you out here. So we could talk."

"Talk about what?"

"About . . . making a deal."

He stepped into the room and closed the door behind him. "What sort of deal did you have in mind?"

"I know you don't want this baby, Simon. I know you have your reasons. I don't even blame you for it—"

He gave a laugh. "Nice of you."

"Just let me have him. I'll take him and move away, out of this state. You won't ever have to see him again."

He smiled. "Wouldn't that be just a little awkward to explain? That I gave my son away to his baby-sitter? What would his grandfather think of that?"

"He's not your son."

"You're full of news, aren't you? Where did you get that—from Nick?"

"From Elizabeth."

Not true, not true. He felt the pain come on, as if she had stabbed him behind the eyes. "Don't be ridiculous."

"Did you kill her? I know you sterilized me at Cook County. If you would do that, I believe you would do anything."

He shook his head. "You're a mess, Marty. You

336

were a mess then, and you're in worse shape now than you know. Everything I did at Cook County was perfectly legal. You signed for it. That scrawl on the form was your signature. Nobody else's."

"Did you kill my baby, Simon? Tell me the truth. Did he die of natural causes?"

"Natural causes? I wouldn't say so. It died of poisoning, due to its mother's heroin habit." He watched this take effect, watched her eyes brim. Good. He wanted her to suffer as he suffered, was still suffering. *Not true, not true. Only he had known for sure about the baby. A blood sample might have told, but no other way. She was lying.*

"I didn't know what I was signing," she whispered. "You knew I didn't know."

"I did you a big favor that day. And I'm about to do you another. Go get the baby. We don't have much time."

"He's not here."

He watched her eyes slide to the closed doors to his right. "You're lying."

"I'm offering to bargain. You took my baby, I take this one."

He shook his head. "You don't understand yet what's been going on here tonight. Actually, all this time, I've been outside in the yard, waiting for my brother to get back with the police. Until I heard what sounded like a shot. That's when I ran in and found you on the floor, the baby smothered in its bed. I know you had your reasons, Marty. I don't even blame you for it. My mother tried to warn me, you'd been depressed ever since Uhler washed up."

"You killed Nicky, didn't you?"

"Monster Man? Maybe you did, Marty. Wasn't

that what you were trying to tell me that day at the hospital? Now, where's the baby?"

"Simon. He's all that's left of Elizabeth."

"Nothing is left of her! That pregnancy killed her, Uhler's murdering brat killed her!"

"We are talking about Elizabeth's baby. About his life—!"

He pulled the revolver from his pocket. "Nobody ever gets it. What about *my life*? That's what I'm looking at!"

She stared at the gun. "You said—"

"I said I wasn't the kind to use a gun. But you are." He seized Marty's arm and jerked her along as he went for the first door and flipped on the light switch. Nothing in the tiny bedroom except a naked cot and a dresser. He stepped back and shoved her toward the other door.

She wrenched free, stepped away from him. "Don't you want to hear how I learned about the baby?" she asked. "Aren't you curious?" Fumbling at her pocket she pulled out a blue envelope. "This is a letter to Nicky. From Elizabeth."

"Old love letters," he said, "prove nothing."

"Not old. This one was mailed last April from St. Cloud. Shall I read it to you?"

"Bitch." He said it quietly. "You scheming bitch. I'm going to tell you something. We've got a lot in common, you and I. We're both sterile. Not only that, we had the same surgeon. I took care of that small job myself after the lab tests came back. I was too fertile for my taste, and it's a very simple procedure, local anesthetic, a day's minor discomfort. There was no reason for Elizabeth to know, and she never would have."

"Except for Nick," she said. "Who was always there."

"You lie and you lie and you don't know anything, do you? We were happy! She didn't need a baby, she didn't need anything!" He looked at his watch. They were on the thin edge of his margin. He only needed to get his hands on the baby; she wasn't going anywhere. He went for the other door, opened it. Bill Hessel stood braced, police revolver outstretched. Simon whirled as the outside door burst open. Charlie stood in the doorway.

"Let me have the gun, Si," his brother pleaded. And so sadly! As if this weren't treachery.

He swung back flat to the wall. "Hessel," he barked, "come through that door and you're dead." To his brother he said, "People getting in my way, Charlie. You know how I feel about that." He looked down at the revolver he held, that blunt instrument. Not the one he would have chosen. He leveled his gaze at Marty. "This is your hand," he said. "Where's the baby?" He lifted the gun to make her stare into it.

His brother lunged forward—a blur of motion at the edge of his vision. "Si, don't shoot—don't!"

He fired. He saw Charlie jerk in midair in front of the girl and fall against the table, saw the yellow suit drop to the floor. On the move now, still he saw it all—Marty's body bent over Charlie's, a show of red, Hessel's two-handed prayer-crouch in the doorway beyond them.

Hessel yelled but he was jerking the door open, was outside it and running. The snow was deep, deeper than he expected, and he plowed through her drifted footprints toward the small woodshed.

Of course she was no fool, she would have hidden it in a place she thought was safe. But he was no fool either. Just this last stitch of business, and he could wash up.

Lights came up suddenly from everywhere, making the yard unnaturally brilliant. An operating theater; all the easier for him to do his job. A small window near the door of the shed beckoned to him; he could almost see the yellow snowsuit from where he stood. He put his hand on the shed door and pulled hard, but the solid wood was wedged, some catch underneath the snow line. All right, then; through the window, an easy shot. One shot was all he needed.

Behind him he heard shouts; he turned to see shadows moving toward him, strange oversize figures looming out of the lights. No time. Never sufficient time. Well, so be it. He raised the hand with the gun. With no waste of motion he placed the barrel securely to the roof of his mouth. He never doubted that he had the angle precisely right.

43

CHARLIE AWOKE TO DARKNESS and to pain. He
was tired. He'd been running for hours, running
through deep snow for his life—was this true? The
pain, being cultured somewhere within his body,
did not seem to have a source. He reached out a
hand to push it from him; felt the hand being
taken by someone. Good; he wasn't alone, then.

"—awake? I think he's awake."

He shook his head, not wanting to encourage
that; he didn't feel at all awake. Would he be asked
to do more running? He knew he wasn't up to it. A
white blur in front of his eyes, vaporlike, thinning
gradually as he strained to see through it . . .
white butterflies. Yes. Tiny Japanese butterflies
floating in front of his eyes. He had seen them
folded out endlessly in a book made like a fan, but
where? In another of his dreams, maybe. Not the
one about the war . . . when he and Nick tried to
get the faces back . . . Simon had stolen all the
faces of the Indians from the Apache Raid puzzle.
He swore he'd never taken them, and Nick kept
saying, "Just give us back Geronimo, that's the
only good one. . . ."

"Charlie? . . . Can you hear me?"

His vision slowly cleared and he could see

Marty's face, a pale circle floating above him in the surrounding darkness. Of all the faces he wanted to see. He opened his mouth to say something, anything, to persuade her to stay.

". . . take back everything I said."

"What?"

Lord, she would have to pay attention. He didn't have energy to repeat himself. Nevertheless, he made the effort.

"Shhh . . ."

He could think of no reply, the pain having declared its location at last, galloping along inside his skull. The face above him came nearer.

"Charlie, I love you."

"Don't have to . . ."

The voice was urgent. "Please say you believe me."

"I do," he said, although he did not. He needed to save his strength. Darkness was again closing over his head. And now he was riding peculiar, solid waves—an earthquake, he guessed. His mother was busy trying to control the furniture as it rumbled from one end of the house to the other, while he grabbed at lamps and falling debris—pointless when the house was about to topple, he tried to tell her. A bureau went flying past, its drawers sliding. Then the floor opened up and he fell into the kitchen. In front of the woodburner was a gaping hole, as if something had torn out the floorboards. Had someone fallen in? Nick! He called out for Simon. An explosion sounded in his ears. He ran back to find Nellie. She was in the dining room, making sure nothing of value got broken. She kept yelling at him, "What's going on here?"—as if it were all his doing. At last he made it to a window, and pushed aside the brown spider-curtains. He couldn't believe his eyes—a calm, sunny afternoon.

And now the darkness again. He felt impatient. Okay, what was the point of this?

A good life is made, not born. Fine. He could understand that one, it was simple enough. Tell that to the baby, though, because he himself couldn't get the hang of it. Chicago . . . Joliet. Could you make that many mistakes and still assume you were headed in the right direction?

He saw Elizabeth, standing off in the middle distance. She looked friendly, but she was waiting for something. From him? He felt a little embarrassed, didn't know how to address her. She wanted to know about Patrick, that much he understood. Hell, he didn't know anything about babies . . . and then, suddenly he did know something, it had come to him the same way he'd understood about the Japanese butterflies.

He understood her as clearly as if she had spoken aloud. *Who will think about the baby?*

"I will," he told her earnestly. "I'm so sorry . . ."

"Shhh, don't, Charlie. Just rest." Her hand reached out to stroke his forehead. When he opened his eyes, Marty's hand was there.

"Marty. I never meant to hurt you."

"You never did."

"Why didn't you tell me about the baby?"

"You weren't around. And it wasn't your problem."

"But it *was*." He tried to sit up; felt pain.

"What is it? What's wrong? You'll hurt yourself."

343

"It was my baby . . . I should have been there with you."

"No, it wasn't. Charlie, have you been thinking—?" She pressed him gently against the pillow. "It was Nick's baby, Charlie. Not ours."

An even greater sadness, then. He would never be that close to her again, and what had come of it? Nothing. He closed his eyes and saw that he was on some kind of long track. White wreaths wrapped themselves thick and cold around his ankles. He guessed he was expected to snap to and start running again. Jesus, but life was an effort. He hoped it would get easier.

44

A SINGLE YELLOW ROSE stood in a vase on Marjorie's desk next to the daily calendar: WED. JAN. 10.

"Got a minute?" Bakke asked him. "Need your John Henry here on this autopsy report."

"Hancock," Bill said.

"Huh?"

"A signature. Is a John Hancock."

"Naah. You sure about that?"

Bill signed and went into his office. Bakke followed him.

"Carmody house just went up for sale," Bakke said. "The one in River Haven. Listing came through this morning. My cousin's husband got it."

"Yeah?" He signed the report, handed it back.

"Talk about weirdness," Bakke said. "What d'you think about the guy vasectomizing himself?"

"Where do you find these words? Vasectomize. There's no such word."

"Creeps me out just to think of it." Bakke shuddered. "But he was a strange one. You must have picked up something, Chief. You knew right where to head with that heel plate."

"Shut the door on your way out, will you? I've got work to do in here."

"You bet."

Marjorie's knock came a moment before she opened the door and stuck her head inside. "Someone to see you."

He rose as Charlie Carmody shouldered in, his right arm in a cast and sling. Above his right eye a neat white bandage.

"Didn't think I'd be seeing you again," Bill said. He felt awkward not extending his hand, and at the same time reprieved. The way he was always going to feel around Charlie.

"Just wrapping things up here," Charlie said, his voice almost shy.

"Have a chair," he said, and waited until Charlie had settled himself. "As long as you're wrapping things up, I got a bone to pick. I went a long way out on a short limb with you that night at the cabin."

"I know it."

"We had a plan, my friend, and you didn't stick to it. I still wake up seeing you jump into my line of fire."

"I got excited. Thanks for keeping your head."

He wondered why he had started all this, what he wanted the guy to say. But he couldn't let it alone. "I had things under control."

"I just blew it after Si pulled the gun. I wasn't much help to you, I know."

"You had plenty to say a while back about getting a raw deal here."

"Look. Could we start over, you and me?" Charlie gave him his grin.

He found himself grinning back. He didn't quite trust it. "So. How's your mother?"

"She made it through the funeral all right. Tom

pulled some strings and got her into Key Row. Maybe she'll do great there with people her own age." He paused. He didn't sound so sure of it. "She said she already raised two boys, and two was one too many. She thinks I did this to Simon, you know. Marty and me, we did him in. I guess it's hard to change stories so late in the game."

"Nothing turned out the way we planned, did it? I'm sorry about Simon."

"He was my brother, that's all I know." Charlie stared out beyond the parking lot. "Too close and too far. I thought for a while things might be changing. Now I have to wonder if he'd have killed us all. It's too hard. I'm not going to think about it."

Bill nodded. What had he heard from Records on Monday? That papers had been filed in the Carmody case. *The Carmody Case.* Jesus, Mary, and Joseph, save him from ever having his name used like that—part of a title in the records department.

"Well, how does it feel being a father?"

"Feels like I got the world around my neck, if you want to know." Charlie smiled. "Kid only weighs six pounds and already I'm walking like a hunchback."

"I was surprised when I heard. Tom and Jeanne declined, huh?"

"Tom did, anyhow."

"Right. You have custody, free and clear?"

"You pumping me, Bill, or what?"

He fought the urge to rise to the bait. "I'm pumping you. Tell me what's ahead."

"We're moving on. Patrick will have enough to

think about without growing up here. Too much stuff to carry up front."

"Lot of people go through hard times and stick around. Nothing wrong with St. Cloud."

"Nothing at all," Charlie agreed. "Just what's wrong with me when I'm in it." He gave him a look. "For what it's worth, I never believed the town was locked up. I just said that to hassle you."

"For what it's worth," Bill said, "I believed everything I ever heard about you."

"So that makes us even, then." Charlie got to his feet. "Well. This leaving part is not my favorite." He stuck out his left hand. "If I'm ever back this way, I'll look you up."

Bill took the hand. "Do that. Sorry to see you go, Charlie."

And it was true. Or at least half true; that was the best he could do.

45

BEYOND THE DARK SILVER VAN in the parking lot was the old St. Cloud Jail, barred and square. Charlie didn't like to think about the view from those windows. After all, it was bound to include the bumpy yellow dome of the Stearns County Courthouse, which topped the list of things he would never understand about this town: a yellow dome?

He'd left the van unlocked, even though it was loaded with everything he owned. A police station lot. You had to put your faith somewhere.

He got in and sat studying the familiar profiles of downtown. Dan Marsh Alley, the old bank building, backlit windows of the funeral parlor. He couldn't stay in St. Cloud. For him everything here felt used up.

"You have your whole history tied up in this place," Marty had told him. "You can't be on the run from something you carry with you, Charlie."

"My history has not been exactly swell to me," he'd shot back. "I'll carry what's mine, but it better pack small."

Hard guy. He was so hard, wasn't he?

The thought of Marty made his heart turn over. During the last week he'd felt things change between them as they fed and bathed and held the baby. He'd found himself thinking: so this is what love looks like. This is how she is when she gives in and feels it. And this is how I am.

A good life is made, not born. He meant to keep that straight—a promise he'd made at Elizabeth's grave yesterday. Standing there with Marty and Patrick at nightfall, the sky black except for streaks of pink at the horizon. A cone of daisies stuffed into the snow to say, *Elizabeth, don't worry, it's all mapped out from now on.*

Beside him Marty had whispered, "I felt a tie with her that I could never explain. Not through Nick. It was Simon. I felt so strange about riding in her car—I couldn't tell you how much it made me think of a coffin. Now I keep seeing her, hoping and hoping all those years to get pregnant while Simon let her think . . . all the things she must have been thinking. That line from her letter, 'on the nights he tells me I'm fertile' . . ." Marty had shivered, and held on to Patrick. "She was never real to him, was she? None of us were."

Charlie twisted the key in the ignition. He meant what he'd told Hessel: he was not going to think about it. Not for a long while. Maybe not ever.

He drove the van to Wilson Avenue and pulled in snug against the curb. The sign above Voigt's Family Store looked faded. Knowing you were leaving changed the way you saw things. He crossed the shoveled sidewalk and made his way around back. He heard the door open above him.

Boz peered over the balcony. "Where you been?" he called down crossly.

Another hard guy.

"I just took the crib apart. Here." As he got

there, Boz shoved a large box into his arms and went back into the apartment.

Charlie looked through the storm door. In her red sweater and jeans Marty knelt on the kitchen counter with her back to him. He stood outside pierced by a sudden thought that he would only be able to look at her; too many of his dreams had ended just that way. He shook his head. What it meant was, somewhere inside this body the high-schooler was still at large. Meanwhile the thirty-year-old managed to balance the crib box against the railing and open the door. "I'm here," he said.

She turned. "Been waiting for you." She pointed to taped boxes on the kitchen table. Their labels read FOOD, FORMULA, BEDDING, EXTRA CLOTHES. A large suitcase stood next to the chair.

Boz came back from the bedroom. Through the open door he shoved a heavy plastic bag into Charlie's jacket pocket. "Here's the bolts and washers for the crib. Leave 'em in your pocket so you'll know where to find 'em tonight at the motel."

"Great." Charlie hoisted the box again.

"There's more stuff in the bedroom," Boz said. "I can help you carry it down."

"I'll come back," he said. "Just hand it out the door." He made six trips up and down, arranging boxes in the van, before he returned to the apartment at last.

Zipping up his jacket Boz said, "Do me a favor, will you? Don't drive over the speed limit."

"What is the speed limit?" he asked, then raised his hand and smiled. "Just kidding, Boz. I won't go over the speed limit."

"You put the car seat in?"

"Car seat. Changing table. The works."

"I don't get this," Boz said. "Why you two can't get married here in town. Where you both grew up. Where she's been making me go to church every goddamn Sunday—"

"Dad, you're not going to start this up again, are you?" Marty came in with Patrick dressed in his yellow snowsuit.

Charlie peered at the somber face. "On the road again, my man." He took the baby, hefted him to his shoulder with his good arm.

"How you gonna drive, anyway?" Boz asked.

"I can drive." He stood jiggling Patrick, who dropped his head against Charlie's left shoulder with a bang.

"Jeez, be careful," Boz muttered. "You want to scramble his brains?"

"If you and Mrs. Finch didn't scramble anything the night you kept him—"

"Do me another favor. I don't want to hear any more about me and Mrs. Finch."

Marty returned, wearing her camel coat. She gave her father a fierce hug. To his surprise Charlie felt Boz's arm go around his shoulders.

"Now you take care," Boz said harshly. "I don't want to have to tell you again."

The three of them trooped down the stairs, Boz carrying the baby. He walked them to the curb and stood with his hands in his pockets while they got themselves buckled in.

Charlie opened his window, gave the old man the high sign as they turned the corner. Then he drove looking straight ahead, conscious of Marty's hair brushing his shoulder as she turned to check Patrick in the car seat.

She said, "You sure took your time on those trips out to the car."

"Your dad was getting ready to bawl. I didn't think I could take it."

"Babies cry a lot," she said. "Better get used to that."

"Babies crying I can handle."

"I saw Mr. C. for Catastrophe cry yesterday evening," she said.

"We were at the cemetery, for God's sake."

"Hard guy. How's your arm? I'll drive, if you want me to."

"I want you sitting right there."

They made the curve where Kilian changed into Minnesota Boulevard, then turned onto County Road 8. Marty spread the stiff map over her knees. She raised her head. "Charlie. You're sure about this, aren't you?"

"Hell, no," he said. "Are you?"

She looked at him and smiled. It was the look he still couldn't believe he would ever see coming from her to him—not in his lifetime. He glanced at the map in her hand, and then out the window at the broad white lay of Minnesota prairie all around them.

"Where to?" he asked.

Sheer terror...
and the uncontrollable urge
to keep reading await you
in the suspense novels of

MARY HIGGINS
CLARK